cruel
CRYPTS

USA TODAY & *WALL STREET JOURNAL* BESTSELLING AUTHOR
BECCA STEELE

CRUEL CRYPTS

GODS OF HATHERLEY HALL
BOOK 1

BECCA STEELE

Cruel Crypts

Copyright © 2023 by Becca Steele

All rights reserved. No part of this book may be reproduced or transmitted in any form or by any means, electronic or mechanical, including photocopying, recording or by any information storage and retrieval system, without written permission from the author, except for the use of brief quotations in a book review.

Editing by One Love Editing

Proofreading by Rumi

Cover design by Opulent Designs

Becca Steele

www.authorbeccasteele.com

This is a work of fiction. Names, characters, businesses, places, events, locales, and incidents are either the products of the author's crazy imagination or used in a fictitious manner. Any resemblance to actual persons, living or dead, or actual events is purely coincidental.

AUTHOR'S NOTE

The author is British, and this story contains British English spellings and phrases.

For anyone who's ever been knocked back due to unexpected circumstances.
You are strong enough to deal with whatever life throws at you.
I promise.

It's not what happens to you, but how you react to it that matters.

— EPICTETUS

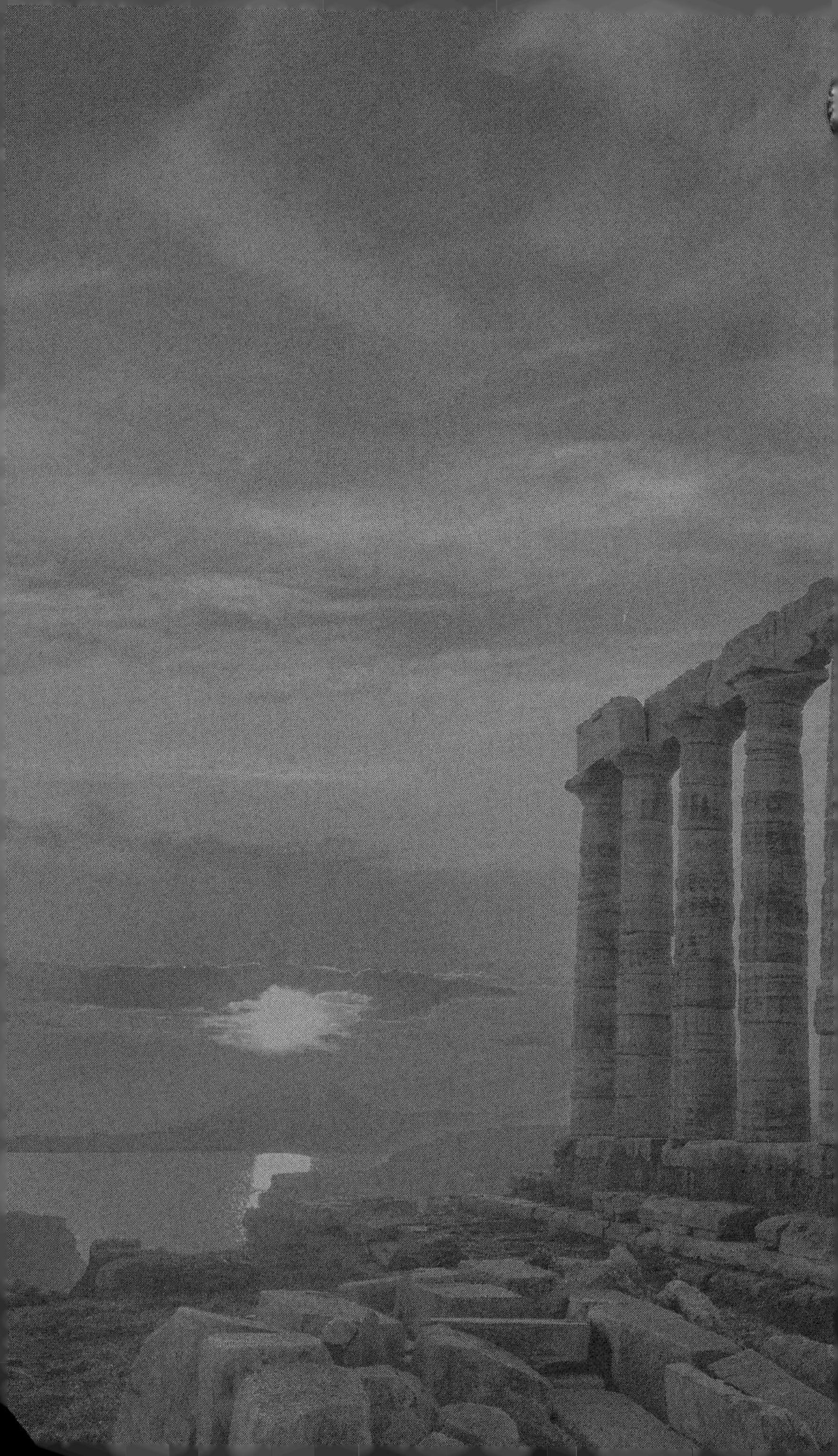

LEGEND

Legend tells of three gods. Zeus, king of all the gods and ruler of the skies, Hades, ruler of the underworld, and Poseidon, ruler of the seas.

The three gods were brothers.

According to legend, the gods grew bored with their immortal lives, and their attention was drawn by the humans who lived in the mortal realm. Each of them took women, and sometimes men, even though it was forbidden.

When the Titans, parents of the gods, discovered what had been done, they threatened the gods with banishment and even death. So the gods agreed never to visit the mortal realm again.

Thousands of years passed, and humans no longer believed in the gods, although the legends remained.

The blood of the gods was strong, though. Every so often, a child would be born who would be faster, stronger, more beautiful than those around them. The inherent characteristics of the gods could be seen in these children too, shaping their personalities and lives.

Did the gods exist?

Legend

Was it all a myth?

No one knows for sure. But eighteen years and one month ago, a dark-haired, dark-eyed boy was born, beautiful and strong, with a magnetic presence.

Some called the boy cold. He preferred to be alone, skulking in dark corners. He had many acquaintances but few true friends. It was difficult to read him—on the surface, he was cool and controlled, but woe betide those who provoked his wrath.

Still, his life was good. He was in a position of privilege, thanks to his family heritage, and he was never short of attention from those who either wished to be him or wished to be with him.

The boy was on top of the world.

Until one day.

A day when his plans crumbled to dust and his world was turned upside down.

The day *she* entered his life…

PROLOGUE

Elena

The interior of the car was deathly silent. Every now and then, the taxi driver's gaze would flick towards the back seat, where my mother and I sat on opposite sides with her small handbag between us, and his brow would crease as if he were concerned. The cab's boot contained a total of two duffel bags—one for me and one for my mother—all that we owned in the world now after everything else had gone.

We'd had no choice but to sell the meagre possessions we had. Every single penny counted now, had done for the past year, in fact.

Ever since it had happened.

One event had bled into the next, a relentless nightmare that we could never wake up from. Never escape.

As the sign for the small town of Nottswood came into view, my mother sucked in a breath. Her hands were folded in her lap, but it didn't hide the tremble of her fingers.

Not for the first time, doubts entered my mind. "Are

you completely sure you want to do this?" I broke the silence, speaking low in the hope that the driver wouldn't pick up on my words.

My mother glanced across at me, and her expression was resolute. She nodded once, sharply. "*Yes*. They're gone, and he needs to pay for his part in it. If it hadn't been for him, we'd still have a life. We'd still have them both."

A tear slipped down my cheek, and I angrily whisked it away. Now wasn't the time for sadness—I'd done enough crying over the past year. I was strong. I'd had to be. My defences were in place, ready for what we had to do.

"You're right." With a sigh, I let my head fall back against the headrest.

The wheels of the taxi rumbled over the tarmac, the headlights cutting a swathe of light through the darkness, illuminating a set of black wrought-iron gates that stood open. Welcoming us in.

Beyond the gates stood a house, bigger than any I'd ever seen up close. A mansion, in fact. Tall, pale gold stone, with white trim and a black front door. Trailing ivy curled up the sides, and soft lights illuminated the sash windows.

It was beautiful.

I hated it on principle.

"Here we are, ladies." The driver came to a stop close to the front door. He tried for a smile, but it came out more like a grimace, thanks to the suffocating tension inside the car. "The Ashcroft residence."

I ran through the names again in my mind, names that had been burned there ever since my mother came up with this plan.

Anthony Ashcroft. Maria Ashcroft. Josephine Ashcroft.

And the name I hated the most. The person I'd been instructed to play my part with. The person that I'd had to study on social media and gossip sites, building up a picture of a spoiled, arrogant, lacrosse-playing rich boy.

Knox Ashcroft.

My mother paid the driver, and I exited the car on autopilot, my battered trainers crunching across the gravel as I moved around to the boot to collect my duffel bag. Squaring my shoulders, I turned to face the house and made a silent promise to myself.

Whatever waited for me inside, I would face it, and I would be the one to come out on top. Justice would be served.

And if Knox Ashcroft tried to get in my way, I'd make sure he'd regret it.

1

KNOX

As I stood in front of the mirror, a slow smile curved across my lips as I ran a hand through my hair, tousling it just the way I liked it. I was feeling on top of the world. And why wouldn't I be? I had everything. I was one of the elite students at Hatherley Hall—an exclusive boarding school in the Cotswolds that you had to be rich as fuck and have the right connections to attend. I was popular, hot—and that wasn't me being arrogant; it was a fact—had a guaranteed job in my dad's law firm after I'd toed the line and finished my years of education, and more money than I knew what to do with.

Then there were my two best mates, Roman Cavendish and Tristan Smith-Chamberlain. Together, the three of us made up the pinnacle of the elite of Hatherley Hall. The gods, as some referred to us as, and I didn't mind the nickname.

This year was my final year at Hatherley Hall, and it was going to be *my* year. Instead of living with my parents, I'd persuaded them to let me board with my fellow students for the first time. I'd attended as a day student up until now because my family lived so close, but fucking finally, I was going to be on-site twenty-four-seven. Roman, Tristan, and I had already worked out a plan, and with the secret place I'd discovered at the end of last term, I was so fucking ready for this year to begin.

Deep underground, through the hidden passageways no one knew about or remembered, was my domain. *The crypts.* My lair. My exclusive place that I could control and only those I invited would ever get to see.

The one place that was mine and mine alone.

After one last glance at my reflection, I grabbed my sunglasses and car keys and made my way through my parents' mansion towards the front door.

"Knox."

My mother's voice stopped me in my tracks.

"Mother," I drawled, turning to face her. "What is it? I'm on my way out."

She tutted impatiently. "You'll have to put your plans on hold. Come with me."

With a sigh and an eye roll, I followed her. There was no point in getting into an argument with her. When I said I had everything? That came with a set of conditions. Namely, my parents got to call the shots. Or at least, they liked to think they did. They gave me enough free rein that it wasn't a problem, but when they gave an order, I was expected to follow through.

We reached the east wing of the house where the staff lived, and I raised a brow. What the fuck were we doing here? Before I could question it, my mother paused in front of an open doorway. "Knox, I'd like you to meet Josephine's new nanny." Without giving me any time to process her statement, she swept into the room and gave a dramatic wave of her hand. "This is Ms. Letitia Greenwood and her daughter, Elena Greenwood."

Outwardly, I showed no signs of emotion. I knew this because my mask was fucking perfect. Inwardly, I looked over the two new arrivals…and found them lacking.

Letitia Greenwood looked to be in her late forties. She was slim, and I could tell that she'd been good-looking once, but time hadn't been kind to her. Her bottle-blonde hair was coiled into a bun, with dark roots peppered with grey forming a band around the crown of her head. Her lips—I knew a bad filler job when I saw one, and that was a serious trout pout she had going on. The make-up she wore was too harsh for her features, and although the staff uniform she wore was neatly pressed, it didn't make up for the rest of her.

Her daughter, Elena…there wasn't even a nice way to describe her. She was lanky, with greasy, nondescript brown hair, dull light brown eyes, baggy grey tracksuit bottoms, and a shapeless grey top covered with a large, fraying, unzipped navy hoodie that hung off her small frame. The kind of girl that faded into the background. There was a shiftiness to her gaze that instantly put me on alert, and when I glanced back at Letitia Greenwood, I noticed the same expression.

I didn't like it.

The feeling intensified when I saw the way my mother was greedily eyeing Elena…this was bad fucking news.

"Nice to meet you," I said, all icy politeness, my lips curving into my practised fake smile. It was usually enough to fool my parents, and it didn't fail this time either, with my mother giving me a genuine smile.

"Letitia will be overseeing Josephine's care," my mother told me. Josephine was my baby sister—a surprise arrival only two years ago when my father's vasectomy had supposedly failed. I shuddered. I did not need a reminder of the fact that my parents had a sex life. I had an older sister—Cora, who was away at university—but JoJo was the baby of the family, and everyone adored her.

My mother was still speaking. "Elena will be attending Hatherley Hall with you, starting on Monday. You'll be taking her to and from school since she doesn't have a car of her own." Her tone left me with no doubt that this was compulsory.

"How can I do that? I'm boarding on-site now, remember?"

She huffed. "Excuse me for a moment, Letitia, Elena." Placing a hand on my arm, she steered me out of the room. When we were out of earshot, she turned back to me. "Elena isn't like you, Knox. She's been taken away from her home and everything she knows, and you only have to look at her to see that she's going to have trouble fitting in with your fellow students. I'm going to do what I can, but your father and I are relying on you to smooth the way for her at school."

I doubted my dad gave a fuck, but equally, I knew that he'd side with my mother if it came down to it. And that could mean the loss of things that I loved…like money. Or my car.

"This is the start of term, and I'm supposed to be boarding with Tris and Ro. You already agreed. What do you expect me to do? Drive here every day from the school, just to go back again? Can't she get a taxi? Or you could drive her?"

"Knox. I am on the board of more than one charity, you know this. I don't take my responsibilities lightly, and I don't have the time to play chauffeur. You will stay here—"

"No!"

"*Temporarily.* Just for a month or so while Elena finds her footing and makes her own friends. During that time, you will take her to and from school every day. I've already spoken to the school, and everything's arranged."

"A week," I countered.

"Four weeks, and that's my final offer. You don't want me to get your father involved. You know what the consequences will be."

Fuck. "Fine." I set my jaw and fumed behind my mask. I could probably get it down to three weeks, maybe even less, if I approached my dad one-on-one, but I'd have to frame it in a way that made it look like there'd be more of an advantage to me being on school grounds than here. Surely, he'd understand, though. He knew how much I'd been looking forward to this. Not only that but he'd also boarded at Hatherley Hall as a student, and he always spoke fondly of his time there.

"Thank you, Knox." She smiled. "I don't expect you to be here all the time—but I'd like you to sleep here on weeknights at least, take Elena to and from school, and look out for her while she's there. That's not too much to ask, is it?"

I shrugged in lieu of an answer, but it was enough for her. She headed back down the hallway and into the room where the Greenwoods were waiting.

Glancing over at Elena Greenwood again, I gritted my teeth. Like fuck was I going to be seen with this girl anywhere outside the house. People might get the wrong idea, thinking she was cool by association or, worse, think that we were involved or something. I shuddered again. To be honest, the most likely thing that would happen would be that my friends would recognise her as another of my mother's charity projects, but they'd be constantly taking the piss out of me, and then I'd have to fuck them up. That wouldn't go down well. Not only that, but explaining how I was being forced to delay my move to Hatherley Hall while my two best mates got to board there without their parents interfering with their fucking lives…yeah, they were definitely going to take the piss.

I tuned back into my mother, who, yeah, was still talking. Something about schedules and Elena being the same age as me and a whole load of shit I wasn't interested in. I tuned out again until her mouth finally stopped moving, and then I spoke. "Are we done here? I'm meeting Tristan at eleven."

My mother nodded, and finally, I was free to escape. Throughout the entire conversation, neither Letitia nor Elena had spoken one word. That was fine by me. The less interaction I had with the staff, the better.

I sent a text to Tristan to let him know I was on my way, then climbed into my matte-black Maserati Levante and got the fuck out of there.

"She not only expects me to move back home for *four fucking weeks*, but she expects me play chauffeur to this greasy girl, who, by the way, is now living in my house for free. It's taking the piss."

Tristan smirked at me, his bright blue eyes full of sadistic humour. *Wanker*. "Didn't your sister's last nanny live there? What happened to her, anyway?"

I sat back, pushing my sunglasses onto the top of my head. We were sitting in a shaded part of the terrace of Nottswood Golf & Country Club. It was pretentious and full of snobby assholes, but there was something about the atmosphere I liked. I usually came here with my dad, but I'd dragged Tristan here because there was a new waitress who was apparently hot as fuck, and he knew my tastes better than anyone. He could be my wingman today.

"Yeah, the last nanny lived there, but she didn't have a kid of her own. No idea why she left either, just decided the job wasn't for her anymore. I don't know, I don't have anything to do with the staff. That's my mother's domain. Back to the important point—we've only just sorted our living arrangements and the crypts, and now I have to stay at home? It's fucking bollocks. And this girl basically gets to live rent-free in my house, plus she's somehow managed to get into Hatherley Hall."

"That's what the Ashcroft name gets you." Tristan tapped his fingers on the edge of his glass. "Instant admission."

I rolled my eyes. "Yeah, well, she'd better stay away from me in school. We don't want her kind hanging around us. And no taking the piss out of me either."

"I'd never do that," he said with a smirk, lying through his teeth. "It sucks that you have to stay home for now, but you know what it means?"

"What?"

"Big party at the crypts when you finally get to board with us. It'll be Halloween, so it's double the chance to celebrate. Good excuse, right? You know the girls will be all over you; might improve your mood." He gave me a smug grin. "Now, are you going to tell me why you dragged me here?"

"I thought you'd never ask." Turning my head towards the glass doors that were currently open, thanks to the unseasonably warm late-September weather, my gaze scanned the bar area. "I have it on good authority that there's a new waitress here. Big tits, long dark hair, long legs, just how I like them."

"You want my seal of approval?"

"Something like that, yeah."

He nodded. "I'm on it."

2

Elena

I didn't recognise the girl staring at me in the mirror. Had I ever looked like this? My long, dark brown hair fell down my back in a glossy, sleek waterfall. Subtle make-up made my golden-brown eyes look huge and my lips look full and pouty. My tailored uniform fit me like a glove—and I'd never understood that saying until now. Fuck, even my underwear was perfectly fitted, so silky and so soft that I barely noticed I was wearing any.

I smoothed the lapels of my blazer down—navy with blue piping—and then traced a finger over the school crest. *Hatherley Hall.* This was going to be a big departure from my previous school, where uniform policy was…lax…let's say, and the combined wealth of the students probably equated to about two of my new classmates'.

Rich people could suck my metaphorical dick. Starting with Knox Ashcroft, the stuck-up, arrogant knob that strutted around this monstrosity of a house like he owned the place. Just like his dad. Like father, like son. I knew the type—a typical spoiled rich kid, thinking they were better than everyone else. I'd admit, I was basing my knowledge on reality TV, but so far, he was ticking every box. The way his gaze had passed over me like I wasn't even worthy of his attention, like I was nothing to him. If anything, he wasn't worthy of mine.

But his mum—Maria, as she'd insisted we call her—she'd actually made an effort. Taken me shopping to be fitted for these new clothes. Given me a phone and told me that I didn't have to worry about data limits. Said I could decorate the tiny room next to my mum's bedroom however I wanted—I just needed to tell her, and she'd order paint in any colour.

It was almost enough to make me feel guilty about what we were here to do.

Almost.

But not quite.

Gripping the waistband of my demure navy, black, and royal blue tartan skirt, I rolled it up, exposing more of my legs, and then added a sweep of eyeliner around each of my eyes. Stepping into my chunky heels, I blew my reflection a kiss before scooping up my new buttery-soft tan leather backpack and heading out of my bedroom.

It was time to go to battle, and I had my war paint on.

In the hallway of the main house, I glanced at my phone exactly once. Maria had told me that Knox hated to be late, so I was expecting him at any second.

He didn't disappoint. There was a creak on the uppermost stair, and then he descended the staircase like a fairy-tale prince turned villain. Beautiful, with an edge so sharp that you knew it would cut you if you got too close. Dark, thick hair. Deep, brown eyes. Angular jaw. A sinful mouth, soft-looking lips with a cruel twist to them. Tall and built, his body flexed and released as he moved, powerful and coiled like a jungle cat, ready to strike at any moment.

For a second, I was intimidated, but I straightened my

Cruel Crypts

shoulders and reminded myself that just because his parents had money, that didn't make him any better than me.

Far from it, in fact. His family would pay for what they'd done. My mum had her part under control. As for me? Now I was at school with him, I was ready to take advantage of every opportunity I could.

When Knox reached the bottom of the stairs, he suddenly seemed to notice me. His eyes widened for an instant, but then his mask dropped back into place, and he was the instantly cool, unruffled eighteen-year-old I'd met two days ago.

"Here's how it's going to work." His voice was smooth and deep, honey combined with rich, dark chocolate but with a vicious bite of venom that he made no effort to hide. "I drive you to school. I'll stop at the gate that leads to the fields. You'll get out, and you'll walk the rest of the way."

I had no idea what or where the fields were, but I'd already gathered that he didn't want to be seen with me, so it didn't take much to deduce that they weren't close to the school.

"Sounds lovely." I gave him a false smile to match his own, and we headed outside into the dull grey morning to his poser car—some black SUV. And when I say it was black, I meant that everything was black. Wheels, trim, back windows...all of it.

"Knox?" I injected as much sweetness as I could into my voice once we were both seated in the black-on-black interior. "Is your favourite colour black? Your car reminds me of a hearse."

His shoulders stiffened, and I had a moment of satisfaction before he shrugged it off, leaning casually back in his seat with one hand on the wheel and the other on the gearstick. He ignored my comment as he started the engine, the muscles in his arms flexing as he reversed out of the parking space, onto the driveway, and then finally, onto the open road.

The deathly silence between us was broken by the sound of the radio, some obnoxious song with a guy rapping about how rich he was. Knox was tapping his long fingers on the steering wheel, and I rolled my eyes.

It wasn't long before I felt the car come to a stop at the side of the road. Glancing out of the window, I saw that we were next to a field, edged with limestone dry-stone walls. In the distance, up ahead, framed by ominous grey clouds, I could see a huge Cotswold stone building. A sandy, golden colour, it was almost castle-like in appearance, the walls studded with large, lead-paned windows, with ivy curling around the bricks. There was a scattering of smaller outbuildings on its fringes. A huge, sweeping driveway bordered by trees led to the road, where a high stone wall and tall iron gates marked the entrance to the property.

It somehow managed to look both beautiful and foreboding at the same time.

So this was Hatherley Hall. I guessed that we'd stopped at the school boundary.

"Out." Knox growled the word, low and threatening.

"Should I mention to your mum that you didn't take me all the way to school?" As I glanced over at him, his eyes flashed with anger, and his grip tightened on the steering wheel.

"You wouldn't fucking dare."

"Fuck you. I'll do whatever I want."

His hand came flying out, gripping my school tie, and yanking it, hard. I fell, sprawling over the seats, one hand flying to the console, the other landing on the hard muscles of his thigh. His face was so close to mine I could feel his hot breaths on my skin. "Listen to me, because I'll only say this once. I'm one of the elite. One of the three fucking gods of Hatherley Hall. That means I'm in charge. I can make or break you in this fucking school, so don't even think about stepping out of line. And if you go telling tales to either one of my parents or any of my family members, your life will become very, very difficult."

When I remained silent, he yanked on my tie, and I reflexively curled my nails into his leg, then dug them in, my own warning. He could try to intimidate me, but he wasn't going to get the better of me.

His hand closed over mine, ripping it away from his thigh as he growled at me. "Do I make myself clear? You don't want to make an enemy out of me."

"Crystal," I ground out through clenched teeth. "But you don't want to make an enemy out of me either."

"Too fucking late. Now, get the fuck out of my car and stay out of my way in school." He released his grip on my tie, and I wasted no time in sweeping my bag from the footwell. Almost as soon as I touched the door handle, the rain started.

"Out," he repeated, gunning the engine.

I got out.

He shot off without a backwards glance.

As I picked my way across the school fields, the rain fell harder. Passing a building that looked like a boat shed, next to a small, pretty lake, I stopped for a second's breather. I ducked into the overhanging shelter above the doorway, but it was too late to save me from the rain. With a sigh, I moved on. By the time I reached the main entrance, I was soaked through, my previously glossy hair plastered to my head, and after a surreptitious glance in the selfie camera of my new phone, I saw that my mascara had also smeared around my eyes.

Drowned rat chic was so 2022. My new look wasn't going to do me any favours here, but I'd have to do what I did best and brazen it out. My previous school had taught me enough tricks, after all. If the sharks smelled blood in the water, they'd bite, and I was going to do my best to avoid that happening.

I walked into the grand school entrance, where I'd been told to go on my first day. Glancing around me, I saw a sign for the visitor loos and quickly made my way inside, my shoes echoing on the Cotswold stone tiles. My tights were soaked through, so I pulled them off and then used toilet paper to blot the insides of my shoes dry. I didn't have a spare pair, but I had my brand-new PE kit in my bag, so I pulled on the white socks, thankful that the waterproofing of the leather bag had been enough to keep the contents dry. Wiping under my eyes, I repaired the damage to my make-up as best I could before sweeping my wet hair into a ponytail.

It would have to do.

When I made my way back into the foyer, the school receptionist glanced up at me, one eyebrow raised. After a moment's silence, she tutted, coming out from behind the desk and directing me towards a cluster of chairs. When I was seated, she handed me a stack of brochures and papers in a folder. "Sit here for a moment, please, while I get Professor Donnelly."

She disappeared, and I began shuffling through the papers, just for something to do while I waited. I didn't have to wait long—a few minutes later, she was back with a tall, dark-haired man in tow, who introduced himself as Professor Donnelly, head of Epicurus house. "It's good to have you here at Hatherley Hall, Ms. Greenwood. Now,

I've spoken to the school administrators, and it looks like the curriculum you've been following is more or less the same as the subjects you'll be studying here. You may have to do some catch-up work, but your individual teachers will advise you of what needs to be done." He went through a whole list of school rules and things I should be aware of, but most of it went over my head.

He came to a halt mid-sentence, his attention diverted. I followed his gaze as he greeted two new arrivals—a boy and a girl who looked to be around my age. The boy had floppy mid-brown hair and an open, friendly smile on his face, and the girl was blonde and beautiful, her pale hair pulled back into a ponytail. When she saw me watching her, she gave me a bright smile, which I returned.

"Elena, meet Katy Peterson and William Fitzgerald-Jones, two of our prefects. Between the two of them, they're taking all the same A-level classes as you, and they'll be taking you under their wing while you get settled in here."

I climbed to my feet, exchanging greetings. Prof. Donnelly drifted away to talk with the receptionist, and I picked up my backpack, tucking the folder inside. As soon as we left the foyer, Katy tucked her arm through mine and began chattering away while William told me to call him Will and began pointing out the various parts of the school as we passed them. I learned that the school had a mix of day and boarding pupils, although the boarding pupils far outnumbered the day pupils, and both of them lived on-site during term time.

After ascending a set of wide stone stairs, our footsteps echoing through the stairwell, we reached the common room of the house I'd been placed in.

Before I could enter, Katy tugged me to a stop. She covered her mouth with her hand, speaking in a low voice.

"You need to know something before you go in there. This school is ruled by the elite…and there are three guys who are top of their hierarchy. Or, as some people refer to them, the three gods." She rolled her eyes. "Just because they all have influential families, and they're supposedly the best-looking guys at Hatherley Hall, they've been named as gods for the past few summer balls. They wish they were gods. First up, we have our head boy, Tristan Smith-Chamberlain, and then there are his two friends, Roman Cavendish and Knox Ashcroft. They're all in Epi—that's our nickname for Epicurus house. Did I mention the houses?" When I shook my head, she glanced up at the sign above the doorway, and I followed her gaze to see "Epicurus" etched into the stone in large letters.

"Oh, yeah. Epicurus, though? What does that mean?"

She gave me a small smile. "We have four houses here, all named after ancient Greek philosophers." Holding up her hand, she began to tick them off one by one, using her fingers. "Aristotle, Democritus, Socrates, and Epicurus—otherwise known as Aris, Demo, Soc, and Epi." Before I could reply, she continued. "Tristan's the head of our house as well as head boy. He's okay on his own… occasionally, but when you put him with Roman and Knox, they turn into typical rich, obnoxious, spoiled boys. Knox is probably the worst of the three, but honestly, I'd avoid all of them if you can. I'm just warning you now because you seem nice, too nice to be corrupted by them. My advice is—stay under their radar."

I sighed. "That's going to be difficult, because I'm living in Knox's house."

Both Katy and Will stared at me, open-mouthed, so I elaborated. "My mum is the new nanny for Knox's little sister. It's a live-in position."

They gaped at me for a little while longer before Will

nudged Katy. She cleared her throat, shooting me a sympathetic look. "Wow. That sucks."

Yeah, it did, but I'd put up with it as long as necessary for my mum's sake. "I know, but there's not a lot I can do about it. Knox has already made it clear what he thinks of me, so don't worry, I intend to stay as far away from him as possible."

Katy gave me a reassuring smile. "I'll be right here with you. I don't like to be on their radar either, believe me. Anyway, Knox is boarding here now, so at least you don't have to see him outside of school."

"Um. His parents kind of made him move home for a bit so he could take me to and from school and help me settle in."

Eventually, after throwing some sideways glances at Will, Katy shook her head. "I hate to say it, but you're the F-word. Um...*fucked*. That's not going to go down well with Knox."

"Believe me, I know. He's made it clear how much he dislikes our current arrangement. But I'm not going to let him ruin things for me." I straightened my shoulders. "Let's do this."

The moment I entered the Epi common room, I saw them.

The three members of the elite were sprawled over the sofas, surrounded by their loyal subjects. Girls were draped across them, and one was even fellating a banana right in Knox's face in a desperate bid for his attention.

I studied the so-called "gods." Knox was seated to the left, but my gaze passed over him to his two friends. Tristan appeared to be the tallest of the three, from what I could tell, with golden-blond, tousled hair and electric blue eyes fringed with golden-brown lashes. Then there was Roman, with jet-black hair and deep blue eyes. Objectively, all three of them were beautiful, and yes, almost godlike, as much as I hated to say so—each with stunning, chiselled features, tall, muscled bodies, and sun-kissed skin. It was easy to see why they were so popular, based on their exterior beauty. But if Tristan and Roman were anything like Knox, their interior didn't match with their exterior.

When a hush stole over the room as people began to notice the new face in their midst, heads raised. Three heads, to be precise, with identical, cold expressions as they caught my perusal.

But I ignored Roman and Tristan, meeting Knox's icy gaze. His eyes dared me to start something so he could justifiably take me down in front of everyone.

Too bad for him, I knew how to bide my time.

My lips curved into a mocking smile.

Knox Ashcroft might think he was a god, but once I was through with him, he'd be worth less than nothing.

3

KNOX

That fucking smile. This girl needed to learn her place, and fast. I'd thought I'd made it crystal clear to her this morning before school, but it appeared not.

When she did nothing but continue to smile, I relaxed incrementally, my gaze sweeping over her. When I'd seen her this morning, she'd taken me by surprise, not that I'd shown it. She'd looked…like she could fit in here. But I'd seen her before my mother had worked her magic, and I knew what she really was. The daughter of one of the staff, who was happy to take whatever handouts my mother deemed worthy, someone else to take advantage of my family's generosity.

Now, with the downpour having stripped away some of her veneer, she looked more like I'd remembered. Except…were her eyes always that fucking big? And were her lips that pouty before?

Whatever, who gave a shit? She was beneath my attention, despite the fact that I had to drive her to and from school. And speaking of…

I tugged my phone from my pocket, dislodging Freya from my thigh. She made a sound of protest, and I smirked, leaning forwards and taking a bite from the banana she'd been suggestively eating. The ways that some of the girls at this school threw themselves at me and my friends were getting old, and truthfully, I was over it. I was bored.

I'd tried setting my sights elsewhere lately, but so far, nothing. I hadn't even managed to get anywhere with the waitress at the country club. She'd been more interested in hitting me up for information about my dad. Another social-climbing leech. She was wasting her time—my dad was completely committed to my mother.

Back to the task at hand. I opened up my messages and started up a new one. My mother had forced me to add Elena's new contact number to my phone, and for the first time, I was actually glad because I could avoid speaking to her in person.

ME:

> Don't even look at me and definitely don't fucking smile at me. I have lacrosse practice after school so you can find your own way home

I watched out of the corner of my eye as she pulled her phone from her bag, her eyes narrowing as she read the message. The stupid smile was finally wiped from her lips. I waited for her to reply, but she just shoved her phone back in her bag.

What the fuck?

Before I knew it, I was up and out of my seat and crossing the room towards her as she stood there, arms folded across her chest and a taunting gleam in her eye.

Wait a minute. This was her plan, wasn't it? I'd told her

not to speak to me when we were in school, but she was trying to manipulate *me* into speaking to *her*.

I was almost impressed.

Instead of going up to her, I walked right past her, out of the doors of the common room, down the stone stairs and out into the grounds, uncaring that the rain was falling. Outside, I leaned against the wall, scrubbing my hand across my face and kicking at the golden gravel underneath my shoe. Why was she getting under my skin this way?

The bell rang, reminding me that the school day was starting, but I waited a minute longer before going back inside, regulating my breathing until I had myself under control again.

When I returned, Elena was gone, as were most of the rest of the students, so I grabbed my bag and made my way to the cavernous hall where our house assembly was due to take place. My shoes echoed on the worn flagstones as I made my way up the centre aisle to where Roman had saved me a seat. Prof. Donnelly, our head of house, did nothing but raise a brow at me from behind the lectern, but Roman gave me a scrutinising look as I dropped into the pew next to him.

"Problem, Knox?"

"Nothing I can't handle," I clipped out. I'd told him about the girl after I'd spoken to Tristan at the country club, but I'd downplayed it. They didn't need to know how she was already getting under my skin. As far as they were concerned, she was beneath the attention of us all. The only thing they were pissed off about was the fact that my parents were forcing me to put our plans on hold for the next four weeks. And that was something we could all agree on.

"What the fuck do you think you're playing at? The ball goes into the net."

"No shit, really? Is that what's supposed to happen?" I turned on Roman, throwing my stick to the grass. "Any other helpful tips you wanna give me, or can we get back to practice?"

He shoved at me but was stopped by the coach, Mr. Saunders, aka Saunders, blowing his whistle loudly.

"Enough! You're a team, and you will play like a team, or I will have every single one of you doing suicides until you drop!"

There was something in the air today. We were all on edge, and I didn't fucking like it. Maybe it was the fact that we had an away game against Beaufort on Friday, who were top of the schools' league, and we needed the win. Maybe there was just something in the air that none of us could explain.

As one of our three attackers, my accuracy skills were expected to be exemplary, and today, they weren't. I couldn't fucking believe I'd missed the goal from my position—a shot I'd made a hundred times before and could do with my eyes closed.

Saunders ordered us to take our positions again, and I got into position behind Tristan, midfielder and our captain, ready to catch the ball to take a shot. I'd barely lifted my stick when he was blowing the whistle again. "Bellingham!" he roared, the veins bulging in his neck. "You're a defender—fucking act like it!"

Lincoln Bellingham climbed to his feet, brushing grass from his knees. "Sorry, sir," he said, grimacing at Saunders. I noticed Roman glaring at him, and I nudged him with my elbow.

"Not just me who's off my game today, huh? Link's fucking up too."

"You're a fucking liability," he hissed, spinning away from me and stalking off, leaving me staring after him.

Fuck. What was going on with everyone today?

After the torturous practice finally ended, I ripped off my helmet and gloves, stalking into the changing rooms to shower the mud and sweat from my skin. As I headed back outside, I was stopped by Saunders before I could escape to the student car park.

"Ashcroft. Got a minute?"

"Yep." It wasn't like I could give him another answer.

He folded his arms across his chest. "Your playing isn't up to standard. You're better than this. I want you to stay behind after school every day this week. We'll work on your catches and bounce shots. I want you game ready for Friday."

"Fine." When he didn't reply, I assumed the conversation was over and walked away.

The second I reached the car park and saw the figure leaning against the passenger door of my SUV, my jaw clenched. I stalked over to my Maserati and came to a stop right in front of Elena, so close that the edges of her blazer brushed against mine.

"What the fuck are you doing here?"

She didn't reply, just stared at me coolly.

"I thought I told you that you needed to find your own way home."

"You told me that you have lacrosse practice, so I'd need to find my own way home. I decided to wait for you." Her voice was sweet poison as she widened her eyes innocently. "Don't think I missed you calling it 'home.' You think of it as my home too?"

My nostrils flared, and before I knew what I was doing,

I was pressing her up against my car with my hand wrapped around her throat. Her pulse beat rapidly against my fingers, and it was fucking mesmerising. I found myself lowering my head to her ear, her pulse stuttering under my fingertips. My nose brushed against her soft skin, and my own pulse stuttered. What the fuck?

"Don't fucking test me," I ground out, releasing my grip on her. She gasped before bringing up her knee in a lightning-quick movement. Too bad for her, my reflexes were honed from years of training, and I easily countered her move, pinning her again and rendering her immobile. Lowering my face to hers again and doing my level best to ignore the feel of her soft curves against me, I spoke in a low, savage rasp. "I said. Don't. Fucking. Test. Me."

Her expression twisted into pure hate, and I drank it in.

Elena Greenwood would learn her place, even if I had to break her to do it.

4

Elena

Wrapping the towel more tightly around my body, I gripped the doorknob and opened the bathroom door, letting a cloud of steam escape. The accommodation we'd been provided with consisted of three rooms and a bathroom, all opening into a central hallway. The first room had sofas, a TV, a bookcase stuffed with books, and a small kitchenette with a microwave, fridge, and sink. Across the hallway was my mum's bedroom and the bathroom. My room was opposite the bathroom. We were on the ground floor of the house, and my sash window looked out onto a corner of the driveway. Not the most exciting view, but this beat our last residence by a million miles. That place…we were lucky to get out of that drug-infested hellhole. Not that we would have been there in the first place, if it wasn't for—

"Elena."

My mum's voice stopped my thoughts in their tracks. I turned to face her. "Mum, hi." I hadn't actually seen her since I'd come back from school—she'd taken Josephine out somewhere, and then she'd fed her and gone through her bedtime routine with Maria, while I'd shut myself in my room and made a start on the piles of homework I'd already been given.

"How was your first day?" She scanned my face, concern in her eyes. "Did anyone give you any trouble?"

I shook my head. "No. There were the entitled rich kids that we knew would be there, but there were one or two that seemed nice. I made two new friends."

"I'm glad." Moving closer, she patted my arm. "I'm sorry you have to deal with the rich kids, but it'll all be worth it in the end."

"I know it will be." My voice hardened as I thought of the way Knox had acted around me earlier. What an absolute arrogant wanker.

"Did you find out any information on the younger Ashcroft?" By "the younger Ashcroft," she meant Knox, because he was the one I had to get up close and personal with. I'd never met their older sister as she didn't even live here—I believe she was attending university somewhere, and obviously, his little sister didn't count.

"Not yet, but I will."

She nodded. "Good. Now, get some sleep." Turning into her bedroom, she closed the door.

Back in my own room, I pulled on a comfy old pair of joggers and hoodie, twisting my damp hair up into a bun on top of my head. After shoving my feet into my flip-flops, I exited the bedroom and made my way down the hallway and through the quiet house.

Maria had told me, in a polite way, that my own clothes were only fit for burning, but now I had them on, I felt more comfortable than I had done all day. Those new clothes she'd provided me with—they were nice, but they weren't me.

Heading into the cavernous kitchen, I faltered. Knox

was sitting at the white marble island, his phone in one hand and a sandwich in the other. As soon as he saw me, he placed his phone and sandwich down, slowly and deliberately, his gaze boring into me the entire time. The kitchen was dim, the only lighting coming from the downlights underneath the cupboards, but it was easy enough to see his expression.

It was completely blank.

Two could play that game. After my sudden stop, I carried on as if he wasn't even in the room, making a beeline for the fridge. Maria had said that I could help myself to food—meals were included as part of my mum's employment package, and I would be doing a little light cleaning in return for mine. The Ashcrofts already had a cleaner—or cleaning crew, probably, but my mum had volunteered me to do this, and they'd agreed.

I'd just closed my fingers around the handle of the fridge when my hand was yanked away.

"Nothing in there belongs to you." Knox's voice was close to my ear, and the heat of his body was all up against my back. "Remember your place."

I spun around, and now my chest was trapped against his, all hard, unyielding muscles. I craned my head back to look up at him, speaking through gritted teeth. "If you've got a problem, take it up with your parents. They agreed that I'd be doing some cleaning in return for my room and board. In fact, they told me I could stay for free, but my mum insisted. We're not freeloaders, despite what you might think of us."

A cold smile curved across his lips. "Is that so? Then earn your fucking place." Tugging the fridge open so hard that I had to jump out of the way in order not to brain myself on the heavy stainless-steel door, he pulled a container out and upended it all over the floor at my feet.

Leftover pomegranate chicken splattered across the tiles, a bright red stain on the shiny white flooring.

"Earn it," he ground out, then slammed the fridge door and stalked out of the kitchen. I was torn between anger and disbelief—he actually just did that? I'd never hated anyone as much as I hated him at that point.

Not even his dad.

Thirty minutes later, the last of the pomegranate seeds had been swept up, and I'd reversed the damage. The floor was spotless once again, the Tupperware was soaking in the sink before going in the dishwasher, and the cleaning products had been stowed away. I took Knox's former seat at the kitchen island, biting into his abandoned sandwich.

I'd just finished up the last of it, brushing the crumbs from my hoodie, when a shadow darkened the doorway again.

Knox was back.

He stalked into the kitchen, his eyes darkening with anger. "Where's my food?"

Sliding off the stool, I reached for the empty plate, but he grabbed my wrist roughly, spinning me to face him.

"Where's. My. Fucking. Food?"

He was so close, his chest rising and falling against mine as he snarled down at me with undisguised animosity. At that moment, I'd never felt more like prey cornered by a predator. But I was no meek little mouse, and his first mistake was to underestimate me. I may have been no match for him physically, but I wasn't going to stand there and take whatever he wanted to dish out.

I thrust out my hand and gripped a handful of what was hopefully part of his dick and/or balls through his joggers. "Let go of me, right now," I hissed. "I cleaned up the mess you made, but you don't get to push me around."

His breath came in harsh pants as he lowered his head,

his lips almost touching mine. "Get your fucking filthy hand off my junk, *now*."

I tightened my grip, my long nails digging into his sensitive parts—I hoped—and he cursed loudly. In a lightning-fast move, he curved his free hand around my throat and squeezed. An involuntary choked whimper tore from me, and I felt him smile.

"Yeah. I thought so."

He loosened his grip as I loosened mine, and to my horror, I felt his previously soft dick hardening under my palm. *What the fuck?* I yanked my hand away as if I'd been burned, my eyes flying up to his. Shock and horror flared in his gaze for a second before he released his grip on me completely, pushing away.

We were both breathing hard, and I was…I couldn't… my mind…

My eyes flicked down to where I'd been gripping him, and there was no mistaking the large bulge there. My cheeks heated, and I took an unsteady breath. When I returned my gaze to his, I expected to find him regarding me with disgust or some other similar emotion, but instead, he looked almost as disconcerted as I felt.

Good.

"Get out." His voice was a low rasp. "Get out of my sight."

I needed no prompting. Spinning on my heel, I left, leaving him standing there frozen in place.

5

KNOX

"You look like you could use a drink."

I slumped back on the sofa in the crypts, accepting the chilled beer that Tristan handed to me. "Yeah, but it's gonna take more than a drink to improve my mood."

He sank down next to me, clinking his own beer against mine. "Cheers."

Thanks to my parents and my temporary change of accommodation, I'd come to the crypts during our lunch break to pick up some shit that I needed. Surprisingly, Tristan had come with me and, even more surprisingly, had offered me one of the contraband beers we'd stocked down here in the mini fridge. Day drinking when we had afternoon lessons, and I had my one-on-one lacrosse practice with Saunders after that—it wasn't the best idea we'd ever had, but he seemed to sense I needed it.

"Do you have a plan?" Placing his bottle down, he turned to me.

I glanced at the archway through which the stone stairs that led back up to the school cellars were just visible, the low, simmering anger in my belly getting hotter at the thought that I'd be away from all this for the foreseeable future. The crypts were supposed to be my domain. My secret place. And now, instead of being here, partying and living my best life in my final year at Hatherley Hall, I had to stay at home and play nice with the fucking help.

The room we were in now was the biggest in this underground haven. I'd stumbled upon it way back in the third year of my time here, when I'd managed to sneak into the abandoned cellars, deep below the school. I hadn't even been looking for anything in particular, but I'd always been drawn to dark, underground places, and I'd wanted to explore. In the very back corner of a tiny unused storeroom, covered in a thick layer of dust and cobwebs, I'd found a door, hidden behind some shelves. It led to a set of stone steps, descending into the crypts.

The crypts themselves were the remains of a much, much older building. Built from solid, ancient stone, with arched ceilings and shadowy corners, they were a haven for spiders and other creepy-crawlies. The steps into the crypts led to a small room that we sometimes used as a kind of waiting area. Beyond that was an archway leading into the room we were in now—the largest of those down here. On the far side of this room was another archway, leading to a small room containing a number of tombstones. I fucking loved the aesthetics. Still, the room was rarely used, except when I passed through on the way to my private area. Behind a locked door, I had a bedroom. There were no windows, and the space wasn't much bigger than the bed I'd installed there, but it was all mine. No one had ever been allowed in there before and never would. It wasn't somewhere I officially slept, but I'd crashed in it occasionally, and I'd planned to make it my home away from home this year, even though I'd officially be moving into the dorms.

Of course, my plans had been fucking derailed. The fact that it was temporary was the only thing that kept me from losing my cool.

I gritted my teeth, forcing myself to remain calm as my gaze swept over the space in front of me. Across from the sofa I was currently reclining on was another door that led down another set of stairs, and down there...well, aside from yet more tombstones and spiders, there was a place that belonged to me, Roman, and Tristan. While I'd discovered the crypts, and while it was my sanctuary, in reality, this place was theirs as much as mine. They'd helped me to break into the school during one of the holidays to clear out the space. We'd furnished it together, and we'd rigged it up with electrics and our Cerberus security system that stopped unwanted people from getting in. Even though there was a risk of being caught and expelled, they'd never once faltered, tirelessly helping me out. We were the gods of Hatherley Hall, and we had each other's backs. Always would.

"Knox? Did you hear me? I said, do you have a plan?"

Shaking myself out of my memories, I shrugged. "I'm going to talk to my dad. But there's something about the nanny and that girl...something I don't trust. Maybe it's better that I'm there to keep an eye on things. You know my parents aren't home much."

"Why do you keep calling her 'that girl'?" Tristan smirked at me. "She has a name. And if you look at her objectively, she's fucking hot." He paused. "Not that it makes up for the fact that she's the hired help, I guess."

Why *did* I keep refusing to call her by her name? It made things more impersonal. Made it easier to treat her with the contempt she deserved. Last night in the kitchen had been—

Fuck. I shook my head. "We all know your taste in girls is questionable, Tris. Maybe you wanna get your eyes checked out."

Laughing, he elbowed me in the side. "I could say the same for you."

"Fuck off." Downing the rest of my beer, I placed the empty bottle on the table and then climbed to my feet. "I'm gonna get the stuff I need from my room. Wait for me?"

"Only if you bring me some condoms. I'm out."

"You should try keeping your dick in your trousers sometime. You're going to run out of girls." I headed to my room, hearing him call, "Where's the fun in that?" behind me.

I grabbed a few of the textbooks I needed, shoving them into my bag, then rummaged in my bedside drawer for the box of Magnums I kept in there.

Back in the main crypt, I threw a strip of Magnums at him. "Bet those don't even last you a week." Laughing, I twisted out of reach of his fist and tucked another strip into my bag. Last night had proved to me that my dick needed some action. As soon as fucking possible.

Walking into my afternoon business studies class with Tristan and Chelsea, a gorgeous but annoyingly whiny girl who I unfortunately had to put up with because of her status as one of the elite—her parents were influential in this town, and I had to play nice—I was met by the sight of Elena Greenwood sitting very fucking close to William Fitzgerald-Jones. They were deep in discussion, their heads bent together as they studied a piece of paper on the desk in front of them. I didn't even think—just headed straight over to the desk and swiped the paper from underneath their noses.

"Give that back!" Elena jumped to her feet, reaching for the paper, but I held it out of her reach easily. William may have been a prefect, but he was a meek, mild-mannered guy, and he knew his place. The only way I could tell he was pissed off was the way he sat back with his arms folded across his chest, his mouth set in a flat line. He wouldn't dare to cross one of the elite, and so I dismissed him. Elena was the one I wanted to piss off, anyway.

"What's this?" I scanned the paper, taking in the lines and notes scattered across it. "Music? Did you miss the part where this is a business studies class?"

"I know. Give it back." Her eyes shot daggers at me. I let the paper fall to the floor, then stepped on it like the dick I was, leaving an imprint of my shoe.

Tristan and Chelsea had witnessed the whole thing, and Chelsea smirked at me but didn't say anything. Tristan looked amused for the most part, although there was a hint of a question in his eyes, and I knew it was one I wouldn't be able to answer. I fucking hated how easily this girl was getting under my skin.

Today, her hair was back to being shiny and straight, framing her heart-shaped face. She'd taken her blazer off, even though we were supposed to keep them on at all times unless it was an exceptionally hot day, and her high tits strained against the fabric of her shirt. Her lips were all pouty and glossy, and her eyes looked huge and luminous.

Fuck. No. Those were things I shouldn't be noticing about her. Ever.

William swiped the paper from the floor, muttering to

himself, but I paid him no attention. Not until he leaned into Elena, placing his hand on her arm and whispering in her ear. My lip curled, and I took a step forwards. He fucking dared to touch—

"Everyone, please take your seats." The voice of Professor Fletcher, our business studies teacher, sounded from behind me, and there was a mad scramble as everyone moved into their places. I took my usual seat at the back of the classroom, kicking my feet out in front of me and leaning back in my chair, the legs scraping on the worn flagstones. My gaze scanned the classroom, purposely avoiding a certain dark-haired girl. Until…what the fuck?

"What the fuck is Chelsea doing?" I hissed to Tristan, watching as she slid into the empty seat on Elena's other side instead of sitting with us as usual. Now Elena was sandwiched between her and William.

He glanced at me with a shrug, the corners of his lips kicking up in amusement. "Fuck knows. Making friends?"

He thought this was funny? Fuck him.

When Chelsea shot me a sly smile, it suddenly became clear. This was payback. I'd turned her down last week, and she thought this would get to me. Rolling my eyes, I shook my head, watching her smile fall.

Then, I spent the rest of the class glaring at the back of Elena's head, and when it ended, I couldn't even say what we'd been studying.

6

Elena

"Seventy-five. That's my final offer."

"It's worth way more than that, and you know it. It hasn't even been used." I narrowed my eyes at the scruffy-looking bearded man, and he grinned, showing me his missing teeth.

"Beggars can't be choosers."

"Two hundred." I held his gaze, keeping my voice firm. "Otherwise, I'll take it elsewhere."

A glimmer of respect came into his eyes. "A hundred and fifty, cash, and you've got a deal."

"Done." We shook on it and made the exchange. I ignored the twinge of guilt that came from selling the Balenciaga bag that Maria Ashcroft had purchased for me. The money was more important. Even though the bag was worth far more than what I'd just got for it, the money would still go a long way.

The man disappeared, and I let my shoulders slump in relief. I knew it was risky and stupid to meet someone I didn't know, especially alone. But a friend of a friend from back home had put me in contact with him, said he'd pay in cash for items, and so far, so good.

I was so absorbed in shoving the cash right into the bottom of my bag, concealing it in an unobtrusive fabric pouch underneath my make-up and deodorant, that I completely missed the large black Lamborghini Urus idling at the kerb. It was only when a throat cleared behind me that I spun around, my eyes shooting between Knox Ashcroft, who was standing right in my personal space with a hard look on his face, and his dad, Anthony Ashcroft, sitting behind the wheel of the Lambo. He was wearing mirrored aviator sunglasses, so I couldn't see the expression on his face, but his mouth was set in a flat line.

Fuck.

"What are you doing in this part of town, Elena?"

It was the first time that Knox had said my name to me, and it slid off his tongue in a way I *really* shouldn't have found hot. Lucky for me, and for him, I wasn't a slave to my baser urges, and it was easy enough to remember what an asshole he was when he was staring at me suspiciously with that ever-present air of arrogance surrounding him.

Lowering the hood of my hoodie and brushing my hair out of my face, I played dumb, widening my eyes innocently. "I borrowed a bike from the sheds around the back of your house, and I somehow managed to get lost." Waving my phone at him, I added, "I was just about to check the map to see where I was."

He stepped closer, all dark and brooding as he folded his arms across his chest, the toe of his shoe prodding at a broken bottle resting on the pavement next to an empty crisp packet. "I don't believe you."

"Well, that's your problem, not mine. What are you doing in this part of town if it's so repulsive to you?"

"Not that it's any of your business, but this is a shortcut to the house from my dad's office. Stop deflecting. What are you doing here?"

"Knox! Bring the bike! You, get in the car!" Anthony had clearly had enough of waiting around, and he snapped his fingers at me as if I were a trained dog waiting to do his bidding. No wonder Knox was such an arrogant dickhead with a dad like that.

I slid into the car, and after much shuffling around, Knox managed to get my bike situated. He climbed into the front and glanced across at his dad, communicating without a word. I was struck by how alike they looked in profile.

"Miss Greenwood."

My gaze shot to the rear-view mirror, where Anthony Ashcroft was watching me, his eyes still hidden behind his sunglasses. There was something in his tone that had me swallowing hard, trying to compose myself. He couldn't have known what I was really doing out there, surely.

His lips curved into a smirk as he manoeuvred the car back onto the road. "May I call you Elena?"

"Of course," I managed.

"Good. You may call me Anthony if you wish." He ignored the sound of protest that Knox made, which made me smile, albeit unwillingly. "We haven't had a chance to get to know each other yet, and I think it's time we rectified that, don't you?"

Remaining silent seemed like my best bet, and he carried on speaking, hardly appearing to notice that I hadn't answered him. "Maria has the charity dinner tonight. We'll go to the club."

"Dad, they're not going to let her in looking like that. There's a dress code," Knox hissed, his lips curling in distaste, probably at the thought of being seen anywhere in public with me.

He hummed thoughtfully as he eyed me through the mirror. "Perhaps not in ordinary circumstances, but she'll be with us. I'll call now." Pressing a button on the dashboard console, he had a short conversation through the tiny headset that I hadn't noticed he was wearing, and around fifteen minutes later, we were turning off the road and passing a large sign that said Nottswood Golf & Country Club in silver metallic lettering. We stopped in a parking area outside a pretty Cotswold stone manor house-style building, and as we exited the car, Anthony cleared his throat, tilting his head towards me while looking expectantly at Knox. Now he'd removed his sunglasses, I could see his eyes were the same shade of brown as Knox's, and there was amusement in them as he took in the hard set of Knox's jaw.

"Knox," he said softly, and suddenly, there was a warm hand placed at my back. I hid my shock with a cough, or I hoped I did, at least.

Knox pushed me gently forwards as Anthony gave him an approving smile, and again, I had to hide my shock. This was the nicest he'd been to me since the day we'd met. The heat of his palm felt like it was radiating through my body, warming me all over.

When we entered the lobby of the club, Anthony stepped over to the desk, while Knox steered me into a dimly lit corner with two high-backed tan leather armchairs facing each other, a low round table between them. He stopped next to the closest chair and lowered his mouth to my ear.

"Don't think for one second that your presence here is wanted. I'm playing nice with you for my dad's sake, but when this is over, you go back to keeping your distance."

His lips brushed my ear, and I suppressed an unwanted shudder.

"Gladly."

"Good. Oh, and Elena?" His voice lowered into something dark and dangerous. "I don't believe your story about going out for a bike ride. And neither does my dad. So you'd better tread very fucking carefully, and if I find out that you've been up to something, you won't like the consequences."

Fuck this guy. I turned my head, our faces so close together that I could see tiny flecks of gold in his dark irises. His long lashes should have softened his gaze, but the way his eyes were reflecting pure hate at me negated their impact. "I'm bored of your threats, Knox. You really aren't as scary as you seem to think."

He exhaled harshly, making his chest brush against mine. "Don't test me."

Then he was gone, stalking away from me, back to his dad.

With a sigh, I followed them.

7

KNOX

The club restaurant was quiet, and my dad had arranged for us to be seated in one of the booths in the far corner of the space, so at least no one would see Elena. On the pretence of acting gentlemanly, I let her slide into the booth first before seating myself next to her, trapping her in place.

She was fucking up to something. I didn't know what it was, but what she didn't know was that I'd seen the scruffy, bearded guy that was walking away from her. No idea who he was, and I didn't think my dad had even noticed him, but there was something really shifty about him.

"As I mentioned earlier, we haven't had a chance to speak properly yet," my dad was saying to Elena when I tuned back into the conversation. "How are you settling in?"

"Well, thank you," she said, putting on her toothachingly sweet polite voice that set my teeth on edge.

How much did we know about this girl? I knew whatever agency her mum had been hired through would have run a basic background check on them both, checking for any criminal records and so on, as per legal requirements, but had my dad bothered with anything deeper?

He must've done. This was JoJo. The baby of our family and the light of my parents' lives. They wouldn't entrust her care to someone they hadn't vetted thoroughly.

But even as I told myself this, I had a feeling in my gut that I couldn't ignore. There was something about Elena fucking Greenwood. Something I was going to get to the bottom of.

Maybe it was time to get my friends involved.

While my dad was occupied with explaining every fucking dish on the menu to Elena, I pulled out my phone, balancing it on my thigh and angling it so that if Elena looked down, she wouldn't see the screen. I sent off a quick text to Tristan, asking him to keep an eye out for anything suspicious, and then I texted Roman. I knew he had a cousin down on the south coast who was some kind of hacker or computer genius or some shit. Someone who could be useful in digging up any dirt on Elena Greenwood.

ME:

> Hey, Ro. Am I right in thinking your cousin is a hacker?

He didn't take long to respond, which was good because my dad was one of those people who hated anyone using their phones at the table—unless he was the one doing it.

ROMAN:

> Yeah, Weston. Not a hacker or so he says, but he might as well be. Why? What are you up to?

Cruel Crypts

> ME:
> I might need some info on someone

> ROMAN:
> I'll ask him. If he can help it'll cost you

> ME:
> You know money's not an issue

> ROMAN:
> OK I'll send your number to him and he'll contact you if he can help. If so I want all the details

> ME:
> Appreciate it. Too much to explain over text, but it involves the new girl

> ROMAN:
> Say no more. I'm on it

We exchanged a few more messages, and then I slid my phone back into my pocket, my dad and Elena none the wiser. It seemed like they were exhausting their topics of conversation, unsurprisingly. My dad was good with people, but there was only so far you could go when the person you were talking to was giving you mostly monosyllabic answers.

The waitress interrupted the dying conversation to take our orders, blatantly simping over my dad—oh, yeah, she was the same waitress I'd tried my luck with before. My dad barely paid her any attention, but Elena glared at her in open hostility. Wait, what the fuck? Did Elena have a crush on my fucking father?

Anger burned through me, and I acted without caring about the consequences. I slung my arm across Elena's shoulders, ignoring her exclamation of surprise as I pulled her into me. Her body was tense against mine, and it felt like she was holding her breath.

From across the table, the fucker formerly known as my dad was eyeing me with unconcealed amusement, and the second the waitress disappeared, I quickly released Elena, sliding across the booth and away from the heat and soft curves of her body. I narrowed my gaze at him, and he took the hint.

"Looks like we're on track to win the Stratford case," he told me, and I relaxed into my seat. I was hoping to follow in his footsteps after I'd earned my degree, and talking about his work always interested me.

"How many cases is that now? Eleven?"

"Twelve," he corrected me with a proud smile. "If I win this one, which is more or less guaranteed, I'll hold the record. George owes me a case of Scotch."

I laughed. George Smith-Chamberlain, Tristan's uncle, was my dad's partner in their law firm, Ashcroft & Smith-Chamberlain Solicitors LLP. They were both criminal defence solicitors, and my dad held the current record in the firm for getting clients acquitted. He'd been on a winning streak until he'd lost one case a year or so ago, but since then, he'd built up his streak again.

I was so proud of my dad. I just hoped I'd be half as good a lawyer as he was one day.

Next to me, Elena sat stiffly, not even attempting to contribute to the conversation. Zero fucking surprise. She only came to life when the waitress came back, and all she did was glare at the waitress as she flirted with my dad again.

I slid my hand onto her thigh and squeezed in warning. Her hand smacked down to cover mine, and she dug her nails in viciously. *Bitch.* I tightened my grip on her thigh, and she just jabbed her nails into my skin even harder.

Cruel Crypts

Fuck this girl.

I slid my hand higher, which was more difficult than it sounded, thanks to the death grip she had on me, and only when I was almost at the top of her thigh, my fingers resting way too fucking close to the juncture of her thighs, did she rip her hand away.

I left my palm there, waiting to see what she would do. My grip on her leg loosened a little, and I slid my finger up, then down. One second passed…then two…then three. After the third second, I heard her breathe in shakily, and my fucking dick jerked in my jeans.

Fuck.

This game was getting way out of hand.

But I didn't stop. I kept sliding my finger up, then down. She sucked in another shuddering breath, and my dick was totally on board with the soft noises coming from her that she kept trying to stifle. I couldn't fucking stop touching her, and she made no effort to stop me either.

"Knox!"

My head shot up, my eyes widening as I took in my dad across the table, all amusement gone from his gaze. Shit, I'd completely forgotten he was there. And from the look on his face, it wasn't the first time he'd tried to get my attention.

What the fuck was I doing?

As smoothly as I could, I removed my hand from Elena's leg, letting my face default to its usual blank mask. "Sorry. I was miles away. Thinking about our game against Beaufort on Friday. Did I tell you Saunders has me doing extra practice every day this week?"

That was enough to distract my dad as he launched into a recount of his time on the lacrosse team at Hatherley Hall, and I breathed out a sigh of relief. I didn't know what had come over me just now, but I sure as fuck wasn't planning on it happening again.

8

Elena

My sociology class was a welcome respite from Knox's presence and that of the other two members of his little gang. I'd been seated at a table with a beautiful girl named Aria. Petite, with long, jet-black, wavy hair, huge golden-brown eyes, and a rosebud mouth, she looked sweet and almost fragile at first glance, but I'd soon realised that looks could be deceiving.

"A party?" I gave Aria a cautious glance. "Tonight? Are you sure that's a good idea?"

She nodded. "Fuck yeah. I can normally take or leave the elite parties, but you're new here, and it's the quickest way to meet people. Everyone will be there. The first party of the year in the crypts."

"I don't think Knox would be happy to see me there."

Tossing her hair over her shoulder, she smirked at me. "Who gives a shit what he thinks? You have every right to be there. He might have claimed the crypts for himself, but he doesn't actually have ownership of them."

"You're right." A slow smile spread over my lips.

"I always am." Her answering smile disappeared.

"Seriously, though. I know what the three of them can be like, so I understand if you're wary. Want to swap numbers in case you want to talk or anything?"

I nodded. "Yeah. Thanks, that would be great."

She input her details into my phone and then texted herself so she had my number before glancing to her left, her eyes brightening. "Gracelyn! You're coming tonight, aren't you?" She grabbed the arm of a passing girl that I hadn't been introduced to yet, pulling her around to face me. The girl had long red hair and pale, freckled skin, and she gave me a warm smile when she met my gaze. Aria waved a hand between us. "Grace, meet Elena. Elena, this is Gracelyn. Or Grace."

"Hi." I returned her smile. "Nice to meet you."

"You too," she said. Turning to Aria, she grinned. "Of course I'm coming. Samira is too." Raising her hand, she beckoned someone from across the room, and I followed her gaze to see a striking girl with cropped dark hair and flawless brown skin heading towards us, who flashed me a bright smile when she noticed me looking. When she reached us, she hopped up onto the table we were sitting at, tugging Gracelyn between her legs. Gracelyn nodded her head towards the newcomer. "Elena, this is my girlfriend, Samira, or Mira if she likes you. Samira, meet the new girl. This is Elena, Knox's new roommate."

Mira grinned at me. "I know."

They all laughed, and after a moment, I joined them. "I guess news spreads fast here."

Tucking her phone back into her bag, Aria looked between us all. "You're the new girl, so you're already the most interesting person in the school. Living with the Ashcrofts makes you ten times more interesting." She clapped her hands. "Now we're all friends, can we talk about this party? Elena, want to come and get ready with us? We're all roommates, so we'll be getting ready together. I might be able to procure a bottle of vodka for the pre-party celebrations." Her expression darkened. "We'll need it to deal with the three gods and their wannabe goddesses."

"Gods and goddesses?"

She rolled her eyes. "Stupid Hatherley Hall tradition. There's a ball every May with a Greek gods and goddesses theme. People dress up and vote for their favourite gods and goddesses. It's a popularity contest, and it's obvious who'll win each year. The votes are separated by groups. We have the first three school years, who all vote together for three gods and goddesses split across their three year groups. Then there's the GCSE students—the next two years, who again vote for three gods and goddesses. And then there's us—the two years of A-level students. Same process. Anyway, it's only September, so we don't need to worry about that now. Tonight, we have the party, where you can see who's who…or who to avoid, and then the next big event is the Halloween party that'll also be held in the crypts. I guess we should probably make an appearance at that too."

"You love the parties, really." Samira eyed her with amusement.

"I love reminding Tristan that I'm so far out of his league I'm in a different orbit."

"That's my girl." Gracelyn gave her a high five, and I watched with a smile on my face. So far, my preconceptions about the students here had only turned out to be partially true. Aside from Knox and his friends and hangers-on, most of the other people I'd met had been nice. Genuine, as far as I could tell. It was unexpected, and if I was honest with myself, it had shaken me. My mum had spent months with me, going over everything I could expect, how I couldn't trust anyone, how rich, elite people were all the same, but…I couldn't help wondering if we'd been wrong.

I cleared my throat. "Thanks for the offer of getting ready with you guys, but I…I've got a few things I need to do beforehand." I probably sounded like I was making excuses, but with the way my head was spinning, I needed time alone to process everything.

Aria's gaze softened, and I had the feeling that maybe she got it. "No worries. The offer stands for any of the future parties, so we'll have plenty of opportunities to make up for it. You're definitely going to come tonight, though, right?"

"Yes," I said decisively. I really did need to find out more about Knox, and this party could be a good opportunity to see how he acted when he was around his friends outside of a school environment. Plus, if I was lucky, maybe I could explore his space when he was otherwise distracted.

A smile spread across her face. "Good. Invite Katy and Will if you want. I doubt they'll come, but they might if you ask."

"Okay," I said. "What's the party for, anyway?"

"Two reasons. Celebrations or commiserations after the lacrosse team's game, and it's Link—Lincoln Bellingham's—birthday. He's on the team." She eyed me with amusement. "Do you want to go and watch them play before the party?"

"*No.*" My reply was instant and emphatic, making Aria laugh. That would definitely be crossing a line with Knox, and why would I want to see him running around, getting all sweaty, his muscles—

I stopped that train of thought in its tracks. Even though he was hot—yeah, I had eyes—it didn't change his abhorrent personality *or* the fact that his family needed to pay.

"I can't believe you talked me into this." Katy shook her head disbelievingly, tugging the hand of a reluctant Will.

"Yeah, me neither." He pulled a face. "To make it clear, I'm only here for the alcohol."

I couldn't help my smile. "Whatever the reason, I appreciate you coming. And believe me, I'm going to need alcohol to get through tonight."

We fell silent as we reached the entrance to the crypts. The thick stone had muffled any sound, but as soon as Will opened the heavy wooden door, I could hear music spiralling up from below. Stone steps led down into the darkness, penetrated by flashes of coloured light. Despite the murmurs of noise that reached us, telling me there was a crowd of students down there, I couldn't suppress the shiver that went through me, a chill penetrating my body as we began to descend. I couldn't tell if it was fear or excitement.

"This place creeps me out." Katy ventured. "I see why Knox and the rest of the elite like it here—the seclusion and the fact that it's deep below the rest of the school, but I wouldn't want to sleep here at night." She glanced up at the low ceiling above our heads, spiderwebs criss-crossing the stairwell. "Really, really wouldn't want to sleep here at night."

"But on the plus side, think of the uninterrupted nights we could have." Will smirked at her, and she laughed.

"Hmm, you do make a good case."

"So neither of you have been here before?" I looked between them both, and they shook their heads. Katy took a step closer to me, lowering her voice a little as she stopped on the edge of one of the rough-hewn stone stairs.

"We've never been invited before. Not until you came along. And here you are, at the end of your first week in a new school, already getting invited to the popular-people parties and getting us an invite in the process."

I shrugged. "Yeah, I'm still not sure how that happened, actually. Aria and her friends seem to like me for some reason, and they insisted that we should come tonight. I don't think it'll be enough for me to escape Knox's wrath when he sees me, though."

Will gave me a look that was almost admiring. "I know we told you to stay under his radar, but I get the feeling that you can handle him."

I wasn't quite so sure about that as he seemed to be, but I'd fucking well try. "I can," I said aloud, and it felt like a promise. "Let's do this."

Tossing my hair back over my shoulder, I entered the elite's inner sanctum.

The first thing that hit me was the noise. The heavy bass of the music thrummed through the huge space, a dark and heady undercurrent to the sound of voices. People were packed into the area in front of me, and it was difficult to make out the features of the room we were in. It appeared to be an open-plan space, all stone walls and arching ceilings. I spotted a couple of sofas pushed up against the walls and a few smaller pieces of furniture, all in shades of blacks and greys—unsurprising, given Knox's penchant for black.

"Drinks?" Will shouted over the noise, and I nodded.

"Just going to look around," I called back. "I'll come and find you." What I wanted to do was to find Knox before he found me so that I could put him at a disadvantage.

I pushed forwards, swallowed up by the crowd, and began my hunt.

There was no sign of him anywhere. I spotted the other two members of the three gods—Roman and Tristan, holding court in the centre of the space, surrounded by what looked to be most of the lacrosse team, with the usual girls fawning all over them, the mood celebratory from the team's win earlier today. Lincoln Bellingham was there too, with a lopsided crown on his head and a garish "18" badge pinned to his T-shirt. But Knox wasn't with them.

Maybe he was busy with a girl. I gritted my teeth at the thought that came from nowhere. No way did I want to walk in on him with someone. My gaze travelled to the far side of the space, to an arched opening. Before I could think it through, I found myself pushing through the crowds and entering the new space.

Another shiver ran down my spine as I looked around me.

This small area was filled with tombs. Some crumbling, some solid, seemingly almost pristine, other than the thick layer of dust coating the surface. I brushed my hand over the nearest one, the inscribed words faded, although I could just about make out a date—1232.

Wow. This was old. Ancient.

I stepped back, taking everything in. Candlelight illuminated the spaces around me, a contrast to the coloured lights in the previous room, dancing and flickering, sending long shadows across the space, throwing the edges of the tombstones into sharp relief. Wax dripped onto the stones, trickling into the dusty cracks.

It was dark, it was eerie, and something about it called to me.

I loved it.

For a moment, I forgot why I was here. Why I'd ventured into this place.

Until I remembered. *Knox*. I was here in his domain.

There was a door set into the stone wall, just visible in the gloom. Was that his bedroom? If the rumours were to be believed, he had a room down here.

The door was firmly shut, so if it was his bedroom, then the likelihood was that he was busy in there with a girl.

Fuck him. I'd just have to stay alert for his eventual appearance. In the meantime, I needed to find Katy and Will again.

My gaze caught on a waving arm, and I turned to see Aria, along with Gracelyn and Samira, all three of them looking in my direction. Abandoning my hunt for Katy and Will, I headed towards them.

"You came!" Mira smiled at me. "How are you finding the creepy vibes of the underworld?"

"It's definitely creepy," I said truthfully. "But I'm glad I came. It can't hurt to find out more about Knox's inner sanctum."

The three of them smiled at me, then exchanged glances. "Yep. Welcome to the crypts. It's…an experience," Aria murmured. "Just remember, no one here has power over you. No one."

"You're right." Straightening my spine, I gave a decisive nod. "Thanks. I'm going to find Katy and Will and make sure they're okay. It's their first time here. I'll come and find you later."

Pushing back through the crowd in the direction I'd seen Katy and Will heading, I cursed my stupidly high heels. My feet were aching, and I wished I'd worn flats, but I'd been told to come dressed up, and I'd had to ask Maria

Ashcroft for help, because fuck if I knew what kind of thing to wear to these kinds of parties.

I was almost too distracted to notice the heavy wooden door at the side of the cavernous main crypt space, but the second it caught my eye, I was immediately intrigued. When I reached it, I studied it for a moment before glancing around me to make sure no one was paying me any attention. Then I took a breath, closed my hand around the handle, and pulled.

It wasn't locked.

The door opened almost noiselessly, in fact, and I slipped through a crack wide enough for my body before carefully closing the door behind me. There were more rough-hewn stone stairs leading down, and I began to descend, my curiosity spiking. This originally would have been a lower level of the crypts, if I had to guess, and another shiver went through my body as I thought about what might await me at the bottom of the steps. Low lighting illuminated my way, activated by tiny motion sensors, and the air was fresh rather than stale, so it was clear that the passageway was definitely in use. There was no noise, though. The sounds of the party had all but disappeared, although I could still feel the rumble of the bass if I concentrated.

The air was much cooler down here, almost cold, and I rubbed my arms as I descended the final few steps to a stone corridor with two wooden doors at the end. I made my way along the short corridor to the doors and tugged on the handle of the one directly in front of me.

Fuck. This door was locked. I turned around to try the second door.

And found myself face to face with Knox Ashcroft.

9

KNOX

The shock on Elena's face would've made me smile if it wasn't for the fact that I was so fucking pissed off that she'd not only had the audacity to come to this party, but she'd gone poking around areas that were very fucking off limits to her. I'd clocked her the second she'd entered the crypts. She was unmissable tonight. Her thick, glossy hair was pulled into a high, sleek ponytail, and whatever she'd done with her make-up made her eyes look huge, framed by long dark lashes, and her lips shiny and pouty. The tiny excuse for a dress she was wearing…fuck. Me. Black, silky, and so fucking short, making her legs look miles long, aided by the towering heels she had on. The shoes themselves were sexy as fuck, gold with straps twisting up her calves.

In short, she looked like someone I'd be down to fuck. All fucking night. Leagues above any of the other girls at this school, in my opinion—and based on the way my dick was straining at the confines of my jeans, she was about to be aware of that fact very soon if I didn't move away from her.

But I could ignore my urges because it was *her*. The girl who'd caused me to leave my friends upstairs, the girl whose only interactions with me had been filled with antagonism, the girl who had something so shifty about her I didn't trust her as far as I could throw her. In fact, I hadn't even had one drink tonight because as soon as I'd lifted my beer to my lips, I'd spotted her, and straight away, my drink was forgotten. I needed a completely clear head to watch out for her in case she tried anything. What it was about her, I didn't know, but she was fucking up to something, I knew it.

I was just about to step back when my dad's words came back to me. Something he used as a mantra in the courtroom. *You catch more flies with honey than vinegar.*

Maybe it was time for a new tactic.

Instead of moving away, I moved closer, pressing her against the door that she'd just tried to open. "Want to know what's behind door number one?"

"W-what?" she stammered out, clearly confused by my tactic.

I let my hips press into her, and she gasped as she felt my erection. Lowering my head, my lips skimmed her ear. "I said, do you want to know what's behind the door?"

She shivered beneath me, and I smiled. Yeah, this girl was as shallow as the rest of the wannabe goddesses, even if she hid it most of the time, and I wasn't above using my looks to get what I wanted.

What exactly I wanted, I didn't know, but I'd figure it out. As long as it ended with me getting one over on her. She needed to pay for thinking she could just stroll in here like it was her right.

In fact... An idea began to form, and my smile widened.

Cruel Crypts

I dug into my pocket and fished out the heavy iron key, then reached around her and slid it into the lock. "Ready?"

Elena remained silent, but her breathing was becoming more rapid. She was either scared or turned on, and I wasn't sure which I preferred. Either way, it proved the power I had over her.

I turned the key and opened the door, using my body weight to push Elena into the large room. The second we were inside, I spun her around, hauling her back against my chest and banding my arms around her so she couldn't escape. I kicked the door shut behind us, and then I took in the room, trying to see it through her eyes. She was still completely silent, probably in shock.

"What do you think, Elena?" My mouth was at her ear again. Fuck, she smelled so fucking good, all seductive and sexy.

She exhaled deeply. "What is this?"

"The lower level of the crypts." As I trailed my mouth slowly down the side of her throat, she pressed back into me, the curve of her ass grinding directly against my cock. *Fuck.* "The tomb of the gods." I swallowed hard.

"This is where the elite bring their conquests to fuck, you mean." Her voice was full of disdain, but there was a breathless quality to it that proved how affected she was. I raised my head, following her gaze to the giant tomb that dominated the centre of the room, carved with archaic symbols, ancient Greek inscriptions chiselled into the surface. There were three other tombs set into the walls, one on each wall, and the fourth wall held the exit, along with a stone shelf carved into the wall and a large wooden chest. The central tomb was lit in a way that threw the carvings into relief, and the muted light penetrated just far enough to dimly illuminate the other tombs. Elena was wrong about the purpose of this room—the other room down here was used when we wanted privacy with girls. This one was where we stored some of our equipment, but most people didn't get off on fucking on tombstones, so it had never been used for the reasons she thought it had.

Although…I glanced down at her wide eyes, and the way she was staring at the tomb, so mesmerised…

"Yeah. This…" I traced my finger down her arm and angled my head back down to her neck, scraping my teeth across her skin. "…is where we come to *fuck*." As soon as I said the last word, I bit down on her throat, and she straight up fucking *moaned*.

Fucking hell. Why had I thought this was a good idea to bring her in here? My dick was throbbing, and the way she was rubbing up against it, I was going to have a very serious problem in about two minutes.

My head began to clear when I reminded myself of who exactly she was. Tightening my grip on her, I backed us towards the side of the room. Holding on to her with one hand, I reached behind me, feeling along the stone shelf carved into the wall until I found what I was looking for.

She was fast, and clever, and I knew I'd only have one shot to get this right. I gripped her wrist, tugging her hand behind her back, and snapped the restraint into place. She didn't even have time to react before I pulled her other wrist behind her, yanking the chain of the restraint through the thick iron ring that was set into the stone behind us, and cuffed her other wrist.

Her cry of outrage was fucking beautiful to hear, and it made me even harder, especially when I walked around the front of her to see her snarling at me with that familiar hate in her eyes.

"You wanted to see what was inside this room. I'd say you'll get an up close and personal show anytime in the next hour or two. Might be Tristan, might be Roman, might even be me if you're lucky. Enjoy."

"Fuck you." She had the audacity to spit at me, although she completely missed, and I fucking loved it. She was helpless, and angry, and scared. Just how I wanted her. "What do you think is going to happen when I don't come back tonight?"

I smirked at her. "Already thought of that. I'll be texting my mum as soon as I get out of here, letting her know that you've passed out and we're staying here tonight. She'll be so happy to know that we're bonding and I'm taking care of you."

"Let me go and I'll fucking take care of you," she growled. "With my fist in your face."

Moving out of reach of her flailing legs, I raised a brow. "Do you even know how to hit?"

"Come here and find out."

I shook my head. "Sorry, baby. No can do. Have a good night."

With that, I left her, her cries of rage filling her ears as I shut and locked the heavy wooden door behind me.

10

Elena

That absolute fucking *bastard*. I couldn't believe he'd left me locked up here. Twisting around, I managed to make out that I was cuffed to a thick iron ring set into the wall that looked like it was incredibly old and incredibly heavy. It was clear that I wouldn't be able to dislodge it, so I needed to think of another way to free myself. The restraints felt like leather, which probably meant they were used for sex. Who was I kidding? There was no "probably" about it. This was Knox.

I experimented with yanking the chains apart, which did nothing except hurt my wrists, twisting my hands against the iron ring, and then I tried to use my feet to reach the shelf to my left in case I could knock anything useful to the floor. Nothing worked.

I'd even left my phone with Will because I had no pockets, and he did. I had the slim hope that he or Katy would come looking for me, but it was unlikely—Knox probably would have locked the door to the basement, and both of them were probably well on the way to being tipsy by now.

It looked like I was stuck here. How could I have been so bloody stupid?

I didn't know how much time had passed when the door was suddenly thrown open, but my throat was dry, and my arms and legs were aching like crazy. Straightening up, I watched warily as two people entered the room.

Fucking brilliant. It was Knox again, with some blonde girl hanging off him. I recognised her from school, but I couldn't remember her name. It was irrelevant anyway—what was relevant was that they were moving towards the bed, which meant that he'd actually been serious when he said I was going to get a personal show.

"Knox!"

At my shout, the blonde visibly jumped, spinning in my direction. Her eyes widened when she caught sight of me. "Knox? What's going on?"

A smirk curved across his sinful mouth as his eyes glittered with malicious amusement. "Elena likes to watch, don't you, baby?"

I glared at him.

"Um." The girl chewed on her lip. "I'm not really into being watched."

His gaze snapped away from mine, and a frown appeared on his face. *Good.* "No?"

She shook her head. "No. Not by *her*."

He immediately released her, like the cold, heartless bastard he was. "Then you can leave. Close the door behind you."

"You're kicking me out because I don't want her to watch us fuck?" The girl's mouth was hanging open as she stared at him in disbelief.

"Yeah. Go."

She spun away from me, stopping dead as she stared at the sight in the centre of the room. Her entire body shuddered, and she screeched, lifting one shaking finger. "You're fucking sick, Knox. As if I'd want to do anything in the same room as *that*. You two are welcome to each other."

I almost laughed, but I was way too angry to find much humour in the situation. The second the door closed behind her, he stalked over to me. I kicked at him, but he stayed out of reach.

"You fucked up my evening. I haven't fucked a girl in over a week, and you cockblocked me tonight."

"That sounds like a you problem." I was still seething, but I couldn't resist riling him up. "It didn't seem like she was into your creepy tombstone aesthetic either. Maybe you should consider redecorating."

His lip curled. Ignoring my second comment, he snarled, "No, it's a *you* problem. You shouldn't even fucking be here. You don't belong."

"Then let me go, and I'll leave."

"I don't think so." Moving to the stone shelf, he dug through the contents, and I heard the clang of metal as he drew his hand back out. "You haven't been punished enough yet."

He held up what looked like a baton. "Do you know what this is?"

"No, but you'd better keep it away from me," I hissed. "I don't want any part in your sick games."

"Too late." With a sudden movement, he was on the floor, gripping me by my ankles and locking restraints around them. How did he move so fast?

I gasped when he did something that made the metal

bar between the restraints widen, forcing my aching legs farther apart.

"This is a spreader bar." Rising to his feet, he grinned at me. "It'll stop those vicious little kicks you keep making."

"I *hate* you." My eyes filled with tears of frustration. He had me completely at his mercy now.

"I really don't care." Sliding his arms around me, he pinned my body in place against the cold stone wall. He took one of my wrists in a powerful, bruising grip, holding it in place while he undid the restraint, and then refastened it around my wrist. I was so immobile I couldn't even struggle against him. "Time for the rest of your punishment."

Then he picked me up, and it was only then that I realised he'd uncuffed me from the wall. My arms and legs ached so much that all I could do was slump against him, a dead weight in his arms. I felt so fucking drained now, all the fight had gone out of me, and all I had left was hopelessness.

A tear spilled from my lashes and trickled down my cheek as he laid me on the top of the tomb, my hands uncomfortably bound behind my back, scraping against the rough stone beneath me. Closing my eyes, I took a deep, shuddering breath and prepared for the worst.

"Hey."

My eyes flew open. That tone...I'd never heard it before.

"Where's your fight?" He almost sounded disappointed.

"You took it all away," I whispered.

He rubbed his hand across his face, muttering some words I didn't catch, and then began to pace the room. When he whirled on me, I steeled myself. His hand wrapped around my throat, his lips almost touching mine. "Fight, or I'll leave you here all night."

"Fuck you," I bit out, blinking back the tears that wanted to escape.

"Elena. I fucking mean it." His grip tightened. "Fight back."

Instead of replying, I closed my eyes again, swallowing around his grip.

He swore under his breath and then yanked me into a seated position. His arms went around me again, his hands going to my wrists, but this time, he removed the restraints. As soon as I was free, he moved to my ankles and undid those restraints too.

Opening my eyes again, I fell back on the cool, solid stone, stretching out my arms and legs, relief filling me at finally being able to move again.

"Now you can fight." His voice came out as a low rasp. "Show me your fire."

My hopelessness was replaced by burning anger as everything he'd done tonight flashed through my mind in vivid relief. He wanted fire? He was going to get it.

Launching myself up to his level, I threw my arms around his neck and pulled down as hard as I could.

He fell, an "oof" punching from his chest as my back hit the tombstone and his body slammed into mine. It hurt, but I barely noticed the pain. Without waiting for him to recover, I wrapped my legs around him and dug in with my heels, hoping that I managed to spear a part of him. As I did so, I grabbed handfuls of his hair and yanked, and his howl of rage was better than anything I could have hoped for.

"You fucking—" His head snapped back, and his deep brown eyes had darkened so much they were almost black.

Fuck, he looked so hot like this, and I hated him even more for it.

"You wanted my fire," I panted. "You've got it."

He lowered his head, so close that I could feel his lips forming the shape of the words as he rasped them out. "Now you get mine."

Before he could act, I arched up, closing the final few millimetres of distance between our mouths, biting the words right off his lips.

Except, when my mouth connected with his, I didn't bite.

I did something far, far worse.

I kissed him.

11

Elena

He froze above me for a millisecond, but then he was kissing me back, and he was really, really into it. Teasing my lip between his teeth, licking over my skin, touching and tasting until I was writhing beneath him, desperate for more, the rough scrape of the stone against my back forgotten as he devoured me. My hands were no longer pulling at his hair, but they were holding his head down. He groaned into my mouth when I raked my nails across the back of his neck, low and dirty, and it was too much but not enough all at once.

"Knox," I whimpered as his mouth moved to my throat while he ground his hips into me, the unmistakeable press of his hard length, covered by rough denim, rubbing against my clit through the thin satin of my underwear in the most delicious way.

"Fuck," he muttered against my neck, his hot breath ghosting over my dampened skin and sending a shiver through me. "Fuck."

He raised his head, staring down at me with his inky pupils swallowing the brown of his irises. He licked his lips, a slow swipe of tongue that made my pussy throb, but then he moved up and off me.

"Get up. I'm taking you home."

I blinked up at him, my brain trying to make sense of his words. "W-what? I thought you said—"

"I'm taking you back. Now."

"Haven't you been drinking? And didn't you text your mum to tell her I was staying here?" Why was I arguing with him? I should have been pleased that he was apparently showing me mercy.

"I haven't been drinking tonight," he bit out, his pupils finally receding and some of that familiar hate entering his gaze. "Now, get up before I change my fucking mind."

I flew up and off the tombstone. "Believe me, I don't want to stay in this STD-ridden crypt any longer." Yanking at the hem of my dress to cover my ass, I glared at him. "Take me home."

"With pleasure," he growled, making a grab for my wrist and tugging me towards the door.

We were back in the main crypt before I knew it, Knox's grip tight and unrelenting as he led me through the crowds. I spotted Katy dancing with Will, and her eyes widened when she caught sight of me. Shaking my head at her, I mouthed, *Talk later*, and she gave me a look that let me know I'd have a lot of explaining to do. She tapped Will on the shoulder, and his head swung to mine. He lifted my phone in the air, and I gave a small nod. As Knox manhandled me through the crowds, he came up behind me, pressing the phone into my hand, thankfully unnoticed by Knox.

Before we could make it to the door at the top of the stairs, we were stopped by Tristan leering at us. "I knew you wanted to fuck her."

"Fuck off." Knox glared at him. "I'm taking her back home where she can't cause trouble."

"You don't want her?" A gleam came into his eye. "Then you won't mind if I take a turn."

My emphatic "Fuck, no" was completely drowned out by Knox's voice.

"You don't fucking touch her. *No one* touches her."

Tristan stepped back, hands in the air, although his eyes were full of amusement. "Calm down, man. I've got a girl lined up for tonight already."

Knox's tense posture relaxed somewhat, and he loosened his bruising grip on me. "Let's go." With a curt nod to Tristan, he pulled me out of the door, carrying me swiftly through the building and out into the night air.

As we made our way down the darkened path, I stumbled on my heels, and I would have fallen flat on my face if I hadn't tripped in Knox's direction. Instead, I fell into him, making him stumble, and his hand automatically came to my waist to steady me.

"My shoes. Stop for a second, let me take them off." I wanted to burn these shoes. High heels were the worst form of torture. It felt like I was walking on knives by this point.

"You'll cut your feet to fucking shreds on the gravel," he ground out, sweeping his arm around me and lifting me up into his arms. I froze, shock racing through my system as he began walking, easily carrying me like I weighed nothing.

Fuck, he really was strong, wasn't he? I gazed at the motion of his bicep flexing, his tight black T-shirt highlighting the lines and grooves of his muscles. Then I tilted my head back, looking up at his sharp jawline, the harsh angles that made up the planes of his face.

He was so beautiful.

But such a massive wanker.

What a waste.

We reached his car, and he lowered me to the ground, leaving me to climb into the passenger seat on shaky legs. The cold hit me all at once as soon as I was away from his body heat, and I rubbed at my arms again, trying to get warm.

The next thing I knew, the engine was on, and a delicious heat was spreading through my body, the seat beneath me turning toasty.

"Thanks," I whispered into the silent car.

"Don't speak to me." Knox's voice was curt, but it only held a hint of its usual venom. Letting my eyes drift shut, I smiled to myself, feeling the warmth that was filling me from the inside and had nothing to do with the heat of the car.

That warmth abruptly disappeared the second we pulled up outside the Ashcroft house.

"Out." He spoke without even looking at me.

"Okay." I unclipped my seat belt. "Are you coming?"

"No."

"Going back to the party to find a girl to fuck?" Why couldn't I shut up? It made no difference to me what he did. I should be glad to get rid of him.

"None of your fucking business. Out." Gunning the engine, he gripped the steering wheel tightly, and I got the message. Exiting the car, I tried to slam the door, but it was a stupid soft-close door, so I couldn't even do that. I could've sworn I saw his lips curve up in amusement as he began to reverse away from the house, but the headlights were blinding me, so I couldn't be sure.

12

Elena

"What have you managed to discover?"

Blinking my eyes open, I rubbed my hand across my face, groaning when I saw my mum standing at the foot of the bed with her hands on her hips.

"Mum, it's too early for this." I'd barely slept last night, tossing and turning, replaying everything that had happened in my mind.

"It's never too early. Don't forget why we're here, Elena. It's not to party and sleep late."

That was unfair. A large part of the reason I'd gone to the party last night was because of her insistence that I needed to investigate Knox. And look where that had led me. Handcuffed to a wall in a room of tombs, and then—

I knew it was my imagination running wild, but I could still taste him on my lips.

"Whatever. I haven't found anything incriminating yet." *Except that Knox is a sadistic bastard who thinks that tying someone up and locking them in a crypt is a great idea.*

"Rich people always have skeletons in their closets. Try harder."

Or literal skeletons in tombs, in Knox's case. Sighing, I pushed myself into a seated position, brushing my tangled hair away from my face and tucking it behind my ears. "I'll do what I can. Have *you* managed to find anything?"

My mum's mouth thinned. "Not yet. I will find something, though. I just need the right opportunity, and I've been making nice with Anthony and Maria in the meantime, becoming indispensable. Speaking of, it's time for Josephine's breakfast. Try to make yourself useful today, please. Remember why we're doing this."

"I know," I whispered. I knew I'd been blowing hot and cold, caught between wanting to stay away from the person who got under my skin and made my head spin and needing to get closer to him for the sake of my mother's plan—the plan that I'd agreed with. Even though…even though I was having second thoughts about the whole thing.

My mum turned on her heel and swept out of the room, a dark look on her face, and I fell back against my pillows with a frustrated huff of breath.

What could I do to make it up to her?

Pulling out my phone, I sent a text.

"Welcome to our humble abode." Aria opened the door with a deep bow, grinning at me. I laughed as I took in the dorm room. The décor was similar to the Epi common room, with stone walls and floors, large leaded windows with thick curtains, and huge, soft rugs. There were four beds—one in each corner, each with a desk, wardrobe, and shelves. One of the beds was empty, and the other three were neatly made.

Aria followed my gaze to the empty bed. "I wish you were boarding with us. We have a spare bed and everything."

If only. For one moment, I let myself imagine what it might be like if this was my life. But there was no use in fantasising because all of this was temporary. Who knew where I'd end up when this was all over?

Pushing that thought away, I attempted a smile. "Where are Gracelyn and Samira?"

"Down at the lake. There's an open-water swim meet today, and they're both on the team. Want to go and watch?" She glanced at her phone. "It starts at eleven, so we have plenty of time. You can tell me where you and Knox disappeared to last night on the way."

I followed her out of the door, shaking my head. "There was no 'me and Knox.' He took me home, then he came back to the party, didn't he?"

"Nope. At least, not that I saw."

"Well, he drove off as soon as I got back to the house."

As we descended the stairs, she shot me a sideways glance. "Why do you sound disappointed?"

"I don't. I mean, I'm not. Hey, can I ask a question? Has Knox ever been in trouble for anything?"

We reached the ground floor, and she headed for the doors that opened onto the path that led down to the lake and sports facilities. "Not that I can recall, other than stupid stuff like pranks and being out after curfew. If you want to talk about trouble, Roman's the one you want to focus on." Glancing around us, she lowered her voice. "Arson."

My brows shot up, my disappointment in the news about Knox temporarily forgotten. "Arson? Really?"

She nodded. "Yep. He doesn't have a reputation as Hatherley Hall's bad boy for nothing. And he was expelled from a few other schools before he came here, or so the rumours say."

A heavy arm landed across her shoulders, making us both jump. I hadn't heard anyone coming up behind us. "Gossiping about my friends again? I knew you were obsessed with us...with me, should I say, but you should know better than that."

"Head boy." Aria shrugged Tristan's arm off, giving him a disdainful look. "You're the one who's obsessed. First last night, and now this?"

"What happened last night?" I stared between them, but neither of them paid me any attention, too busy glaring at each other. Clearing my throat, I tried again. "What happened?"

Tristan broke the little staring contest, drawing his finger across his throat and pointing at Aria as he stepped backwards. She rolled her eyes and gave him the finger before tucking her arm through mine. "Come on. Let's get to this swim meet."

"What happened last night?" I repeated yet again.

"Nothing notable. Tristan was being Tristan."

It was clear that she didn't want to talk about it, so I didn't pry any further, and I also dropped the subject of Knox. If he hadn't been in any serious trouble, then that was another dead end. It was possible that there could have been a situation with a cover-up, but if there was, Aria didn't know about it.

We reached the lake, which had been split into lanes for the swim meet. Apparently, there were four schools taking part today in various heats. Samira was in the women's 50-metre and 100-metre heats, and Gracelyn was in the relay race.

"Roman got kicked off the swim team and diving team after the arson incident." Aria nodded towards the sprawl of beautiful people filling the front row, two rows down from our position on the tiered seating. Right in the middle, in prime position, was Knox. The girl from last night was next to him, along with Chelsea and a couple of other girls who were hanging on to his every word. Roman Cavendish was to his left, his arms folded across his chest and his shoulders tense as he stared out at the water. "I don't know why he tortures himself by coming to these meets."

"Hmm." I was only half listening, my focus on Knox. One of the girls was now in his lap, and I gritted my teeth as he chuckled at something she was saying into his ear.

Tearing my gaze away, I scanned the rest of the stands, which were beginning to fill. Out of the corner of my eye, I spotted Will and Katy making their way up the stairs, and I waved to get their attention. They were deep in conversation with a tall, pretty blonde with a sleek ponytail, but when Will saw me waving at them, he lifted a hand in acknowledgement, touching Katy's elbow and indicating towards us.

"Who's that girl with Will and Katy?"

"That's Penelope. She's the head girl. Probably talking to them about prefect shit. She normally hangs out with the elite." Aria leaned back in her seat, crossing one leg over the other. "She's not bitchy like some of the others, but she is close to Freya. I think they're related somehow. Third or fourth cousins or something."

I watched as Penelope split off from Will and Katy, making her way down to the front row, while they shuffled into the empty seats next to me. As soon as they were seated, both of them turned to me with expectant looks on their faces.

"Nothing happened last night," I said before they could ask the inevitable questions. "Knox pissed me off, I pissed him off, he took me home and drove off the second I got out of the car. The end."

"But—" Katy began.

"But nothing. Please can we talk about something other than Knox Ashcroft? Please? Anything?"

"As long as you're okay," she said.

I gave her what I hoped was a reassuring smile. "I'm fine. I can handle him, I promise." Turning my gaze to the lake, I noticed the first swimmers were lining up at the edge. According to the information board, the first event was the women's 50-metre race. "Samira's in this one, isn't she?"

The conversation was forgotten as everyone focused on the lake.

Aria disappeared to congratulate Gracelyn and Samira on their respective victories, and I decided to take my chance. Now that I knew where the entrance to the crypts was, it was a perfect opportunity to explore while everyone else was occupied. With a quick goodbye to Will and Katy, I slipped back into Hatherley Hall and made my way towards the cellars.

When I opened the door that led to the cellar storeroom with the hidden entrance to the crypts, I was faced with a problem I hadn't considered but should have because it was obvious. Next to the entrance was a tiny electronic pad with a glossy square sensor in the centre and "Cerberus" written underneath. A fingerprint sensor. *Fuck.* I tried the door anyway, just in case, but nothing happened.

Now what was I supposed to do? I couldn't go back

empty-handed—my mum was relying on me to find something we could use against the Ashcrofts, but I had no idea how to disable a security system.

Not for the first time, I wished my life was normal. I didn't care about being rich or popular or any of those things. I just wanted a normal life, where bad things hadn't happened, and all I had to worry about was schoolwork and friends and guys who I liked and liked me in return.

As I exited the abandoned cellars, I ran straight into a wall.

No, not a wall. A person.

"Whoa. Watch where you're—" The tall, dark-haired guy I'd run into broke off as he looked down at me. His mouth curved into an easy grin. "Hey. You're the new girl. Elena, right?"

I returned his smile hesitantly. I recognised him from my business studies class, and I knew he hung around with Knox and his friends. "Yes. Hi. Graham, right?"

He planted an arm on the wall at the side of my head as he leaned in. "You know who I am. That's good news for me."

"Is it? Why?" My smile morphed into a real one. Knox might be an arrogant asshole, but maybe not all of his friends were.

"Hmm. It means you've noticed me, and it means you're going to say yes when I ask for your number."

"Does it, now?"

"Get the fuck away from her, Graham."

An arm wrapped around my waist, pulling me back into a large, solid body. A mouth dipped to my ear. "What are you doing down here, Elena?"

Knox raised his head, holding me in place, his arm like a steel band, trapping me. Graham's eyes widened, but he held Knox's gaze.

"You said you'd never demean yourself by touching her."

That fucking bastard. It shouldn't have even surprised me that he'd said something like that, but it still hurt to hear the words coming from someone else.

"She's off limits to you. You don't touch her. You don't even fucking look at her."

Graham folded his arms across his chest. "What, so you don't want her, but you don't want anyone else to have her? That's fucking unfair."

"Tell someone who cares. Don't push me. Elena Greenwood is untouchable. Do I make myself clear?"

"Whatever, man. Why don't you just admit that you want her? She's the hottest girl at this school, by far."

A growl rumbled from Knox's chest, and my breath hitched. Why was I standing in his grip placidly, letting him argue about me like I wasn't even here?

"I have—"

Knox's hand clamped over my mouth. "No. You don't get to speak. Graham, get the fuck out of here, now, unless you want me to make you."

Graham threw his hands up. "Fucking fine." He stalked past us, shooting Knox a dark look, but Knox only laughed before manhandling me backwards into the abandoned cellar.

Pressing me up against the wall, his hand around my throat, he lowered his head to mine. His dark eyes were glittering with rage, and I realised right then just how angry he was. I swallowed hard around his grip. Something told me that his anger wasn't to do with Graham.

"Explain," he ground out, his breath hot on my skin.

"Explain what?" Normally, I'd fight back, but I didn't

want to provoke him without knowing the source of his rage.

A phone was thrust in my face. I blinked at the screen, bright against the dimness of the cellar. When it came into focus, I couldn't stop the gasp that fell from my lips.

"Yeah. You were caught on camera." He shoved the phone back into his pocket. "Imagine my surprise when I had an alert to say that someone was trying the door to the crypts. Then I pulled up the camera feed and saw you there. What are you doing, Elena? What the fuck is down there that interests you so much that you tried to break in to get to it?"

"I was curious."

He laughed humourlessly. "If you're so fucking curious, take a look." Releasing my throat, he wrapped his fingers around my wrist, tugging me into the storeroom. Stalking over to the door, he slammed his thumb down on the fingerprint sensor. There was a click, and then he pulled the door open. "Go ahead."

I stared down into the darkness. This wasn't what I'd had in mind. Far from it. But something about the crypts called to me. Last night…the tombstone… I suppressed a shiver.

Knox tightened his grip on my wrist in warning. I straightened my shoulders and stepped forwards.

13

KNOX

As we descended, the automatic lighting flicking on and illuminating our way, I loosened my hold on Elena's wrist, but I didn't let go of her. I couldn't let go. I wanted to know why she was trying to break into my haven, but overriding that was the urge to remind her of her place, to wipe away the memory of that sweet fucking smile she gave to Graham, a smile she'd never given to me.

We reached the bottom of the stairs, and Elena immediately tore herself away from me, running straight to the far side, darting through the archway into the smaller area with the tombstones. I let her go—it wasn't like she could go far. There was no escape from me down here.

When I reached the tombstones, I found her standing in front of the locked door that led into my private bedroom. Coming up behind her, I pressed up against her back, brushing her silky hair away from her ear as I lowered my head.

"That room's off limits."

"Why?" Her tone was sharp, interested. Too interested.

"It's off limits to everyone, not just you."

Her head turned, her lips almost touching mine. "Even Roman and Tristan?"

"Mmm, yeah. Even them. It belongs to me, and me alone."

"Show me what you're hiding," she murmured against my mouth. Fuck. My dick was hardening in my jeans at her proximity. I'd been too angry earlier to think about the effect she had on me—too caught up in the knowledge that she was trespassing, and then the unexpected and very fucking unwanted interaction with Graham. But now, there were no distractions to remind me that messing around with this girl was a bad fucking idea. I slid my arm around her waist, pulling her into my side, my other hand already reaching into my pocket for the key. What the fuck was I doing?

"You can look, but you can't touch. You don't even get to step inside. Do you hear me?"

As I swung the door open, she nodded, her gaze scanning the room.

A small spider scuttled into a crack in the wall, probably startled by the creak of the wood. A cool breeze blew in from somewhere way above, from whatever ventilation system had been installed here. There wasn't much to look at. The bed filled the centre of the space, covered in black sheets and soft pillows. A chest of drawers, a wardrobe, and a small desk were the only other pieces of furniture in here.

"How did you get all this stuff down here?"

I shrugged. "If you have enough money, you can make anything happen." It had been a huge undertaking, but with the assistance of friends in high places, anything was possible.

She rolled her eyes. "I wouldn't know. How many girls have you had in here?"

"None. Why, are you jealous, baby? Do you want me all to yourself?" I smirked down at her, and she bared her teeth at me.

"You wish. What's the purpose of the room, then?"

My jaw tightened, and I released her, folding my arms over my chest as I turned to face her. "This was supposed to be my sanctuary, until *you* came along and fucked up my plans."

One delicate brow arched. "You're really that pissed off about having to wait a few extra weeks? It's barely any time."

I took a step closer, narrowing my eyes on her as I spoke from between clenched teeth. "I spent a long time planning this. I don't like anyone fucking up my plans, Elena."

She glared up at me. "Spoiled rich boy, used to getting whatever you want whenever you want. Guess what? Life doesn't always work out the way we want it to. Get over it."

Lowering my head, I unfolded my arms. My breath skated across her lips. "What the fuck did you just say?"

"Get. Over. It. And welcome to the real world, where things don't always go to plan."

"This is the real world. My world. You don't belong here."

She laughed without humour, her huge eyes glittering with barely suppressed ire as her body pressed forwards, her soft curves moulding against my hard lines. "I know that. I want to be here even less than you want me here." Her soft, pouty lips were almost brushing against mine. "But I—"

I cut off the rest of her words with my mouth, slamming it down on hers. She made a soft noise of surprise but almost instantly kissed me back, her arms winding around my neck as I backed her up against the nearest tombstone.

Fuck. I was already so fucking hard, and I resented her even more for this effect she had on me. Tearing my mouth away from hers, I stepped backwards, dragging a hand across my mouth. "Fuck you."

She stared at me with wide eyes, breathing hard, her mouth open.

"Get out," I said, my voice low. When she didn't move, I slammed my palm out onto the wooden door, making it judder. "Get. Out. *Now.*"

Her mouth snapped shut, and she turned on her heel, stalking out of the room. I heard her footsteps on the stone stairs and then the slam of the entrance door as she shut it behind her.

With a frustrated groan, I entered my bedroom, throwing myself onto the bed on my back. Even though I hated myself for it…and her, my hand was already opening my jeans and shoving my underwear down. When my fingers wrapped around my hard, aching cock, I gritted my teeth, stroking myself hard and fast to thoughts of the last girl I wanted to think about but couldn't get out of my head.

14

KNOX

I drove aimlessly through Nottswood on autopilot. Last night had been such a fuck-up. I should've been on a high—Hatherley Hall had won our lacrosse game, beating Beaufort 13-9, and I'd scored a hat trick, which left Saunders grinning smugly at me afterwards, telling me that the extra practices I'd done had paid off. It was Link's birthday, I was back in the crypts where I belonged, and I could guarantee a fuck by the end of the night.

Until Elena had come along and ruined every-fucking-thing.

I'd only taken Freya into that room to fuck with Elena's head. I'd planned to taunt her and then take Freya next door so she could suck my cock, which had been hard most of the fucking night. But my plans had been completely derailed, as they had been today, both times thanks to Elena fucking Greenwood, and now I was here instead of with my friends.

My phone buzzed with a text, interrupting my thoughts, and when the message preview appeared on my watch, I immediately pulled off the road to read it properly.

> **UNKNOWN:**
> This is Nitro. I was told you wanted information

I raised a brow at the nickname. Clearly, this was Roman's cousin Weston. Whatever, I guessed hackers had to have code names, so I played along with it, saving the number in my contacts as Nitro.

> **ME:**
> Yeah. My parents hired someone as a nanny to my sister and she has a daughter. Something about them is sus, I need any info I can get

> **NITRO:**
> OK. I'll send you a link to a secure server. Upload anything you can get me. Employment records, passport, birth certificates, photos. The more info the better. I'll see what I can do

> **ME:**
> Appreciate it. I'll send through everything I can

He replied a minute later with a link, and that was all the motivation I needed. Starting up the car again, I turned around and headed towards home.

The house was silent when I returned from driving the empty streets, and my mind was no clearer than it had been before I left. It was late enough that everyone should be asleep by now, and so I made my way to my dad's home office, where I was hopeful that most of the information I needed would be located. Shit like passports and birth certificates would probably be with Elena and her mother in their accommodation, but there should be copies here at least.

Because of his law background, my dad liked to keep huge amounts of paperwork for everything, and not only that, but he also didn't trust computers, so he had paper copies of everything. Environmentally friendly, he was not. This time, it worked in my favour because I wouldn't have to waste time trying to figure out his computer password.

Heading straight over to the filing cabinet, I punched in the unlock code on the keypad and grinned when it clicked open. My dad should really know better than to use JoJo's birthday as his unlock code, and I knew it was the same one he used for his phone. Someone really should give him a heads-up about changing it.

Thanks to his meticulous organisational skills, it was easy to find the file for the Greenwoods. I shuffled through the papers—standard criminal disclosure check for Letitia Greenwood, headshot photos of them both, references from Letitia's previous employer. I noted down their previous address details, unfamiliar with the area—somewhere in Surrey, south of London—but noting it down for research. There were medical reports for both of them, too—height, weight, blood pressure, cholesterol, STDs… It looked as if every one of my parents' standard employee health checks had been covered at the time of employment. Clipped to the health check pages were papers noting medication details—Elena was on the pill, and her mother was taking a low dosage of prescribed mild anti-anxiety meds.

There were no passports. But there were copies of their birth certificates, so I took those too. Once I had everything I needed, I spread them out on my dad's desk, switched on his desk lamp, and began photographing the papers, then uploaded them to the secure server.

After I'd put everything back in its proper place and switched off the desk lamp, I sent a text to "Nitro" to let him know it was all uploaded, then made my way upstairs to my bedroom. I gritted my teeth, angry all over again that thanks to Elena, I was in this situation, skulking around my own fucking house and trying not to wake anyone when I could have been balls-deep in a willing girl or passed out in my bed in the crypts after a good night.

When I reached my bedroom door, it was ajar, and I paused on the landing. It shouldn't be open. I distinctly remembered closing *and* locking it before I left the house earlier.

All my senses were on high alert. Fuck. If we had an intruder, I didn't have a weapon. But I had the element of surprise, and I was strong. That was all I had to work with.

Treading noiselessly, I eased the door open and looked inside.

I saw them straight away. Although my room was dark, the tiny torch light they were currently shining inside my fucking bedside drawer gave away their position, and I wasted no time slipping into the room and closing the door softly behind me. Using all my speed and strength, I launched myself at them and took them down in a tackle that would've been highly illegal if I'd done it on the lacrosse field. We hit the bed, hard, and it took me a second to get my bearings before I realised just who I had pinned underneath me.

Elena fucking Greenwood.

"What the fuck do you think you're doing sneaking

around my room and digging through my shit?" I roared. "First you go poking around the crypts, trying to get into places that are off fucking limits, and now you're in my bedroom? What the fuck are you playing at? I'm going to wake my dad up right now and tell him what you've been up to, and you and your mother can kiss this job goodbye and get the fuck out of our lives!"

"W…w…" she wheezed, and only then did I notice how hard her heart was hammering and how her breath was coming in short pants. Her eyes were wide and panicked, and fuck if I'd be responsible for crushing the girl to death, so I moved back a tiny bit, just enough for her to suck a few deep breaths into her lungs.

"Wait." Her lip trembled, and her eyes shone with unshed tears, and it did things to my cock that it really shouldn't. "Wait. *Please*. Don't tell him."

"Give me one good reason. Because I already caught you in the crypts, *twice*, and now I've caught you red-handed, going through my fucking stuff. As far as I'm concerned, there's *no* excuse for that." I pressed her down into my mattress. Just my fucking luck that I'd never had a girl in this bed before, and here I was, with the one girl I hated more than anything lying underneath me.

"I wanted to pay you back for being such a bastard to me all week," she said eventually, and I fucking *knew* she was lying.

"Guess what. I don't believe you."

"Believe me or don't, it's the truth." Her voice was toneless, and her eyes had taken on a blank expression that I knew all too well because I'd perfected it.

"That's not reason enough. Get ready to pack up your shit because you'll be out of here in the morning."

"Knox. *Please*."

Something about the way she breathed my name and

begged me for mercy went straight to my already half-hard dick.

I looked down at her and threw down the gauntlet, a cold, taunting smile curving over my lips. "Convince me not to tell him."

15

Elena

Convince me not to tell him.

Knox's words seemed to suck all the air out of the room. When he'd tackled me, after my initial moment of panic, I couldn't help the flare of relief that the fact that he was here meant he wasn't out somewhere with another girl.

I didn't even want to unpack what was happening, but I was overflowing with adrenaline and shock, and even though he was the enemy, he was so fucking gorgeous and strong and here, and, well…you didn't have to like someone to sleep with them. Hate fucking was a thing, after all. And it would make it all the more sweeter when we brought his family down, knowing that part of him wanted me, even though he clearly resented that fact.

There was a taunt in his smile, and I knew that at least part of him had expected me to back out immediately. But that was because he didn't know me.

"Okay." I licked my lips, and I didn't miss the way his tongue followed the movement. "You want to be convinced?" I'd noticed how his pupils had dilated when I begged him, as they had last night in the crypts when I'd been helpless. He clearly got off on being the powerful one, like the arrogant asshole he was, but he also liked it when I fought back.

I could give him helpless damsel with an edge of fire. If this was my one shot at convincing him, then I needed to push as many of his buttons as possible.

It wouldn't exactly be a hardship.

"Hmmm." I widened my legs so he was settled between them and hooked my bare leg over his. I was in a black cami and pyjama shorts set, which covered just about as much as my dress had done last night, but this time, I had no instruments of torture strapped to my feet. Sliding my heel up the back of his calf, I reached up and threaded my fingers through his hair, scraping my nails across his scalp.

His eyes flashed with fire, and he lowered his head to mine, but I released my grip on his head and placed my palm across his mouth.

"Not yet. You're wearing too many clothes."

Amusement entered his gaze. "Yeah?" Fuck, his voice was so raspy, it did things to me.

"Yeah."

"Do something about it, then." He suddenly moved back and up, dislodging my leg, and cocked his head at me.

Okay, so this wasn't going to be me acting like I was helpless. "Um. Stand up." My mouth was so dry.

When he immediately moved off the bed, I couldn't hide my gasp of shock, and a smirk curved over that cruel, sexy mouth. "What are you waiting for? You're not convincing me of anything yet."

Oh, he was asking for it. I was going to be the best fuck he'd ever had.

I rolled over onto my stomach and pushed myself up

Cruel Crypts

onto my knees, then prowled across the bed towards him. He watched me, his gaze dark and hungry, tracking me like a predator who knew that they had their prey exactly where they wanted them. My nipples were hard, my breasts ached for his touch, and my pussy was wet, and somehow, I was not only pushing his buttons, but he was pushing every single one of mine.

When I reached the edge of the bed, I rose to my knees and placed my hands on his hard chest. I ran my palms down his body, feeling him flexing beneath my touch. Then, I gripped the hem of his T-shirt and slid the fabric up his torso, exposing all those defined, sexy muscles for the first time.

When I'd relieved him of his T-shirt, I took a second just to absorb the godlike body in front of me. His jeans dipped low on his hips, exposing a V-line that I wanted to lick, and the thick denim couldn't disguise the bulge of his hard dick. I leaned forwards, placing my hands at the top of his jeans, and took one of his nipples between my teeth.

"Fuck," he hissed out above me, his hand coming down to my hair and pushing my face into his defined pec. I got the message, lightly biting at his nipple again, then alternating with licks and soft puffs of breath before I switched to the other one, before moving my mouth down his body. He panted and groaned and growled, a litany of sexy-as-fuck sounds, while his abs flexed and his body shifted beneath my touch. I'd never known anyone so responsive before, and it was so fucking hot.

When I finally undid his jeans, it felt like we were both holding our breaths before I let them fall to the floor. His black boxer briefs were strained to their limit with the huge erection they were barely managing to conceal.

Fuck, this boy was packing.

I ran my finger lightly across his hard length, swirling it

in a circle when I got to the tip, and his dick jerked beneath my touch. His boxer briefs were damp with precum, and the thought that he was that turned on by me sent a fresh wave of arousal through my body. I tried to rub my thighs together to relieve some of the ache, but it didn't work.

"Elena. Little fucking cocktease," he ground out. "Stop playing."

I stared up at him from beneath my lashes as I lowered my mouth to the head of his cock, closing my lips around it over the fabric. He groaned, his grip on my hair tightening, and I smiled as I released him from my mouth.

"Am I convincing you yet?"

His only answer was to tug at my hair and glare down at me, so I took that as my cue to continue. I curled my fingers around the top of his underwear and eased it down, exposing his dick for the first time.

Fucking hell. I was up close and personal with the biggest cock I'd ever seen in my life. Long, thick, the head glistening with precum, and a vein running up the underside of his shaft that I was dying to lick.

My formerly dry mouth watered. I needed a taste.

When I glanced back up again, he was smirking down at me, clearly used to getting a reaction from the sight of his huge erection.

"Cocky," I murmured, and his smirk widened into a grin.

I took my time just dipping my head and letting my breath skate across the tip before I lowered it farther, down to the bottom of his shaft, almost touching his balls. Then I dragged my tongue up the underside of his cock and over the head, swirling my tongue the way I'd done with my finger.

He groaned low in his throat. "Fucking *fuck*. Such a little cocktease. Suck my dick, baby."

I needed no more encouragement. Opening my mouth wide, I took him in.

He was way too big for me to be able to swallow his full length, so I shifted lower on my knees for better balance, gripped the back of his thigh with one hand, and wrapped the other around the base of his cock, as far as my fingers would reach. Then I used my tongue and lips to drive him wild, humming around his length as he pushed my head forwards until tears were tracking down my cheeks and I was gasping for breath.

"You think a blow job is going to be enough to convince me?" he rasped, pulling my head back. His hand cupped my chin, and then he used the pads of his fingers to wipe away my tears. "I can get my dick sucked whenever I want. Try harder."

I glared up at him, and he smirked down at me, but I knew that he liked what I was doing. There was no way he could fake his reactions.

Slowly and deliberately, I licked my lips, holding his gaze. "If you want me to stop, say so."

A low growl came from his throat. "Remember why you're doing this. I'm going to fuck you now, and you'd better make it worth my while."

Arrogant asshole. He loomed over me, and suddenly, I wasn't sure who had the upper hand anymore. With a press of his hands to my shoulders, he pushed me, and I fell back on the bed.

"Get naked, now."

16

KNOX

Elena lay there for a second, stunned, before she took a deep, shuddering breath and moved up the bed so she was lying with her head on my pillows. I didn't miss the way her nipples were poking through the fabric of her top and the way she kept rubbing her thighs together. Her hair was all messed up from where I'd had my hands in it, her eyes were huge and bright with the tears that still filled them, and her pouty lips were even more swollen than usual from being wrapped around my cock.

I needed to fuck her, right now. Swiping my discarded jeans from the floor, I pulled a condom from my wallet and began rolling it over my dick. Fuck, I was so fucking hard, and I needed to come while I was inside her. Needed to know how she felt, even though she was the last girl I should be doing this with.

She began drawing her top up her body, and it was way too fucking slow for my liking. My patience was at its limit, and my dick wanted in. I crawled over her, pushing her hands away and tugging her top all the way off. When her full, lush tits were exposed, I forgot everything else, running my palms over them, rubbing my fingers over her nipples, touching all that soft fucking skin that felt so good under my hands. Her breathless moans had my cock throbbing, and I rubbed it against the apex of her thighs in an attempt to give myself some relief.

It was an effort to tear myself away, but I forced myself. This wasn't supposed to be about her pleasure; this was about me and her efforts to convince me to stay quiet. I moved back, pulling down her shorts, and that was when I got a first look at just how fucking affected she was by me.

She was so fucking wet. Glistening, dripping, begging for a taste. Fuck, I needed to get inside her, but first…

I lowered my head, mimicking her by just breathing across her wetness, knowing how frustratingly hot it was. Her fingers curved into the duvet cover as she arched up, trying to get her pussy into contact with my mouth. I laughed, but then I scooped up her thighs, hooking her legs over my shoulders and widening them, and then I licked a long line all the way up her soaked pussy.

"Knox. Oh, fuck. *Please*."

The begging sounds falling from her lips were so fucking addictive, and I needed more. I tongued her clit, then back over her pussy, licking into her wetness, getting her ready for my cock.

When I raised my head, her eyes were closed, and her chest was rising and falling rapidly. She already looked fucked out, and I hadn't even managed to get my dick inside her.

"Ready for my dick, baby?" It wasn't a question, more of a warning that I was about to fuck her. She moaned in response, and then I was finally lining myself up with her and pushing inside her.

Fuck. She was so fucking tight and wet and hot. As I

buried myself all the way to the hilt, she threw her head back with a cry.

"So...big...Knox...need..." She was almost incoherent, and fuck, my balls were already drawing up. This was going to be over way too quickly, but I couldn't stop myself from thrusting harder and harder as she hooked her legs around me, her nails digging into my skin as she met me thrust for thrust.

"Knox." Her voice was urgent, and I angled my hips, judging it perfectly, making her moan and arch up into me. Her body began to shake, pulsing around my cock, and it felt like seconds before I was spilling into the condom, coming deep inside her and fucking wishing I could go bare so I could fill her with my cum.

"Fuck." I collapsed down on top of her, breathing hard, feeling her shudder with aftershocks beneath me.

She mumbled something that I didn't catch, and I lifted my head from her throat. "Huh?"

Her cheeks, already flushed, darkened further. "Doesn't matter. Did I convince you?"

I withdrew from her, sliding off the condom and tying it in a knot. What should I do?

Keep your friends close but your enemies closer.

Did that include fucking them?

Maybe I should wait until I had the background check from Weston. Just so I had all the information before making a decision.

"You've convinced me...for now," I said, lying through my teeth. "But know this. I don't trust you, and I definitely don't fucking like you. What happened tonight—that's not happening again."

The hazy afterglow disappeared from her eyes, replaced with defiance. "Everything you just said, the same goes from me to you." She sat up on the bed, uncaring that her body was completely bared to me, and gathered up her clothes. Pulling them on, she shot me another glare before making her way to the door.

She paused with her hand on the handle. "By the way. If you don't want me snooping around your room, you might want to get new locks. You do know these ones have a safety feature on them to stop children getting locked in? You might as well not bother with a lock at all."

I gritted my teeth. "Get the fuck out of my room."

In reply, she bared her teeth and then finally left me alone.

I groaned, rubbing my hand over my face. This weekend had gone from one fuck-up to an even worse one, and I couldn't help thinking that fucking her had been a big, big mistake.

But it was too late to go back.

17

Elena

"Look at the duck, JoJo. Shall we give it some bread?" My mum affected the high baby voice she used to talk to small children, and I smiled. I'd come with them to the park today. Anthony and Maria had some brunch to go to, so my mum was taking care of Josephine until they returned.

Josephine's face broke into a wide smile as the ducks came closer, her little feet kicking in excitement as she strained against the pushchair straps, trying to get closer. Her dark brown curls bounced around her head as she stretched out her hands. My mum threw a piece of bread towards the duck, and Josephine squealed in delight as the duck scooped up the bread, clapping her hands.

Being here brought back memories of a life that seemed so long ago now…

"Careful near the lake, Elena!" My uncle pointed to the water as if I hadn't seen it. "Don't fall in."

"I won't." I picked my way along the lake edge with all the confidence of a fifteen-year-old who thought they were invincible.

He shook his head with a smile as he pulled my aunt, my mum's sister, closer. She smiled up at him, but his gaze had turned towards my mum, who was standing a little distance away from us.

"Letitia? Want to feed the ducks?"

A small smile appeared on my mum's face. "I think I'm a little old for that, Jason."

"Never too old," he insisted. "Let's all feed them."

Together, the four of us moved to where the ducks were congregating, and my aunt dug into the picnic hamper for the remains of the sandwiches we'd had for our lunch. It was so nice of my aunt and uncle to take the time to give us this day out together. More and more, we relied on them, and I honestly didn't know what we'd do without them.

When we began to throw the bread, my uncle met my mum's eyes over the top of my aunt's head, and he winked at her. Her cheeks pinkened, and she smiled.

I smiled too, happy.

When was the last time I really felt happy? A long time ago now, before everything had happened. Those idyllic summer days with my uncle and aunt almost felt like a dream.

"How are things going?" We began to walk away from the ducks, taking the path around the small lake.

My mum frowned. "Nothing. I'm beginning to suspect that if there is anything, it's well hidden. We might need more money to dig further."

I thought of the hundred and fifty pounds I had stashed in my room. I'd been saving it for afterwards, but… "I have the money I got from selling the bag if you want it."

"You're a good girl." She took one hand off the pushchair to pat my arm. "Maybe we can kill two birds with one stone. Why don't you see if there are any part-time jobs going at the country club? That'll give us extra money, and it'll be another chance to keep an ear to the ground."

I thought about it for a moment. I didn't love the idea of working there, but at the same time, it did make sense. And I was pretty sure I could fake it enough to fit in. "Okay. After the park, I'll go down there and see if there are any jobs available." I'd have to cycle there. I wish I'd learned how to drive, but the year I'd turned seventeen had been a complete shitshow, and there was no time or money to learn. Now I was eighteen, and it didn't look any likelier that I'd be learning. We had far more important things to worry about.

My mum nodded, satisfied, and that was that.

We wandered around the park for a little while longer, and then my mum and Josephine left to go and meet Anthony and Maria while I started the walk back to the house.

I was jerked out of my thoughts when the low rumble of an engine sounded close to me. A black SUV pulled to a stop at the side of the road, and the next thing I knew, the passenger window was sliding down and Knox was leaning across from the driver's side, one hand on the steering wheel.

"Get in."

"Huh?" I stared at him.

"I won't ask again."

Well, if he wanted to waste his time driving me around, I wasn't going to complain. My feet still ached from Friday's party, even though I was now wearing trainers with a cushioned sole. I climbed inside the car, snapping my seat belt into place.

"Where are we going?"

"Home. I assume that's where you were headed since there's nothing else in this direction?" He tapped his fingers on the steering wheel in time with another one of his obnoxious rap songs.

"Yes. Thank you." I leaned back against the headrest. As much as I hated to admit it, this car had really grown on me. I mean, it could definitely use a splash of colour, but it was so comfortable. I shouldn't get too used to it, though.

"Why don't you have a car?" he asked suddenly.

"In what universe can I afford a car? Anyway, I can't drive, so it's irrelevant."

"You can't drive?" His voice was incredulous, and I rolled my eyes.

"No. Funnily enough, I couldn't afford driving lessons either. It might have escaped your notice, but my mum and I aren't exactly rolling in money." Someone like him could never hope to understand what it was like to have to prioritise your spending, to make every penny count, to choose between going hungry or paying the gas bill.

There was only silence at my words, and I didn't bother to try and fill it.

When we reached the house, he glanced over at me. "What are you doing today?"

Oh. I suddenly realised what this was all about. His suspicions had been raised when he found me going through his room, and he was here to keep an eye on me. Well, too bad for him I had no nefarious plans today.

"Why? What are you doing here anyway? Shouldn't you be hanging out with your little group of friends? You spend way too much time here as it is."

Cruel Crypts

He lunged across the car, right into my space. "Yeah, and whose fault is that?"

"*Not* mine. I didn't ask your mum to take me to and from school every day. Believe me, if there was another option, I'd take it."

"Another option." A thoughtful look came over his face. "How quick are you at learning new things?"

I stared at him. "What? I don't know. Why?"

A slow smile curved over his lips. "You're going to learn how to drive."

18

Elena

I must have misheard him. Surely he didn't mean that he was going to teach me?

As if he'd read my mind, he smirked at me, shifting back into his seat. "Yeah, not me. No, what's gonna happen is I'm going to contact a friend of my dad's who does intensive one-week driving courses with a test at the end. As much as I dislike the thought of you taking even more money from my parents, this'll be worth it because it means that when you pass, I can move into the crypts like I'd planned and stop playing fucking chauffeur to you."

"But I still won't have a car," I pointed out.

"There's an old one in the garage that I used when I was learning. I'm sure you can use it. Come with me. You need to pass at the end of the week, which means you'd better be prepared."

"I was going to cycle to the country club."

That stopped him in his tracks. "Why? You're not a member. The only reason you got to go there the other evening was because you were my dad's guest." He spat the word "guest."

"I want to look for a job."

"What the fuck?"

The shock on his face made me smile—I couldn't have hidden it if I'd tried. He narrowed his eyes at me. "They'll never give you a job."

I reached for the door handle. "We'll see."

"Fucking fine. Come with me now, and I'll drive you to the club after. Even though it's a waste of your fucking time and mine."

For someone who was so resentful of driving me around, he sure seemed happy to offer to take me everywhere today. I wasn't above taking advantage of the situation, especially because I knew he was doing it for his own reasons, and they had nothing to do with being nice.

"Okay."

The "old car" turned out to be a one-year-old shiny black Nissan Juke. It was in immaculate condition, and I was immediately wary of doing anything that might cause it to get a dent or scratch. I sat in the driver's seat while Knox began reeling off a list of various parts of the car too fast for me to keep up.

"Now you're gonna start the engine," he instructed. "Foot on the clutch p— No! For fuck's sake, what are you doing?" Yanking my hands away from the button I was about to press, he shot me an impatient, frustrated look that made me want to slap him. Or maybe punch him.

The next thing I knew, he was out of the car and throwing the driver's-side door open. "Get out."

This guy was really pissing me off now. I hadn't even asked for any of this—although I couldn't deny the idea of having some independence and being away from him was incredibly alluring. Climbing out of the car, I glared at him. "Now what?"

He ignored me, sliding into my vacated seat and

pushing it back so it was arranged to his liking. Then, he threw his arm out, grabbing my jumper and pulling me into the car.

On top of him.

I swallowed my gasp of shock when he positioned me on his lap, his feet on either side of the pedals in the footwell.

"Pay attention because I'm not gonna fucking repeat myself. Got it?" His breath hit the side of my face as he angled his head to look over my shoulder.

"Got it." The sooner this was over, the better because he was pressing all my buttons, but with his hot, hard body beneath me, my brain was throwing me increasingly mixed signals.

"You push down on the clutch before you start the engine, otherwise it won't start. It's a fail-safe."

I concentrated very hard on the instructions he was giving me rather than the way his voice was a low, sexy rumble in my ear. "Which is the clutch?"

He gave one of those annoying-as-fuck irritated huffs of breath, pointing down to our feet. "Left to right. Clutch, brake, accelerator. C, B, A." His left hand came down to cover mine, and before I could pull it away, he was curling it over the gearstick. "Make sure it's in neutral before you start."

Somehow, I managed to start the car to his satisfaction. Then he made me do it again and again until I got the hang of putting it into gear and getting it to move a few metres down the driveway.

"Looks like you're not completely useless after all," he murmured when I'd brought the car to a smooth-ish stop —the first one I'd managed, the others having been jerky movements that sent me rocking back against him.

"Believe me, I have many talents that you'll never get

to see," I said under my breath, shaking out my hands, my fingers aching from where I'd had them tightly clenched around the steering wheel.

"What did you say? Stop fucking mumbling all the time. You did it last night too. What is it you're too scared to say?"

Last—what? It took me a minute to remember, and then I could feel my cheeks heating. But I ignored that. I wasn't going to let him think I was a coward. Angling my body forwards and twisting as much as I could with the very limited space I had, I narrowed my eyes. "First of all, I'm not scared to say anything to you."

He raised a brow, clearly disbelieving, and it made my blood boil. "Last night, I simply made a comment that we didn't kiss when we, you know."

"I think the word you're looking for is 'fucked.'" He smirked at me, but then his smirk died away, and his lip curled. "Don't tell me you actually *wanted* to kiss me. You made that mistake already in the crypts. Twice."

"What? You—huh? I didn't want to kiss you. *Ever*." I silently cursed the unsteadiness of my voice.

"Good. Because we may have fucked—and believe me when I say that I've dicked down plenty of girls who I don't even like, so don't go thinking you're anything special—but kissing you was a mistake that won't ever happen again."

"Glad we're in agreement," I spat out between gritted teeth.

We glared at each other, the tension between us thickening, neither of us willing to be the first to look away.

He suddenly gripped my waist and more or less threw me into the passenger seat, then started up the engine with a roar. I barely had a chance to clip my seat belt into place before we were swinging out into the road.

I didn't even attempt to talk to him, and he remained silent all the way to the country club. When we arrived, he kept the engine running and indicated towards my door with a nod of his head.

I got the picture. Climbing out of the car, I smoothed down my jumper and shook out my hair, then made my way inside, relieved to escape the oppressive atmosphere between me and Knox. Time to focus on what was important and see if I could talk my way into a new job.

19

KNOX

"What happened on Friday night?" Tristan smirked at me as we sprawled out on the leather sofas in the crypts after school on Monday. I rolled my eyes as I swiped one of the beers from the coffee table, passing Tristan the joint I'd just inhaled. It was surprising that it had taken him so long to say anything, if I was being honest. He hadn't said anything all day in school nor during our lacrosse practice afterwards.

"You said you were taking her home, and then you never came back," he added, lazily exhaling out a curl of smoke, when I remained silent.

"What's this about?" Roman flung himself onto the sofa next to Tristan with a deck of cards in hand. After cocking his eyebrow at me and receiving a nod in return, he began dealing the cards between the three of us.

"Knox left the party with Elena," Tristan informed him, handing him the joint.

After inhaling, he placed the joint down on the ashtray I'd placed on the coffee table, replacing it with his beer. He raised his brows, turning to me. "You fucked her? I would."

I gritted my teeth. I didn't want to talk about my ill-advised moment with that fucking lying little temptress. At least I'd done one thing right—getting my dad to pay for her driving lessons meant that I no longer had to give her lifts home from school because the instructor was picking her up daily.

I still had to take her to school, but it was a relief to be able to chill with my best mates after school instead of playing fucking chauffeur.

"I caught her in my room, going through my stuff," I told them. It was the truth, and it would stop them asking questions I didn't want to answer.

"What the fuck?" Tristan leaned forwards in his seat, his sly smirk wiped away, replaced with anger.

Roman froze in the process of dealing the cards, staring at me. "Yeah, I echo that. What the fuck?"

"She picked the lock, and she was going through my bedside drawers when I found her. Thing is, I don't even know what she was looking for. What the fuck do I have that she would want?"

"Condoms?" Roman suggested, and I rolled my eyes again.

"Yeah, no. You don't break into someone's bedroom for condoms."

Shooting Tristan a sideways glance, he grinned. "Tris tried to break into your room here during the party to get some."

I turned on Tristan. "You what? What the fuck happened to the ones I gave you?"

He shrugged unrepentantly. "Used them."

"Fucking hell, if you're getting through them that fast,

maybe you should think about keeping your dick in your trousers."

"You already said that, and I said, where's the fun in that?" he reminded me. "But yeah, I wasn't seriously trying to break in. Ro's making it sound worse than it was. I only tried the door."

"Okay, whatever. She wasn't looking for condoms. That's not the only thing either." I gave them a rundown of the details of the shady guy I'd seen leaving, her sudden interest in working at the country club that I frequented, and how she gave off a vibe that I couldn't really even articulate, but it put me on edge. There was something about her and her mother that I didn't trust.

Tristan picked at the label on his beer bottle, his eyes meeting mine as Roman finished dealing the cards. "Fuck. That's a lot to take in. I don't get it, though. What would she be looking for? Why would she be meeting up with random men in the shit part of town?"

Taking a long swig from my beer, I shrugged. "Fuck knows. That's the problem."

"We didn't want you to be away from us, but maybe it was for the best," Tristan mused, picking up his cards and examining them. "This girl needs to be watched closely so we can work out what she's up to."

I nodded my head as I swiped my own cards from the coffee table. "We'll keep an eye out, but for now, I'm just gonna wait and see what happens. I've got someone looking into her background too. Maybe they'll find something, maybe they won't, but I *know* there's something going on with her."

I fell silent as we began to play, pushing the shit with Elena to the back of my mind. Finally, I began to relax, appreciating this moment with my friends, talking about inconsequential, irrelevant shit, dissecting our most recent lacrosse match, betting on who Tristan would fuck next… just having this bonding time that I'd missed out on ever since Elena had dropped into my life.

Roman and Tristan had both made plans to meet up with girls—something I'd usually be doing too, but for some fucking reason, I wasn't feeling it—so I ended up leaving earlier than I'd planned. I checked the time—my dad would probably still be at the office, workaholic that he was, so I headed into town to see if I could catch him. Maybe he wanted to head down to the country club for a drink.

On the way to his office, I passed a bookshop that was still open, and I paused for a second outside the door before ducking inside.

When I exited ten minutes later, I shoved my purchases into my school bag and then dug my phone out of my pocket to silence the incessant buzzing.

Wait.

Fuck. It was ringing, and the caller display said *Nitro*.

I immediately swiped to answer. "Hello?"

"Finally. You're a hard man to get hold of," came the voice from the other end. "Thought I'd better call you with an update. Are you somewhere you can talk?"

"Yeah. I'm out, but it…there's no one really around." There wasn't, just a few late shoppers.

"Good. You might wanna sit down for this, mate."

A feeling that I was unaccustomed to shot through me at his words. Something that felt a whole fucking lot like dread. Ducking into an alleyway between two buildings, I leaned back against the wall, letting the rough surface ground me.

"I'm listening. Tell me what you know."

20

Elena

Something was going on with Knox, and I wasn't sure what it was. Despite the fact that we clearly disliked each other, he hadn't been outright ignoring me. Now, though, I'd been frozen out. He hadn't even looked at me, not once, the entire journey to Hatherley Hall, and every time I'd seen him in school today, he'd be looking away from me, paying extra attention to the girls who hung around him constantly, but never once glancing my way.

It made me…uncomfortable. I should be pleased, but there was something inside me, a part that I really hated, that had enjoyed his attention and the verbal sparring… and the rest of what we'd done.

I was good at compartmentalising, though, so I pretended like it wasn't there. There was too much going on with me anyway. I had school, my driving lessons, and a new job at the country club that was starting tonight—it appeared that the Ashcroft name really did open all kinds of doors. My mother had instructed me to watch out for Knox, but after going through his room and observing him with his friends and how he was with me, I was of the opinion that trying to uncover anything about him was a dead end. He was just a typical shallow rich boy.

"Elena? Elena?"

I blinked, Will's face coming into focus. "Sorry, I was miles away."

"You don't say." He grinned at me. "Come on. The music lesson's over now, and we need to get to business studies."

"Yeah. Right. Business studies." I gathered up the sheets that I'd been scribbling lyrics on, handing them to Katy. "Here. You can have these, maybe see if you can put them together with your music. I think we're almost there."

She smiled as she took the papers from me. "Great, thanks. I'll work on it now during my free period. I'll see you both after business studies."

Will dropped a kiss on her cheek, and then we left her to it, leaving the music block and making our way to our business studies classroom.

The classroom where Knox would be.

When we entered the room, there were only a few people inside, and I made a sudden, snap decision, heading straight for the back where Knox usually sat.

Will stopped me with a hand on my arm, his eyes wide. "Where are you going? That's where Knox and Tristan sit."

I shot him a glance. "I know. That's why I'm going to sit there. Don't worry, I'm not expecting you to sit there too."

"Do you really think that's a good idea?" His brows pulled together in concern as he released my arm.

"Good? No. Just promise me one thing, though."

"What?"

"If Knox kills me, bring flowers to my funeral. Lilies, please."

"Noted." Shaking his head, he stepped back. "I really hope you know what you're doing."

I didn't, but it wasn't going to stop me. Pulling out the chair next to the one where Knox usually sat, I took a seat, pulling the books I needed from my bag.

Less than five minutes later, a shiver went down my spine as I heard Knox's low, smooth tone, accompanied by the voices of Tristan and Chelsea. I kept my gaze on my textbook, taking my time flipping through the pages, my whole body on high alert, even though I was projecting a casual image.

"What do you think you're doing sitting here?"

Slowly, I raised my head, meeting Tristan's gaze. His eyes were dark and angry. Next to him, Knox's jaw was clenched, and his fists were balled up at his sides, but he was still playing the silent game.

"Are there assigned seats?" Tapping my pen against the desk, I affected a bored tone.

"That's my seat," Tristan hissed. "Move."

"No, I don't think I will. There's a free seat next to your girlfriend, look." I pointed helpfully towards Chelsea, who narrowed her eyes at me and then waved at Tristan.

"Tristan, come and sit next to me." Her voice lowered, and she slowly and deliberately licked her lips. "I'll make it worth your while."

He flashed her a wide grin. "Yeah? How can I turn down an opportunity like that?" Turning back to Knox, he muttered, "The little thief's all yours." Knox remained silent, staring at me with a stony expression.

Thief? Knox must've told him about catching me in his room on Saturday. That would explain his hostility, at least. But I was still at a loss with Knox.

Professor Fletcher entered the room at that point, breaking the tension. "Everyone, take a seat, please! There's time to gossip later. Mr. Ashcroft, stop looming over Miss Greenwood and sit down."

Knox threw himself into the chair next to mine, yanking his books from his bag, and then he paused. I heard him exhale, long and slow, and then he gently placed them down on his desk.

Tilting my head towards him, I studied his profile. "Did you take a vow of silence? Or is this special treatment just for me?"

He finally turned to me, and the look in his eyes sent ice trickling through my veins. So cold. So callous. I thought I'd seen hate from him before, but it was nothing compared to the way he was looking at me now.

"Knox?" I whispered, cursing the shake in my voice.

"Don't speak to me. Don't even look at me," he gritted out. "As far as I'm concerned, you don't exist."

Now I was really confused. What could have possibly changed in the period between yesterday and this morning? After school, I'd had back-to-back driving lessons that had left me so mentally tired I'd fallen asleep in my bedroom watching a film, and so I hadn't seen him come back to the house, but I couldn't think of anything that had changed between yesterday and today.

I was drawing a blank.

"Can you tell me what I supposedly did to deserve the silent treatment?"

No response.

"Fine. If that's how you want to play it. As far as I'm concerned, you don't exist either." I hated that I was stooping to his level, but even more, I hated the tiny part of me that felt hurt by his words and actions. Why should I care what he thought? I was here for one reason, and one reason only. Soon—or so I hoped—I'd be away from here and getting on with my life.

Whatever that life looked like.

Later that night, when I stumbled, exhausted, into my bedroom, I blinked, trying to make sense of what I was seeing. My brain was so tired after three hours of driving lessons, followed by my first four-hour shift at the country club, washing glassware and cleaning tables, that it took a moment for me to register what I was looking at.

Someone had been in my room.

On my bed lay four books, shiny and new, with no creases on the spines.

They were all driving guides. *Learning to Drive. Theory Test Made Easy. The Highway Code. Pass Your Driving Test.*

Carefully, I picked up the books and placed them in a neat pile on the little table next to my bed, trying and failing to stop the smile that was spreading over my face.

Surely these could only be from one person?

When I climbed into bed, my smile still hadn't faded, and I both hated and loved the warm feeling that went through me every time I looked at the books. I flipped on the lamp next to me and picked up the book on the top of the pile. Might as well get started.

I'd only managed to get through a few pages when my phone chimed. Swiping it from the table, I glanced at the screen.

A stuttered gasp fell from my lips, and my heart began pounding so fast I had to take several deep breaths just to get myself back under control.

The message blinked up at me.

Four words on a screen.

Individually, they were nothing. Innocuous. Meaningless, even.

But together…they meant that everything was about to change.

UNKNOWN:
> I know your secret

21

KNOX

Saturday at last. I would've been happy about that fact, except I was hungover as fuck and up way too fucking early after a night of partying. The lacrosse team had won our latest game, and celebrations had followed—this time, with no Elena in sight. That was the upside, along with the alcohol and the weed and the girls, of course…except, fuck, here I was, alone in my bed in the crypts after crashing here after the party.

Last night. What had been my problem? There had been no shortage of willing, hot girls, and yet I couldn't find it in myself to even pretend to be interested.

I stretched, groaning. My dick was the least of my worries at this point. What to do about Elena…that was the biggest problem. I'd done my level best to ignore her ever since I'd received the information from Nitro, aware that if I let her provoke me, I'd end up showing my cards too early. But I was no closer to making a decision than I had been on Monday.

She was very fucking hard to ignore, though. Especially now that I knew what it was like to see her fall apart for me, to feel her tight little pussy squeezing around my cock, her gorgeous tits bouncing as I pounded into her…

I wrapped my hand around my dick, letting the memories of that night flood through me while I wanked myself hard and fast. It felt like no time at all before my balls were pulling up and I was coming all over my hand and abs. It was an empty orgasm, full of resentment, because how the fuck did a memory of a girl I fucking hated make me come so quickly?

"Fuck you," I said aloud, glaring down at my dick like it would make a difference. Grabbing a tissue, I wiped away the evidence of my moment of weakness, then stumbled out of bed with a yawn to shower and get ready to meet my dad.

"Nice one." Shading his eyes with his hand, my dad followed the trajectory of the ball with his gaze. He'd tried to talk me into playing a round of golf, but I was too hungover to traipse all over the golf course, so instead, we were at the driving range.

"Yeah. I've been working on my swing," I told him.

He turned to flash me a quick smile. "It shows."

I couldn't help returning his smile. My dad's approval meant a lot to me, even if it was for something that was relatively unimportant, like this. The smile fell from my face quickly, though, when I thought about the information I was sitting on.

As we continued to play, my mood grew darker and darker, until I couldn't hold it in anymore.

"Dad."

My tone must've conveyed something serious because

he placed his club down and turned to face me fully. "What's up?"

I cleared my throat. "How much do you really know about the Greenwoods?"

His brows pulled together. "What's this about, Knox?"

"I… Have you investigated their background?"

"Of course I have. I wouldn't allow them in my house otherwise. Letitia has impeccable references. Why—"

"Anthony!"

My mother's voice cut off the end of his sentence, and the next thing I knew, I had a squealing toddler hanging off my legs.

"Hey, JoJo." I swung her up into my arms, kissing her cheek while she beamed at me. She began babbling away, waving her arms around and almost sending my sunglasses flying off my head.

"Knox." My mother came over to us. "Sorry. She was too quick—as soon as she saw you, she went running."

"I don't mind." I didn't. My baby sister meant the world to me. Glancing down at her smiling face, I stuck my tongue out, and she laughed, clapping in delight. It made me grin. She was so easy to amuse.

After my dad had finished up with his final swing, we made our way to the restaurant where my mother had made brunch reservations. It didn't often happen, us all together like this—we normally only made an effort when my sister was home from university. But it was nice. Occasionally.

My mother took a small sip from her champagne flute and then glanced between me and my dad. "Did I interrupt something earlier? You both looked quite serious."

I met my dad's gaze and saw a clear question there, so

I shrugged. What could I say now? I needed to talk to him, alone, preferably.

A thoughtful look came over his face, and then his gaze cleared, his lips curving into a smirk. Fuck, no. Whatever he was thinking was *not* good.

"Knox was asking me about the Greenwoods. What their background was like." He tried to communicate something with his eyes to my mother, who instantly seemed to get it, her smile widening.

"Oh, I see."

They did not fucking see. At all.

"Knox," she continued, blithely unaware. "It doesn't matter to us if you want to be with someone that hasn't… had the same opportunities in life as you, let's say. When I met your father, I was a struggling model, living in a tiny, cramped flat with three other girls, and he never made me feel like I was less than him. I know there are certain expectations placed on you, especially with our position of influence, but it would be hypocritical of us—"

"*No.* That's not—"

My dad interrupted me before I could finish my sentence. "Well, you were hardly a struggling model, darling. As I remember, you had a huge billboard up in London, and your flat was in Chelsea." They both laughed, and I groaned, shaking my head.

"Seriously, whatever you're thinking, it's so wrong."

"But your mother is right. If you're interested in Elena, you don't have to worry about our acceptance. We just want you to be happy. Now, I know that she's a little different from the other girls you've been around all your life, a little less…polished, but maybe that could be a good thing. She doesn't appear to be interested in our money, seems very independent, in fact…" His words died away as the object of our conversation appeared from the restaurant kitchen doorway, because that was just my fucking luck.

She glanced over at us, biting down on her pouty lip, and my traitorous dick jerked. Even in the kitchen staff uniform—sensible black with a white apron, hair tied back into a neat ponytail—she looked good to me. Fuck my fucking eyes. And brain. And everything in me that wanted her when I didn't want to want her. Wanted to hate her. *Did* hate her, in fact.

"Elena!" My mother was already waving her over, ready to make my life even more hellish. Elena had no choice but to come over to us, giving my mum a small smile and completely avoiding my gaze. *Good*.

"I'm not really supposed to be talking with the patrons," she confided before crouching down so she was level with JoJo's high chair. Her smile softened, tugging at something inside me. "Hi, JoJo. Would you like to do some colouring?"

"Yesss." JoJo nodded enthusiastically, and Elena straightened up.

"I'll be right back."

The second she turned away, my mum cleared her throat, and she and my dad had a whole conversation with their eyes. My dad nodded, pulling out his phone and showing her something on the screen.

"What are you two doing?"

They both ignored me, and I didn't have a chance to say anything else because Elena returned, placing some sheets of paper and a set of crayons in front of my sister.

My mother placed a hand on her elbow, drawing her attention. "Elena, what time does your shift finish? Do you have a driving lesson afterwards?"

"Twelve, and my driving instructor is picking me up from here after that."

"Do you have any plans for this evening?"

Elena shook her head slowly. "No…"

"Wonderful!" She gave Elena a bright smile. "One of my charities, the Benhall Foundation, is holding a dinner tonight. I'll arrange for you to be collected after your driving lesson, and my stylist will find you something appropriate to wear. You'll attend as Knox's date."

"What the f— What?" I stared at my mother in horror. She had to be joking, surely.

"I-I can't. Um. I don't think Knox——" Elena bit back the rest of her words, sliding her gaze to me, then back again, a pink flush appearing on her high cheekbones.

"Knox would be honoured to have you as his date. Wouldn't you, Knox?" My father's voice was steel, but his eyes twinkled with amusement. Fuck him, and fuck my mother for coming up with this plan.

"I did have plans——"

"Cancel them." He turned to Elena. "Maria and I will be attending the dinner too, but Knox will accompany you."

Her wide-eyed gaze darted between the three of us, and then her shoulders slumped in resignation. "Okay. Thank you for inviting me. I…I'd better get back to work."

"Of course. We'll see you later." My mother threw her another bright smile. As soon as Elena was gone, she gave me a thoughtful look. "I don't know why I didn't see it before. It's clear that you're into her."

"You're right," the traitor, aka my dad, chimed in. "And the same goes for her. Reminds me of the way you used to look at me, back in the beginning."

As the food arrived, they began reminiscing, and I did my best to tune them out. This day was going from bad to fucking worse, and the worst was yet to come.

22

Elena

The chauffeur-driven black car pulled up outside the building where tonight's function was taking place. It was a huge country manor house, Cotswold stone with a sweeping gravel driveway, surrounded by manicured lawns. Guests milled around, expensively dressed and poised in a way that I could never hope to emulate.

I'd never felt so out of place.

I climbed out of the car, the silky sapphire-blue material of my dress sliding down over my thighs as I did so. The dress I'd been given to wear was simple in style—long, form-fitting, with a low back and a sweeping neckline that had required some strategically placed tape to hold it in place. A slit ran up the side of the dress, almost to the top of my thigh, and my look was completed by strappy black heels and a borrowed choker necklace that I was fairly certain was made of real diamonds.

I was almost tempted to sell them. If they were real, the money would go a long way towards our future needs. But I wouldn't. I wouldn't steal. My conscience may be eroded after everything that had happened, but there were lines I'd never cross. As it was, I was beginning to have my own misgivings about my mum's plan...or, more truthfully, I'd been having misgivings for a while now. It had seemed like a good idea when my mum had come up with the idea, but the more I got to know the Ashcrofts, the more I realised they were actually decent people, and the less I wanted to hurt them. With the exception of Knox, of course. I was even beginning to lose my dislike of Anthony Ashcroft. Despite his arrogant persona, he seemed like he might be a decent man underneath.

I just had to hope that my mum didn't find anything on the Ashcrofts. If there was nothing to be found, maybe we could finally move on. Put the past behind us and start a new life, preferably somewhere far away from Knox Ashcroft.

"You came, then."

A figure stepped out of the shadows, exhaling a cloud of smoke that curled through the night air, obscuring his features.

"It didn't really feel like I had a choice," I said honestly, taking a step closer to him.

"There's always a choice, Elena."

The way he said my name, his voice so smooth but dripping with venom, had me burning up inside. Even though I shouldn't want it, I craved the attention he was giving me after days of being iced out.

My next step took me into his space. I could feel the heat radiating from his body. His sexy, muscled body, which was encased in a midnight-blue suit that was tailored for him so perfectly it made my breath catch in my throat. "If that's true, why didn't you say no?"

His hand came up, skimming across the jewels at my throat. He ignored my question, his eyes darkening as he stared at the line of diamonds. "A diamond collar for the little bitch. I'm surprised my mother trusted you with this."

"Maybe I am a bitch. You're a bastard."

He laughed without humour as his hand slid around the back of my neck, underneath my hair. I shivered as his fingers brushed over my skin, and then they hooked into the back of the choker.

The cool diamonds bit into the skin of my throat as he pulled them tight. I gasped for air as he lowered his head, his whiskey-scented breath hitting my lips. "You're right. I am a bastard." His mouth moved to my ear as his grip tightened even further, sending spots dancing across my vision. "I'm the bastard who's going to ruin you, Elena *Black*wood."

Then, abruptly, he released me and was gone. The only sign that he'd been there at all was the glowing embers of his cigarette that he'd tossed on the floor behind him.

My whole body was shaking, and I slumped against the stone wall of the manor house, sucking in deep, gasping lungfuls of air. *He knew*. How? How had he found out?

Fuck. *My mum*. I couldn't even tell her because I hadn't brought my phone with me. I didn't even have a bag because the stylist had convinced me that I wouldn't want to carry one around with me. Stupid, stupid Elena.

When I could breathe again and I no longer felt like I was in danger of fainting, I analysed his words and actions. He couldn't know everything. If he did, there was no way I'd still be here, and neither would my mother.

I had to find out how much he knew. Tonight.

During the entirety of what felt like hundreds of courses of food—some completely unidentifiable—Knox ignored my presence. We'd been seated at a table with people that, as far as I could tell, were all of university age, doing cleversounding degrees, and I was completely out of my depth. Every time I went to speak to Knox, he'd flirt with the woman next to him, who was lapping up the attention. Unsurprisingly, since Knox could lay on the charm when he wanted to. I'd made an attempt to do the same with Richard, the man sitting on my other side, but when he started throwing out words and phrases such as "japes" and "a jolly good lark" while talking about his university misadventures, I zoned out.

When the meal was finally over, Richard leaned closer to me. "Time for my favourite part of the evening. The dancing. Would you do me the honour of being my first dance partner?"

"She's with me." Knox's voice was a low growl at my side, his hand wrapping around my waist as he tugged me closer to him.

"I— My apologies. You hadn't spoken to each other during the meal, and I thought—"

"You thought wrong. Elena here isn't a good conversationalist, are you, baby? She puts her mouth to use in other ways." He made an obscene gesture to which Richard gave a scandalised gasp, clapping a hand over his mouth. My cheeks heated, not in embarrassment but in anger. This fucking bastard thought he could humiliate me?

"Knox, I thought we spoke about your delusions. Your penis isn't big enough to satisfy me, remember? And don't be so rude to poor Richard." I turned back to Richard, who was looking like he'd rather be anywhere than here. I took pity on him because I knew that if I accepted his offer to dance now, he'd be torn between me and the son of one of the most influential families here. "Thank you for the offer, but I think I'm going to get some air."

He nodded, relief written all over his perspiring face. I dug into the skin of Knox's hand with my freshly manicured fingertips until he let go of me with a hiss, and then excused myself, making my way through the groups that were milling around and up a set of stairs. Through an open door, I spotted another large room, this one with a small bar and clusters of tables and chairs scattered through the space. Swiping a champagne flute from the bar, I made my way through the room towards the doors on the far side. They were covered by curtains, but when I pulled them apart a little and tried the handles, one of the doors opened. I slipped outside, pulling the curtains closed behind me.

Leaning against the stone balustrade, I sipped my champagne. I needed a moment to myself to process what had happened, and then I needed to confront Knox.

I didn't get a moment to myself.

The door opened behind me, and I turned around to see Knox standing there, with a dark look on his face.

Fuck.

23

Elena

Knox closed the door behind him and stood there, his gaze fixed on me. I was cornered with nowhere to run. Leaning back against the balcony balustrade, I attempted to look relaxed, although I didn't think he was buying it.

His hand went to the inner pocket of his suit jacket, and he pulled out a slim black flask, which glinted in the dim balcony lighting. Opening the cap, he tipped it to his lips.

"Can I have some?" As soon as the words were out of my mouth, I wished I could take them back.

"You want some of this? Come and get it." It was a challenge, and I took it. Crossing the balcony to him, I reached up, curling my fingers around the smooth metal flask.

But he didn't let it go. Instead, he wrenched it out of my grip and lifted it back to his lips. His dark gaze flicked down to my mouth, so quick that I almost missed it.

"Taste." His voice was a low rasp as his mouth came down to mine. It wasn't a kiss, because he'd told me he wouldn't kiss me again. It was a slow slide of his tongue across my bottom lip that left a lingering heat when he drew away. I licked my lips, tasting a hint of the fiery burn of the whiskey, craving more. More of him. I shouldn't. But I *wanted*.

"More," I whispered.

"A question for a drink." He stared down at me. "You answer a question to my satisfaction, I let you have another taste."

I sucked in a breath. This was a dangerous game, but maybe I could even the odds and find out more about what he knew in the process. "What about a question for a question? I answer to your satisfaction, and I get to ask you a question."

One eyebrow raised. "What about the drink?"

"I have my champagne." I held up my glass. "And you have your whiskey. How about if we skip a question we don't want to answer, we drink?"

He was silent for a long moment, but then he gave a single nod. "Okay. Go inside and get a bottle. You're going to need to drink more if you want to keep up with me."

"I can't just take a bottle."

"You fucking well can. There's plenty behind the bar. Just get one. Unless you're too scared to play with me." His lips curved into a smirk. I wanted to slap it off his face. Or maybe kiss it off his face. At this point, it was fifty-fifty.

"Scared is the last thing I am." When he moved to the side to let me through the doors, I re-entered the room, heading straight over to the unmanned bar and ducking behind it. No one paid me any attention as I slunk back to the doors with a bottle in hand.

On the balcony, Knox had taken a seat at the tiny wrought-iron table and chairs set that stood in the corner. Ivy snaked up the wall behind him, dark, glossy green against the midnight blue of his suit. After placing my bottle and glass on the table, I sat in the unoccupied chair. The metal was cold against my bare skin, and I shivered.

Knox didn't miss it. In fact, he smirked at my discomfort. It didn't surprise me—it wasn't like I'd expected him to offer me his jacket or anything. His calf brushed against my leg as he shifted in his seat, and I was suddenly aware of how close we were.

His dark gaze met mine. "I'll go first."

I nodded, apprehension swirling inside me.

"Did you really think that my dick wasn't big enough to satisfy you?"

My mouth fell open, and the corners of his lips kicked up in amusement. "Wasn't what you thought I was going to ask, was it? Don't worry, we'll get to the hard questions soon enough. That's a fucking promise."

Drink or tell the truth? Fuck it, I might as well say it. If I drank, it was as good as an admission anyway. He knew the truth. "What do you think?"

"That's not an answer. Tell me the truth."

"Oh, fuck, okay. Look, you know you've got a huge dick. Obviously, it's big enough to satisfy me, bloody hell. I was just making a comment earlier."

He grinned at my words, and butterflies came to life inside me. I tried to tamp down these unwanted feelings, but I knew it was too late. Picking up my champagne flute, I gulped it down viciously, draining the rest of the glass.

I went to open the new bottle, but Knox stopped me with a hand on my arm. "Let me. I doubt you know the correct way to open a bottle of champagne, do you?"

I couldn't have stopped my eye roll if I'd tried. Who cared how it was opened?

"Go on, then. Impress me with your rich-boy moves." I sat back, folding my arms across my body, underneath my boobs. Knox's gaze slid from the bottle to my breasts, and he licked his lips. My nipples pebbled under his stare. What were we doing here? I needed to get us back on track. "Knox? Are you going to open it?"

He blinked slowly, and then he cleared his throat, tearing his gaze away from me. "Yeah." His fingers worked the twisty metal bit off the top of the cork, and then he grasped the cork with one hand and the bottle with the other. "Twist the bottle, not the cork."

"That's it? I thought it would be more impressive than that."

"You wanna see impressive?" He placed the bottle down and then pulled out his phone, tapping at the screen with his brows pulled together in concentration. When he stopped tapping, he handed it to me. "Watch this."

I watched as a video started playing. A hot blond guy appeared on the screen, surrounded by cheering people, holding up a bottle of champagne. "Is that a sword?" I heard someone screech close to the phone speaker as the guy pulled what looked like a katana from the wall. He placed the bottle on the mantelpiece and then whistled loudly to get everyone's attention. Then he suddenly swung the katana at the bottle, slicing the top off like it was nothing.

"Okay, I'm impressed. Who is that?"

Knox shrugged. "Fuck knows. Roman sent it to me ages ago. One of his cousins sent it to him—think it's one of their friends." He frowned down at the screen, then scrolled the video back a bit, watching intently. He tapped his finger on the corner of the screen. "Yeah. That's Roman's cousin there. Weston."

And now I had my first question—a nice, easy one to hopefully get him to drop his guard. Handing his phone back to him, I refilled my glass. "My first question. How long have you known Roman?"

"You really want to waste your first question on that?" He raised a brow as he took a swig from his flask. When he lowered it, he shrugged again. "He's one of my best mates. We knew each other as little kids, but he moved around a lot, so we lost touch for a while, other than sporadic texts. But when he came back to Hatherley Hall, we continued where we left off. It's easy. Him and Tristan…they're my closest friends."

As he spoke, I realised that we'd somehow ended up in a fairly civil conversation. It was bizarre, and I had no idea how it had happened.

"My turn. Tell me about your friends. Who are they?"

We were starting to edge into dangerous territory already. I stalled for a moment, thinking about whether I should answer. If I didn't, he'd get suspicious. "I guess…I lost touch with people when we came to Nottswood, so there's no one I'm close to. Katy and Will have become my friends here…" Trailing off, I realised how pathetic that sounded. It was, in fact, the truth because although I'd thought I had plenty of friends in my previous life, the last year had shown me that those friendships were fickle at best. No one had made the effort to stay in touch with me. Not that I had either. I was too busy trying to navigate the world I'd been thrown into, to keep my head above water, to survive.

"That's fucking pathetic." His lip curled, and I was reminded all over again why I hated him.

Sipping from my glass, I savoured the feel of the chilled, bubbling liquid sliding down my throat rather than focusing on the hurt that went through me at his words. When I was composed enough to speak without snapping at him, I asked, "What do you want to do when you finish school? After university?"

Leaning his head back against the wall, he stared up at the night sky. He sighed. "I'm planning on becoming a criminal defence lawyer. Barrister. My dad…he's one of the best in the whole country, and if I can be half as good as him, I think I'll be happy."

I bit down hard on my lip to stop myself from saying anything I'd regret.

"What?" Knox shot me a dark look. "Stop fucking judging. What are your plans, anyway? I bet you haven't even applied to uni."

"No, I haven't. I don't know what I'm going to do." The truth was, I'd probably end up working out of necessity as soon as I'd finished school. University wasn't for people like me.

He didn't comment, returning his gaze to the stars as he drank from his flask. Studying his profile, I let the words fall from my mouth. "There was a text from an unknown number on my phone, saying that they knew my secret. Was it you?"

His eyes snapped to mine, cold and hard. Then he ground out, "Pass," and drained the contents of his flask.

It was as good as an admission of guilt.

When he slammed the flask down on the table with a loud clang, he leaned right into my space. "What were you doing with that man the day my dad found you?"

I sucked in a shaky breath, and then I picked up my glass, bringing it to my lips.

"Pass."

24

KNOX

As soon as I'd asked the question, Elena's eyes went wild, her gaze bouncing all over the place, and I was sure I could get her to crack with a bit more effort. I needed to up the game, to get her to pass on the questions I knew she wasn't going to answer, therefore getting her to lower her inhibitions enough via alcohol so I could ask the questions that I really wanted the answers to.

Climbing to my feet, I looked down at her, all tumbling waves of dark hair, big eyes, and pouty lips, her gorgeous body poured into a dress of the silkiest fucking material that I wanted to run my hands all over. But my dick wasn't running the show, and contrary to some of my previous actions, I did possess a brain.

"I'll be back." Without waiting for a reply, I headed back inside and swiped a bottle of vodka and two shot glasses from behind the bar.

When I returned, she was rubbing at her arms, the October air obviously getting to her. It had been amusing to begin with, but now I needed her warm and compliant.

So I shrugged off my jacket and draped it around her shoulders.

"What are you doing?" Her wide eyes flew up to mine, her long lashes fluttering as she studied me.

"I can't have you getting cold and deciding to go inside just when it's getting interesting."

"Of course," she said flatly. But she pulled my jacket tighter around her shoulders, and I bit back a smile as I took my seat. Pouring out two shots of vodka, I placed one in front of her.

"Your turn to ask a question."

She tapped her fingers against her almost empty glass, thinking. Her gaze lowered, and her voice was soft, almost hesitant. "Okay. Did you like kissing me that night in the crypts? Or…or the next day?"

Hard fucking pass. I picked up the shot and tipped it back, welcoming the burn of the vodka. "My turn."

The wild look in her eyes faded, replaced with barely concealed lust. "Oh, Knox. The fact you didn't answer that question tells me everything I needed to know."

My fucking dick was responding to her, and it needed to stop. "It tells you fuck all. Remember what I said to you? Kissing you was a mistake that won't happen again."

Before she could respond, I asked my own question. "Did you like it when I tied you up in the crypts? Spread your legs with the bar?" I leaned closer, trailing a finger up her throat. "Choked you with my mother's own diamonds tonight?"

Her breath hitched, and my cock hardened even further, straining at the seam of my trousers.

When her tongue darted out to swipe across her lips, leaving them glistening in the low light, I fucking wanted to kiss her, but I wouldn't. She glanced down at the shot glass, the edges of her fingers brushing against it.

Her whispered reply cut through the silence as she picked up the glass, tilting it to her lips. "*Yes.*"

My hand curved around her throat, and I tugged her towards me, sending her sprawling across my body. She gasped, throwing out her hands to land on my shoulders and balancing herself on my thighs. The split in her dress gaped open and showed an obscene amount of smooth, long leg.

I lowered my head, my mouth brushing against her hair. "I knew you did. You were practically begging for it."

"I wasn't," she hissed.

"Little liar." Sliding my hand up her exposed thigh, I felt her shudder against me. "Look at you. You can't hide the fact that you want me."

"What about you?" She shifted on top of me, her thigh rubbing against my hard dick. "It feels like you want me. You do, don't you?"

"Remember what I told you before, baby." I skimmed my teeth down her throat, enjoying her unsteady breaths and her pulse beating frantically beneath my lips. "I've fucked a lot of girls I don't even like. You're nothing special."

"B-but—" Her words cut off on a moan as I sucked a dark mark into her neck. A sign of me that she would be forced to see the next time she looked in a mirror. "That was…wasn't my question."

"Let me make this crystal fucking clear," I growled against her skin. "My dick wants you, but *I don't.*"

She stiffened against me, and then she was pulling out of my grip so fast that I didn't even have a chance to react. Staggering backwards, she put the table in between us. Her chest was heaving, and it just drew all my attention to those gorgeous, full breasts with those peaked nipples teasing me through the silky fabric of her dress. My cock was pounding in my trousers, and it took everything I had to not lunge for her and bury myself inside her.

"Message received," she said, a tremor in her voice. "I think this game has gone on for long enough."

Spinning on her heel, she turned to leave.

I only let her get as far as the door. Before she even touched the handle, I was out of my seat and pulling her back against me. One of my arms wrapped tightly around her waist, holding her securely in place. I ran my hand up her arm, up to her hair, brushing it away from her shoulder so I could dip my head to her ear.

"No, Elena." I bit down on the shell of her ear, making her shudder against me. "The game isn't over until I say it's over."

25

Elena

His low rasp in my ear, combined with the way his hard length was digging into my ass, did things to me. My pussy was soaking my underwear, my skin was so sensitive that every touch set me on fire, and I ached for him. I was fully out of my depth here—I'd never, ever been in a situation where I was so into someone that was so incredibly wrong for me. But I couldn't help feeling like it might be the same for him. He'd said that he'd been with other girls he didn't like, but from my observations, the girls that he didn't flirt with, he treated with disinterest. Not with active hostility, the way he did with me.

I didn't believe that he didn't want me either. And his excuse about his dick wanting me was ridiculous. I believed that he didn't *want* to want me, which was the same way I felt, but that was different to not wanting me altogether.

"Tell me the truth, then," I managed to gasp out as his hand slid around my throat, then moved down, tracing the curve of my breast where my dress dipped down low. He eased a finger inside, carefully peeling away the tape that held it in place, and then his hand was cupping my aching breast, his thumb stroking over my nipple. "Fuck, *Knox*." Throwing my head back against his shoulder, I lost myself in his touch, forgetting that I'd even asked a question until his mouth was at my ear again.

"I want you tonight. Only for tonight."

"Only for tonight." My whispered agreement was barely out of my mouth when he was spinning me around and pushing me back against the wall. His hands skimmed down my sides, down to my hips, and then lower. He grasped the fabric of my dress, his touch surprisingly gentle, and began pulling it up.

"Wait, what? Are you—"

"I'm not fucking you here. *Yet*. We're still playing the game." He dragged the skirt of my dress all the way up so that my underwear was exposed, then pulled me with him so he was sitting back on his chair with us both face to face and I was straddling him properly, my legs on either side of his thighs and my pussy directly in line with the hard length of his erection, with just a few layers of material separating us.

I gasped and immediately clamped down on my lip. He'd had far too many reactions from me tonight, reactions that I'd been unable to control.

But from the smirk on his face, he hadn't missed it.

Bastard.

"My turn." There was amusement in his tone as his hot breath hit my cheek. His fingers dipped down between us, and then he was stroking across my clit, sending bursts of sensation across my body.

"Knox…please…" I didn't even know what I was saying.

"Take a shot, baby. You didn't answer the last question properly."

Cruel Crypts

A cool glass was pressed against my lower lip, and I tipped my head back, opening my mouth and letting the vodka slide down my throat. Smooth but fiery, just like him.

"You didn't either." My brain was getting a little fuzzy around the edges, but I knew that he hadn't answered me truthfully, not until I'd pushed him for an answer.

"Okay." The hand that had been on my hip released me. I leaned back a little, watching as he threw back the shot, his throat working as he swallowed.

When he'd drained the glass and refilled both mine and his, he fixed his dark gaze on me. "It's still my turn." His finger brushed against my clit again, and his mouth went to my throat, his teeth clamping down on my skin and sending pleasure-pain through me that I couldn't get enough of. "What were you looking for in my bedroom?"

A whimper fell from my throat when his large hands arranged my body so I was arched back against the tabletop. His head lowered, and he lightly bit down on my nipple. He followed it up, licking and sucking, before turning his attention to my other breast. I barely remembered that he'd asked me a question, lost in the sensation of his hot mouth on my skin, until he raised his head.

"I asked you a question."

"Evidence." The word fell from my lips before I could even stop it. His body stiffened against me, and he drew back a little to meet my gaze, his brows pulling together. There was confusion in his gorgeous dark eyes.

"Evidence? Of what?"

"No." I shook my head. "I answered. It's my turn to ask you a question." My head was already a little cloudy from the alcohol, and I knew I had to tread carefully. I wanted to find out what he knew about me, but at the same time, I didn't want to make him any more suspicious by asking the wrong questions.

Angling my head forwards, I brushed my lips across his, but he immediately turned his head to the side. *Right*. No kissing. With a sigh, I pressed against him, kissing across his jaw, feeling the drag of his stubbled skin beneath my lips. He exhaled against me, tilting his head slightly farther away, and I took it as permission to continue.

"My question," I whispered after pressing one last kiss to the side of his face. "Why exactly do you hate me so much?"

There was a long moment of silence, and then he shook his head. "Where the fuck do I even start?" he muttered, reaching around me, picking up his shot glass and tipping it to his lips.

When he'd downed the vodka and refilled the glass, he gripped my hips, sliding me over his thick erection, and I moaned. "Knox…fuck."

"You want it so bad, don't you, baby?" He moved me again, and I suppressed another moan.

"Oh…*fuck*. Is…is that…is that your question?"

His laugh was low, vibrating over my skin as his mouth went to my throat. "That was an observation. My question is the same as yours. Why do you hate me so much?"

That was something that I couldn't even begin to answer, and at that moment? Feeling him against me, his hot mouth trailing fire everywhere he touched, the evidence of his arousal between my legs, I didn't think I hated him at all.

"Pass." I started to twist my body around for my shot glass, but he held me in place with one hand.

"Open." His knuckles nudged my chin up, and then when my lips parted, he tilted the vodka bottle to my mouth. The liquid burned as it slid down my throat, and I swallowed, trying not to cough. A few drops escaped, dripping from my lip as he angled the bottle further, and he dipped down, following their path with his tongue, a long, hot line down my neck.

When he reached my breasts again and his mouth closed over the tip of my nipple, I gasped. My skin was overheated and oversensitised, even though my arms were currently bare. His suit jacket must've fallen from my shoulders at some point, and I hadn't even noticed.

"Next question." I didn't care how shameless I sounded; I wanted him too much. "Are you going to fuck me?"

He glanced up at me again, his pupils so dilated that they were almost fully black. A slow smile curved across his lips, and his finger stroked downwards, just above my clit, teasing me with his touch. "I will…if you beg me."

My breath hitched, and we could both hear it.

"Elena. Are you going to beg for it?"

I gave him what we both wanted. "Fuck me. Knox, *please*."

His eyes flashed, dark, hungry fire, and I wanted to kiss him so badly. Wanted him to snap and kiss *me*. But he didn't. He bit down on the skin of my throat, hard, making me gasp. I pulled him closer, sliding my hands across his muscular back, until there was no space between us.

"Wait." He pulled back. His hand went to his pocket, and as my hands went to his tie, undoing the knot, I heard the unmistakeable sound of a foil packet tearing. I yanked the tie from his collar, and then my fingers went to the buttons of his shirt, the sound of our breaths accompanied by the soft whisper of fabric as I parted his shirt and the metallic sound of a zipper opening.

When I kissed down his throat and then lower, letting my teeth scrape across his collarbone, he groaned. "Fuck, baby. Need to be inside you." His hands went to my hips, and then he was shoving the delicate silk of my underwear aside and lifting me, impaling me on his huge, thick cock. It burned, but it was *so* good.

"You. Feel. So. Fucking. Good." He punctuated his words by thrusting up against me, and I rolled my hips down, meeting him thrust for thrust. Our bodies seemed to move together effortlessly, like we'd been fucking for years.

"Knox." All I could do was pant out his name as he took me apart with his cock and his fingers, sending me spiralling towards the edge.

"How…long…have you been wanting to do this?" I managed to gasp out my question.

"Since the first second I saw you tonight. Then when that fucker dared to ask you to dance earlier, I knew I was going to make you mine," he growled, thrusting up harder, his powerful thighs flexing underneath mine as he hit that spot inside me with perfect accuracy.

I moved faster against him, gripping onto his shoulders, kissing every part of him I could reach except his mouth, hot and wet and messy. "Knox. I'm so close."

"Fuck, baby." He moved his hands to grip my ass, palming it as I rolled my hips again and again. "One last question." His tongue traced over the shell of my ear, a soft touch contrasting the frantic movements of our bodies.

"Why did you change your name?" As he rasped out the words, his tone low and dangerous, he gave one hard rub of his finger against my clit. I was done for, soaring over the edge, my body shaking.

My vision blurred, and my mind was gone—caught between the blissful pleasure of my orgasm and the panic that his words had brought on. So much so that I barely registered him coming inside me, his hard length throbbing as he filled the condom.

I didn't know how I managed it because my entire body was completely wrung out, drained and satiated, but I somehow got my shaking legs to work, lifting myself off him and stumbling over to the other side of the table.

"Pass," I whispered. "This game is over."

26

KNOX

Elena stared at me from across the table, still breathing hard. Somehow, between the start and end of this game, I'd lost sight of my objective. Something at the back of my mind had reminded me to ask her the question I'd really wanted the answer to, but by then, it was too late. Her pussy clamping down on my cock felt so good, the curves of her body so hot under my hands, that I couldn't even bring myself to care about the questions anymore. I knew that I'd kick myself tomorrow —it was a fucking guarantee—but for now, my dick was satisfied, and my mind was wiped blank, thanks to a superior fuck. The way this girl was leagues above anyone else I'd been with, including the older women, should have and did make me rage. Usually. But not tonight.

The sound of a key made us both startle, and I was at the door in three swift strides, rapping on the glass.

"My apologies, sir." One of the members of staff inclined his head as he swung the door open. "I wasn't aware that anyone was out here."

"Give us five minutes," I instructed, closing the door in

his face. Heading back over to the table, I swiped my discarded tie from the floor. I buttoned my shirt back up and threaded the tie back through my collar, tying it in an easy, practised movement. Glancing over at Elena, I saw that she was leaning against the table, holding on to it with a white-knuckled grip. Her hair was dishevelled from where I'd had my hands through it, and her dress gaped open where I'd removed the tape that had been holding it in place.

I picked up my jacket and strode over to her. No one else got to see her so undone. Only me. "Put this on."

She met my gaze, her pretty light brown eyes luminous in the low light. "What?"

"Put it on unless you want everyone to know what we were doing out here. I certainly don't want anyone to know that I was fucking someone like *you*." My lip curled as I threw the words out, designed to be cruel and cutting.

She visibly flinched, but then she gathered herself, glaring at me. Yanking the jacket out of my hands, she thrust her arms into it, then did up the single button.

It would do. She was covered enough that no one would notice the state of her dress underneath. Except… her hair…

Reaching out, I slid my fingers through the silky soft strands. "Hold still," I murmured, hating the way my voice betrayed me, coming out almost gentle. When I'd finished smoothing out her hair as best I could, I took a step back, then another, needing to create some distance between us. "We should go."

When I opened the door, she followed me inside in silence. The room was busier than it had been earlier, and when I glanced at the time, I saw that it was close to midnight. The party would probably wind down in around an hour or two, but I had zero desire to stay until the end.

Pressing a hand to the small of Elena's back, steering her through the room, my mouth opened, and I couldn't fucking believe the words that came out of it.

"We said tonight. Only tonight. It isn't midnight yet. Let's go home."

Her eyes widened. She stopped dead in the middle of the room and stared at me for a long moment. Then she nodded.

"Okay. Let's go."

What the fuck was I doing? What were *we* doing? We couldn't stand each other, couldn't trust each other, and yet, here we were, exiting this dinner event like we were a fucking couple or something.

We were almost at the door when I heard my mother's voice from behind us. We both spun around, and I locked down my expression fast, affecting my usual blank look.

"Knox. Elena." She eyed us with one delicately raised brow, and as I met her gaze, I was suddenly aware of the fact that she wasn't alone. My dad was there with her too, smirking at us both.

Fuck my parents.

"Are you going home?" My mother smiled, and it was way too shark-like.

"I'm tired," Elena volunteered, and somehow, she managed to sound genuine. Maybe she actually was tired.

Fuck. Maybe she was expecting that we'd go our separate ways when we arrived back at the house.

Something inside me rebelled at that thought, but I kept it on lockdown.

"Elena's tired, and so am I," I said brusquely, not wanting to prolong the conversation any further than necessary. "Enjoy the rest of the evening."

"Oh, we will." My dad leered at me as he slipped his arm around my mum's waist, and I almost gagged. At least his attention had been diverted, and consequently, so had my mother's. We made our way past them and outside without any more comments, and in less than three minutes, the car that Elena had arrived here in was in front of us. Gareth eyed me with amusement from the front seat—he was my parents' preferred driver for events, and it was more or less guaranteed that he knew everything about us, although he wouldn't ever share anything, thanks to the NDA he'd signed when my dad had first employed his services.

The ride home was silent, and after I'd said a muttered goodbye to Gareth, Elena and I were alone.

It took a minute for me to invite her to my room.

Another minute to divest her of her clothes and jewellery.

And under a minute for me to press her into my mattress and sink my cock inside her.

When we were finished, long after I'd got rid of the condom and pulled her into my arms, I spoke. "This is nothing."

She curled into me, her palm stroking over my chest, where my heart was beating way too hard. "I know. It's nothing. I hate you, and you hate me."

"Yeah." Fuck my voice for going all husky. "Glad you realise that this means fuck all."

"It means nothing." She yawned against my chest. "We hate each other."

"Yeah, we do."

Despite everything, despite the fact that Elena was right here when she should be in her own room, far away from mine, somehow, I fell asleep.

27

Elena

My eyes blinked open. There was a heavy weight across my back, and…was that fingers sliding through my hair?

I turned my head, and the hand fell away from my hair.

"What time is it?" Last night came flooding back to me. I'd fallen asleep in Knox's arms, and here I was, still, and he wasn't kicking me out.

Yet.

"Around five thirty." Knox's voice was a soft, sleepy rumble. "Too early."

I shifted on the bed. I was on my stomach, the side of my body pressed up against Knox, who was on his side. His arm lay across my back, his fingers now resting on my bare skin instead of stroking through my hair.

"Elena. Tell me why you changed your name."

Here in his bed, in the early hours of the morning, cocooned in a blanket of darkness, it was easier to speak. And I was tired. Tired of pretending. Maybe here, we could have this tiny sliver of truth. Even if it wasn't the whole story.

"My mum raised me as a single parent because my dad didn't want to have anything to do with us. But she had help. Her sister and her husband—my aunt and uncle—supported us. You... Well, it's hard to explain to someone who's never been without money." I held my breath, wishing I could take those words back as soon as I'd said them.

Surprisingly, he didn't get angry. "Help me to understand."

"Okay. Well, my aunt, um, she couldn't have any children, and she looked after me so my mum could work. My uncle used his connections to get my mum a job, and he did so much else for us. Took us on holiday, paid for things I needed for school, everything that my mum couldn't afford to pay for. It was...good." For the most part. I didn't mention my aunt's dependence on a cocktail of pills just to make it through the day because Knox didn't need to know that.

Turning my face into the pillow so that I was out of the direct line of his gaze, I continued. "Then one day, they were gone. We were...we were left with nothing. We had nothing, and we couldn't bring them back."

My voice cracked, and I felt Knox's hand smooth down my spine. He remained silent, which I appreciated more than he'd ever know. I couldn't talk about it, how my aunt had taken her own life and how my uncle had lost everything he'd ever loved. How they were both taken from us.

My tears soaked the pillow beneath me, and I sniffed, trying to get myself back under control. "We... My mum decided we needed a fresh start." This was the point where

I was going to have to lie to him because the truth would bring down hell on us. "It was…too painful. So she changed our surnames. It was…a way to disassociate, I think. It didn't matter to me at the time. We were struggling to get by at that point, trying to prioritise bills, working out if we could afford to eat and heat the house at the same time, that kind of thing."

I heard his sharp intake of breath, but he covered it quickly, clearing his throat. "Where did you live? Your birth certificate said you were born in Cirencester. Not too far from here, really. Maybe twenty-five or thirty miles."

Fuck. He'd seen my real birth certificate? My heart rate picked up, and I wished I hadn't started because the lies had to keep coming. I just hoped he'd believe them. The information my mother had made me memorise was thankfully fresh in my mind, and after taking a deep breath, I managed to reply with a mostly steady voice. "We moved to Bristol to be close to my aunt and uncle when I was born."

We *had* lived in the city of Bristol, just not since I was born. Only for the past year.

He opened his mouth, and I spoke before he could ask me anything else. "How did you get my birth certificate? *Why* did you get my birth certificate?"

"I'm not answering the how, but as for the why…" Shifting closer to me, he pressed a kiss just below my ear. "I don't trust you, and I knew you were hiding something."

Fuckfuckfuck. "Well, now you know my big secret. What are you going to do? Tell your parents? Make it look like we've been lying so my mum loses her job, and we end up back on the streets?" My voice shook.

There was a long, long silence, but eventually, he shook his head. "I'm satisfied with your mother's employment record, and I've seen that despite my misgivings, she really is good with JoJo. But if either of you step out of line, I go straight to my dad."

He was going to hold this over my head, wasn't he? He'd have me at his mercy with the perfect blackmail material. It seemed like he didn't know anything else, but if he went digging…if his dad went digging…

"I understand," I said quietly. "I'm not here to cause trouble. I just want to finish this school year, and then I'll get out of here, and you'll never have to see me again." Maybe it would be even sooner if I could convince my mother that her plan was pointless.

Another soft press of his lips against the side of my face. "Is that a promise?"

"That you'll never have to see me again? Yes."

"Good," he said, but he didn't sound satisfied. What did he want from me?

I needed to get out of here. I felt too exposed, laid bare for him both figuratively and in reality. "I'm…I need to go back to my bed."

"Yeah. I'm not stopping you." He shifted back, his hand falling away from me, and turned his head away. I slipped out of bed and pulled on last night's dress, balling up my ruined underwear and grabbing my heels. The diamond choker was on his bedside table, next to his phone, and I hesitated, then rounded the bed, stopping at his side. Trailing my fingers over the diamonds, I looked down at him.

"Would you feel more comfortable giving this back to your mother yourself, or should I take it?"

He stared up at me, heavy-lidded and gorgeous, and I wished for a minute that this could be real. That there weren't so many secrets and lies between us. That we weren't polar opposites in all the ways that mattered.

"Leave it with me," he murmured, and I nodded.

"Thank you." Leaning down, I stole a kiss from him because I knew he wouldn't give me one. It wasn't even really a kiss, just the barest brush of my lips over his before I straightened up, and then I left him alone.

28

Elena

My mother and I hadn't crossed paths at all yesterday—I'd had a full day of intensive driving lessons, and she'd been out somewhere until quite late. So I'd made sure that I set my alarm for an hour earlier on Monday morning, and now here I was, ready for school in my perfectly pressed uniform, my hair neatly tied back, and light make-up enhancing my features. I entered the kitchen, where I knew my mother would be giving JoJo her breakfast, hoping that there wouldn't be anyone else around.

I was in luck. We were alone, other than JoJo, who was digging into a bowl of Cheerios, half of it ending up on the floor around her high chair.

Before my mother could say anything, I slid into the seat opposite her at the kitchen table. "Mum, I need to talk to you."

She glanced up at me, her eyes narrowing as she took in my serious expression. "What's wrong?"

I'd spent all night thinking about this, and yet I still struggled to find the right words. "I think…I don't want to do this anymore. I don't think we should do this. We should leave and let the Ashcrofts live their lives."

Her mouth fell open as she stared at me. "Elena, why are you saying this? Don't you remember why we're doing this?"

"I know, I just think—"

"It's the boy, isn't it?" She shook her head, her lips thinning. "Don't allow your head to be turned by a handsome face. He'll feed you all the lines you want to hear, and then you'll end up pregnant and alone. Is that what you want?"

I sighed. "Mum, are we talking about me or you here? Anyway, Knox isn't the reason. Do you think that it's worth it? If you find something and use it, you'll be ruining a family. What about JoJo? Isn't it better that she grows up with both her parents in her life, parents who clearly love her and love each other? The Ashcrofts...they're good people. Yeah, I know they're rich and sometimes arrogant, but that doesn't mean they deserve—"

"How *dare* you." Her words were like a slap, a stinging mark that flew through the space between us, and I recoiled at the sheer venom in her voice. She'd never spoken like this to me before. "Our family has already been ruined. Anthony Ashcroft deserves everything that's coming to him."

JoJo was now staring between us with wide, worried eyes, and her little bottom lip was starting to tremble. My mother smoothly plucked a banana from the fruit bowl, peeled it, and broke off a piece, handing it to her. She was immediately distracted, thankfully.

"Mum, please. Think about it. Seriously. Because I have. When it was all planned in your head, it...I guess it seemed like a good idea. I was angry, like you. I wanted payback. But now we're here, and these people have done nothing but make us feel welcome…" Except for Knox, of course.

"It's not that simple. If we just gave up, where would we be? I know you've saved some money, but it isn't enough for us to start again."

"Okay, then can we at least forget about revenge and stay here until we have a decent amount saved? I can sell some more things and increase my hours—wait, what's happened to the money you've been earning?"

My mother closed her eyes, pinching her brow, and when she opened them again, there was something calculating in them. Something I didn't like. "My money has been paying back my contact. His interest rates are… excessive. But that's beside the point. You tell me to forget about revenge, but who will pay for what happened?"

I steeled myself, forcing out the words, although I knew she wouldn't want to hear them. "Why does Anthony Ashcroft need to be the one to pay? I don't think you're going to dig up any skeletons because he's a good man. What happened wasn't his fault, not really."

The betrayal in her face was almost too much to bear. "*Yes it was*. He was supposed to be the best, and he failed. I lost *everything*."

She lost everything? It hadn't been just her that had been affected.

"Your aunt's life is over. Your uncle's life is over. Our lives are over. What do we have to look forward to, Elena? There's nothing left for us anymore."

"Please," I begged. "Please just think about it. No more lives need to be ruined."

"If you're not with me, you're against me." Her tone was final.

I stared at her, the woman who'd raised me from birth, and yet, at that moment, it felt like I didn't know her at all.

"Of course I'm with you," I said, but the words were bitter on my tongue. They tasted like a lie.

"What's wrong?"

Knox's voice pulled me out of my dark thoughts. As usual, he was tapping along with his obnoxious music, the rhythm of his fingers on the steering wheel strangely soothing.

I glanced over at his profile, struck all over again by his looks. It wasn't fair that he affected me so strongly. It wasn't even just his looks anymore—the tiny glimpses he gave me of his real self only served to make me want to know more.

There was no point in thinking like that, though, so I ignored the butterflies in my belly and attempted to answer him in as normal a tone as possible. "Nothing, just tired. I thought you liked it better when I didn't speak."

His gaze slid to mine, then away again, amusement glinting in his eyes as a smirk curled over his lips. "I think you and I both know that I like it best when you're moaning my name, coming all over my cock."

I gasped at his unexpected words, shifting in my seat and rubbing my thighs together. "We agreed…I thought we said it was a one-night-only thing on Saturday?"

"It was. One hundred fucking percent. It's not about wanting a repeat, believe me."

"Okay. I believe you." I slumped back in my seat as he turned the Maserati into the Hatherley Hall student car park, the tyres crunching over the gravel. When we came to a stop, I grabbed my bag and made to leave, but Knox stopped me with a hand on my arm.

"Don't tell anyone what happened on Saturday night."

I rolled my eyes. "Why would I want to? I have no

interest in making myself a target for your groupies. Or joining their ranks, for that matter."

His mouth twisted. "You could never be one of those girls. Fucking *never*. You're—"

Before he could say anything hurtful, I threw the door open and slid out of the SUV. "I know. You don't have to remind me again of how I don't fit in here." I managed to close the door without slamming it and walked away. Lucky for me, Katy was up ahead, meandering along the path that led from the lake to the main school building, and I waved to get her attention, detouring to catch up with her.

When she was next to me, she greeted me with a smile. "Hi. Perfect timing. You just caught me at the end of my morning walk. How was your weekend?"

I shrugged. "Busy, I guess. I worked on Saturday morning, then I had a driving lesson, and I had driving lessons again all day on Sunday. How was yours?"

She tilted her head, eyeing me as she slid her arm through mine. "Haven't you left something out?"

I thought of Knox's warning. "No?"

A laugh burst from her mouth. "You should see your face. I wasn't trying to scare you or anything. I just heard from one of the girls in my dorm that you were at an event on Saturday night. With Knox."

"Um. It wasn't like that." As we headed in the direction of the school, I slowed my pace, and she matched me. "It was actually his mum's idea, and both his parents were there. I…I'm not sure why she invited me, to be honest with you, but she wouldn't take no for an answer. She even sent me to her stylist and gave me a dress and shoes, and, oh! She lent me this gorgeous diamond choker to wear. I was pretty sure the diamonds were actually real, and I was honestly scared to wear it." Thoughts of that choker led me to thoughts of Knox... My face heated as memories flashed through my mind. He really was unforgettable, wasn't he?

"Wow. That's really nice of her. Do you have any photos?"

"I took a couple of selfies before I left. I'll show you in a minute." We pushed inside the large doors and headed up the stairs to the Epi common room, dropping into what had become our usual seats. I did my best to ignore the other side of the room where Knox and the rest of the elite held court with their usual crowd. As I showed Katy the photos, Will joined us.

"Morning, ladies." He threw himself down next to Katy, slipping his arm around her waist. Leaning around her, he eyed me with raised brows. "What have you done to elicit the undivided attention of Knox today?"

"What?" My eyes darted in the direction of the elite, and sure enough, Knox's dark gaze was fixed on me. I inhaled sharply, unprepared for the intensity of his stare.

With an effort, I tore my gaze away from his and back to Will's. "I honestly have no idea." It was the truth.

All day, whenever we were in the same room, I felt Knox's eyes on me. By the time I reached my afternoon free period, I was climbing out of my skin, restless, needing to get away. My after-school driving lesson couldn't come quickly enough.

One more hour to go.

During the last period of the day, my phone buzzed with a text.

> ARIA:
> Is everything OK? I didn't get a chance to speak to you, but you looked stressed every time I saw you today. Is it Knox?

I sighed, rubbing between my brows, trying to stave off the headache that was forming. What could I tell her? He'd told me not to say anything, and I took his threat seriously because I knew he meant it.

ME:

> I'm just having a bad day I think. I had a charity thing with him on Saturday night. Not sure what's happening. He's confusing

That was as much as I dared to say.

ARIA:

> Believe me, I know the feeling. If you want to talk, I'm here x

ME:

> Thanks. That means a lot x

If only I could speak to her about what was going on, but I couldn't risk it.

Swinging my bag over my shoulder the second the final bell sounded, I made for the door, aware of Knox's voice in the background telling his friends he'd catch up with them.

I reached the door. Almost free.

A hand wrapped around my wrist, forcing me to a stop, and then an arm came around my waist, hauling me out of the common room and around the corner to an empty corridor.

I was pressed back against the stone wall, and when I raised my head, Knox was there, still looking at me again with that dark, heavy stare.

We were frozen in place, his body holding me against the wall, his face so close to mine we were almost sharing the same breath.

He exhaled, and then he brought his mouth down on mine.

Heat flared, fire racing through me as I opened my mouth to him, letting him take what he wanted from me, his tongue sliding against mine, his hand curving around the back of my head to hold me in place, his fingers tangling in my hair.

This was so much more than just a kiss. It left me breathless, my head spinning, unable to process how the person who professed to hate me could kiss me with such fucking passion.

"You…you said you'd never kiss me again," I gasped out against his lips.

He kissed me again.

And again.

When he finally released me and took a step back, both of us were breathing hard. He slid his tongue across his lower lip, his dark eyes scanning over every inch of my face.

"Maybe we're both liars," he said.

29

KNOX

My phone blinked at me.
1 new message.
When I thumbed open the screen, though, it wasn't the message I was waiting for. Instead, it was from Erin, one of the girls at school and a wannabe goddess, asking if I was free to meet up.

How about fucking never? I ignored her message, scrolling back to the conversation thread with Nitro, staring at it as if it would make a reply magically appear. I'd sent him the information Elena had told me to see if he could find any evidence to corroborate her story, because as much as I wanted to believe it, I didn't. I still didn't trust her, but I wanted to. Too fucking much, and I wasn't prepared to examine the reasons why.

It was bad enough that I'd kissed her again.

I made my way into the kitchen to grab a late-night glass of water and stopped dead at the sight of the girl currently occupying my thoughts, her back to me, wiping down the already spotless countertops.

"What are you doing?"

Elena startled visibly before spinning around to face me, her hand over her heart. "You scared me."

I almost cracked a smile, but I didn't. Instead, I moved closer and closer until I was right in front of her. Her breath hitched, her lips parting and her eyes going wide, and I fucking loved it.

"What are you doing?" I asked again, gripping her chin and tilting her head up.

"What does it look like I'm doing? Use your eyes. I've got a cloth and this cleaning spray. Take a guess."

This time, I did smile, lowering my head and ghosting my lips across hers, not quite touching. "It looks like you're up to no good in my kitchen."

"Your kitchen, is it?" She smiled too, her lips moving under mine, and fuck it. I'd been denying myself for long enough already. I closed the remaining two millimetres of distance and kissed her.

"If you can't work it out," she said when I eventually managed to tear my mouth away from those fucking soft pouty lips, "I'm cleaning for your parents, like I promised I would."

"It's late."

"Yeah, I know that. But I had my driving lesson, and then I had an extra shift at the country club, then homework, and this was the only time I could fit it in." She clapped her hand over her mouth, stifling a yawn. "I still need to revise for my driving theory test after this. It's happening tomorrow and I need to be ready."

"Baby, you're going to make yourself sick piling all that on yourself. Stop the cleaning; you know my parents won't care. They pay cleaning staff, remember?"

"Why do you care?"

Good fucking question. One I didn't have an answer to. "I'll help you in here, and then I'll test you on the theory questions, okay?" What the actual fuck was I saying? I couldn't believe the words that were coming out of my mouth.

"You will?" She stared at me, stunned.

I shrugged. "Yeah. I'm bored. You can entertain me."

"Oh, Knox. You really should get out more if you think that cleaning and helping me revise counts as entertainment." She smirked, and I couldn't help my grin.

"Maybe you could sing for me to make it more fun. You're writing a song with William, aren't you? I saw it in our business studies class."

"Yeah." Her voice went quiet, and I knew we were both remembering how I'd acted towards her that day, grinding the paper under my foot because I was so fucking pissed off with her. Now here I was, with the taste of her still on my lips, fucking bantering with her like we were friends or something.

She slid away from me, and I thought for a minute that I'd fucked up this fragile truce we had going on, but after ducking down behind the island, she reappeared, throwing me a cloth.

"You can do the worktops by the oven, and I'll finish these ones." There was a pause, and then she added, "You're right, I am writing a song with Will. Him and Katy, actually, for our music coursework. I'm more of a lyricist, I guess, although I can play the guitar, but Katy's a genius at finding the melodies, and Will—he writes the music too, but you should see him when he gets in front of a laptop. Mixing the sounds, making something amazing. Creating magic."

My jaw clenched as something curled inside my gut at her tone of admiration. No fucking way was I jealous of *William Fitzgerald-fucking-Jones*.

She glanced at me cautiously as I tried to unclench my

jaw. "You know, there was a song you played in the car this morning. It was a little bit softer than the stuff you normally listen to." Her fingers tapped against the worktop as she thought. "I wondered if it might work with the song we're writing. We have to do an original version and a remix, and…I think it could work for the remix. Something about getting lost." Stepping a little closer, she hummed a few bars, and I immediately recognised it.

"That's 'Lost in the Moment' by NF. If you use it, do I get producer credits or something?"

Shaking her head, she laughed, and I swallowed whatever reply she was going to give me with a kiss.

Fuck. I had to stop doing this. It had been easy to convince myself not to kiss her after the first time, but now that we'd started again, my willpower was way too fucking low to resist.

I'd somehow ended up lying on Elena's bed, stretched out across the length, quizzing her on driving theory practice questions. Every now and then, my willpower would break, and I'd have to fucking kiss her. I'd managed to hold back from anything more, even though my cock had been severely put to the test tonight. She was so close, dressed in simple grey joggers that hugged her legs and a tight plain blue sleeveless top that clung to her tits in a way that drew my eyes every time she took a particularly deep breath. It was so late, considering we both had to be up for school, and yet neither of us suggested moving.

Her eyes grew heavier, and she curled into my side, her voice getting soft with sleep as she answered my next question. When I glanced down at her again, she was fully asleep, relaxed and looking so innocent compared to what I actually knew of her.

It was then that my phone buzzed.

I didn't want to look. Didn't want to face the truth that was at the back of my mind, that she'd lied to me that night when it felt like she was sharing something important with me. Something of herself.

My hand fucking shook as I forced myself to pull my phone from my pocket. I stared at the darkened screen for a long time before thumbing it open.

Even though I'd known she'd lied, something inside me fucking cracked when I read the words.

NITRO:

> I did my best. No records of either Elena or Blackwood or Greenwood at any schools in Bristol or the surrounding areas until a year ago, where I found an Elena Greenwood. I widened my search and found an Elena Blackwood in two Cirencester schools—primary and secondary. Date of leaving matches up with Bristol school. Might be a coincidence but I don't think so. Age corresponds with birth cert. Let me know if you want me to search for anything else

> Good luck mate

I stared at the screen and then at Elena, asleep next to me. Rubbing my hand across my face, I groaned under my breath. Fuck. Why did everything have to get so complicated? Why was she lying to me? What was she hiding?

I had to find out, and I wouldn't stop until I'd uncovered the truth about what my little liar was hiding from me.

30

KNOX

"Are you gonna tell me what this is all about now?" Tristan adjusted his sunglasses, scanning the streets to his left as we hit the outskirts of Bristol, passing the turn-off for IKEA. "Not that I mind skiving off school with you, but you've been suspiciously secretive."

"There's a reason I picked you for this. You're good at chatting shit with girls."

"This is about girls?" He immediately perked up, the horny fucker.

"Down, boy. Your dick isn't getting involved in this little mission." I laughed at his whining sound of protest. "All you need to do is talk nicely to a few of the girls coming out of the sixth form of the school we're going to. Show them Elena's photo, find out what they know about her. I have…suspicions, and I need to see if they're right."

"Okaaay." His head turned towards me. "I can do that."

"Thanks. I appreciate it."

"Anytime, man. You know I've got your back. Ro has too." His gaze returned to the windscreen, his fingers tapping on the dashboard. "So Elena's involved in some shady shit, is she?"

"I don't know. It's a fucking mess."

We fell silent as the satnav directed us towards one of the more run-down suburbs, and finally, we were pulling up in front of a school. It was 1970s-style concrete blocks, with peeling green paintwork. A sign outside, almost obscured with graffiti, pronounced it as St. Catherine's Academy. After parking the Nissan Juke—which I'd purposely used today, knowing my Maserati would stand out like a sore fucking thumb—we exited the car and made our way to the gates.

"Sixth form girls only. They wear different clothes to the rest of the school. No proper uniform—anything in black, grey, or green."

"I'm on it," he promised me, and I trusted that he'd play his part right. As for me, I was going to attempt to sweet-talk the school receptionist, utilising all the tricks I'd picked up from my dad.

After clapping Tristan on the shoulder, I made my way inside the school with confident strides. Eighty percent of getting what you wanted in life was being able to bullshit—to act like you deserved it, to look the part, to be able to talk the talk.

I stopped in front of the reception desk. The woman behind the desk looked to be in her mid-twenties, which made things easier.

"Hi." Leaning on the desk, I gave her my most charming smile, knowing that my biceps were straining against the fabric of my shirt. Thank you very fucking much, lacrosse.

"H-hi." Her cheeks flushed as she took me in. "How

can I help you?"

"Well." Glancing at the nameplate she had affixed to her cardigan, I allowed my smile to widen. "Kayla. I was wondering if you could help me with a little project I have. One of your former students is up for an award for services to the community. She's a good friend of mine, and I promised that I'd announce the award."

Angling my body further, I lowered my voice conspiratorially. "As soon as I'd agreed to announce the award, they asked me to make a speech. I'm supposed to pepper the guests with anecdotes and stories about her life." With an exaggerated sigh, I rolled my eyes. "They want so much from me, Kayla. What can a poor man do?"

She stared at me, her cheeks still pink and her pupils dilated. "What can I do to help?"

"I was wondering if you had any anecdotes about her time here. Maybe any awards, notable achievements, anything like that?"

"I—I'm sure I can find something." Her fingers went to her keyboard, poised and ready. "What's her name?"

"Elena Greenwood."

She tapped away, immediately professional, and I pushed down my unwarranted impatience while I waited for my answers.

"Oh." Her face fell. "I'm sorry. She was only a student here for one year, her first year of sixth form. Although…" Her brows pulled together as she studied the screen. "She did receive an outstanding achievement for music in February of that year. Would that be any good?"

"That would be perfect. Thank you." I gave her another smile, waiting as she hit a button and the printer next to her desk juddered to life, eventually spitting out a single sheet of paper. She handed it to me, Elena's name jumping out as if it were highlighted in neon letters. Folding it carefully, I nodded at Kayla.

"Thank you. Wish me luck with my speech."

"Good luck," she was quick to say, and I shot her another grin as I backed away from the desk before turning on my heel and exiting the building.

Outside, I had to drag Tristan away from some girl he was leering all over, and once we were safely inside the car, I turned to him. "What did you find out?"

"Most of the girls I spoke to recognised her. Said she never fit in at the school. She was a loner, and they said they didn't think she had any friends."

Something in my chest fucking twisted at his words. I could picture Elena here far too easily, alone, away from everything she knew. And then she'd gone through it all again this year, except she'd gone from this shithole to the fucking elite. Where did she fit in?

"They said she was only here for a year. But you knew that already, didn't you?"

I nodded slowly. "I had my suspicions. But I needed them to be confirmed. Now they are, and I need to check out some other shit."

"For what it's worth, whatever suspicions you have about her, she's hot as fuck."

I laughed, steering the car back into traffic, following the satnav and pointing it towards Nottswood. "Yeah. Looks aren't everything, though."

"They are," he argued. "You're under the same roof. Make the most of it."

Instead of replying, I turned the music up. There were some things I didn't want to share, even with my best friends, and whatever was going on between Elena and me was one of those things. No one needed to know how fucking sweet she tasted, how she looked when she came apart underneath me, the way she wasn't afraid to challenge me, to fight back, like no one ever had before.

How the fuck did I reconcile all that with the information I'd just found out?

The only thing I could do was to keep digging, until I'd uncovered every one of her secrets.

31

Elena

I held the piece of paper in my hands, confirming what I'd already been told. I'd passed my driving theory test. Now, I just had the practical test to go at the end of the week, and if I managed to pass it, I'd officially be classed as a driver.

For some reason, all I wanted to do was to tell Knox. He shouldn't have been on my mind. My mum should have been the person I wanted to tell, but she wasn't.

Maybe it was the memory of him with his head on my pillow and the book propped open in front of him while he read out questions in his smooth, sexy voice. Even during the test, my mind had gone back to that moment.

Or maybe he was just stuck in my head. Permanently. And he shouldn't be.

I got back to the Ashcroft mansion at the same time as Knox pulled up. He was driving the Nissan Juke for some reason instead of his Maserati.

After I'd said my goodbyes to my instructor and reconfirmed tomorrow's driving lesson, I found Knox waiting for me outside the front door.

"Guess what. I passed my theory test, and my instructor pulled some strings so that I could have my practical test at the end of the week. There was a cancellation or something." I was aware I was babbling while he just stood there, unnaturally still and completely silent, but I couldn't seem to make myself shut up. "So maybe you'll only have three more days of driving me to school."

That sentence shocked him out of his stupor. With a growl, he closed his fingers around my wrist and yanked me into him.

"You're coming with me."

He dragged me inside, and I definitely wasn't complaining. No matter how ill-advised this situation between us was, after our interactions, I craved more. I wanted everything he would give me.

We made it up to his room, and the second the door had closed behind us, he was pushing me up against it, grinding his hard length into me, making me gasp into his mouth as he attacked me with hot, hungry kisses. His hands gripped my ass, pulling me even closer, and before I knew it, he had me stripped out of my school uniform, leaving me in just my skimpy underwear.

Taking a step back, he stared at me, his gaze raking over my body as he palmed his cock over his trousers. The heat in his eyes set me on fire, and I launched myself at him, ripping at his clothes until he was pressed up against me with his godlike body on full display.

I could barely get the words out I was so fucking gone for him. "Knox. Need you."

"Fuck, baby. You're so fucking hot." His low growl vibrated across my neck as his hands went to my back, undoing the clasp of my bra and then sliding lower, removing the rest of my underwear until I was as naked as him. "Tell me you're on the pill."

"Y-yes. Fuck."

The words had barely made it past my lips before he was lifting me up and thrusting inside me, his thick cock filling me, making the breath catch in my throat.

"*Knox*." My head fell back, hitting the wood of the door as I moaned his name. It was irresponsible to go without a condom, but in that moment, I didn't care. With his huge dick bare inside me, better than anything I'd ever felt before, there was no way I was going to stop.

I squeezed around him, and he groaned against my throat, his teeth scraping deliciously over my skin. His fingers clasped my thighs, digging in, and I hoped that the marks would be visible tomorrow.

"So fucking tight, baby. Feels so good." He thrust up again and again, the angle and grind of his body sending me soaring towards the edge. My back pressed up against the solid door, holding me in place as he pounded into me. It took barely any time before I was falling right over it, my head tipping forwards, moaning into the crook of his neck.

"Fuuuuck," he groaned, thrusting again, then again, and then I felt the hot pulse of his cock as he filled me with his cum.

When he withdrew from me, helping me to stand on wobbly legs, he glanced down between us, his gaze dark and hot and a satisfied smile on his face. "My cum dripping out of you is the sexiest thing I've ever seen." He dropped into a crouch, tracing a line up the inside of my shaking thigh with his fingertip and then gently pushing it inside me. "Feels so good."

"Mmm," I agreed breathlessly, still coming down from the high.

When he withdrew his finger and climbed to his feet,

he studied me for a moment, then tugged me towards his bed. "Round two as soon as we've rested. I want to fill you with my cum."

"You already have." I followed him onto the bed with a smile, collapsing down against the soft pillows.

His gaze scanned me from head to toe and then returned to my eyes. Rolling onto his side, he ran his fingers down my arm. His own eyes were wide, his brows pulled together as he huffed out a disbelieving breath. "Fuck. It feels like I've lost my mind. I've *never* fucked anyone without a condom before."

"Me neither. We probably should have talked about it before. Do I need to worry about catching anything?"

He shook his head. "I get regularly tested. Can't afford to fuck anything up. Do I need to worry?"

"No. I…uh, they made us have a full health check thing before we came here, and you're the only person I've been with since we arrived."

The smile on his face widened, and I couldn't help pressing closer to him, tilting my head in an invitation for him to kiss me. He took it, sliding his lips across mine, slowly and thoroughly, tugging me into him until we were completely wrapped in each other.

Much, much later, after round two was over and we'd both cleaned up and taken a quick break to eat, we collapsed into his bed. He'd shown no signs that he wanted me to leave, and I'd stay for as long as he wanted me. I didn't want this night to end. I wanted to pretend that what we had was something real, that he actually cared for me like I did for him. Something I could no longer deny to myself.

Running my hand over the firm, defined lines of his abs as I rested my head on his bicep, I looked up at him. "I didn't see you in school today. Where were you?"

His jaw tightened, just briefly, but I saw it, and it made my stomach clench. But then I wondered if I'd imagined it because he smiled down at me and said, "I was working on a class project with Tristan. Why, did you miss me?"

"No."

"My little liar." His voice was so soft as he angled his head down and kissed the tip of my nose. He pulled me closer into him, kissing me again, and everything inside me warmed.

32

KNOX

I had a problem—the girl who was curled into me right now, making herself at home in my bed like she was my fucking girlfriend or something. Technically, *she* wasn't the problem. The problem was the way I didn't want her to leave. It was concerning in every way. One: I didn't do repeats. Two: I didn't let anyone into my bed. Ever. Three: we'd fucked without a condom. Although I knew from snooping in my dad's office that Elena was on the pill—and if I hadn't had that information, I wouldn't have taken her word for it when I'd asked her if she was on it—it was still completely fucking reckless. Four: as fucking spectacular as the sex was, it didn't negate the fact that she'd been lying to me, and I knew she was hiding something. And that meant I didn't trust her.

Did I kick her out of my bed like I knew I should?

No.

Instead, I made things worse for myself, pressing my lips to the soft skin just below her ear while I wrapped her in my arms. "Tell me something about yourself."

She drew back, but I didn't let her get very far,

tightening my grip on her body. My dick stirred at the feel of her smooth thigh sliding against it, but I ignored that—we'd already fucked twice, and we both needed a break before we went again.

"What do you want to know?" There was a wary edge to her tone.

"Dunno. Something about you. Something from when you were a kid."

Curling back into me, she sighed. "Okay. Happy or sad?"

I thought about it for a minute. "Both."

Her hand resumed stroking across my abs, and I flexed them beneath her touch, feeling her smile against my skin. "Sad first, then. So you know I told you that my mum was at work all the time, and my aunt looked after me? Well, that wasn't exactly true. I mean, it was, but she was, um, addicted to some prescription pills. I don't know what they were, and she just kind of sat around, and I was normally left to fend for myself unless she was having a good day—which didn't happen very often. That was okay—like, I could deal with it, and I learned how to use the oven and make myself basic meals on the days when I knew my mum wouldn't be there. But she got into these states sometimes—"

"States?" I questioned, fighting to keep my tone even.

"Um, yeah. She had intermittent explosive disorder, or at least that's what my uncle said. She'd be fine for ages, then out of nowhere, she'd just have these moments where she'd rage...almost like how a kid might have a tantrum? It's kind of hard to explain, but that's the easiest way to describe it, I think. There wouldn't really be any warning; it would just happen. Not very often, and it never lasted for long, but yeah. That was it."

I ran my fingers through her silky hair. "I've never heard of that."

"I'm not sure how common it is. She was on medication for it, but then she started taking these other sets of pills, and I'm not sure if they were even legally prescribed to her, to be honest, but I think they interfered with the other ones she was taking because the episodes started happening again. One time, when I was about eight or maybe nine, I was in the kitchen at her and my uncle's house, and I was washing up some glasses. My aunt was sitting at the kitchen table, reading a newspaper. I'd put too much washing-up liquid on the sponge, and my hand slipped when I was holding one of the glasses. It made the glass bang against the tap, and it broke. I didn't mean for it to break."

Her voice wobbled almost imperceptibly, but it was enough for me to tug her even closer and kiss the side of her head. "You don't have to tell me what happened."

"No, I want to." She took a deep breath and then continued. "About two seconds after the glass broke, my aunt appeared next to me and yanked me off the step stool I was standing on. I fell over, and I had to curl myself into a ball next to the cupboard to try and protect myself while she went into this rage. She threw some of the glasses, and they smashed. Then she started slapping me and shouting at me, saying I was stupid and couldn't be trusted to do a simple task and I'd ruined her favourite glass. When it was finally over, she stormed out of the kitchen to lock herself in her room, and I managed to cut the bottom of my foot quite badly while I was cleaning up the mess. My uncle got home just after that happened, which was lucky because I ended up having to go to A&E to get stitches, and I couldn't walk on it for ages because the cut would've reopened."

I wanted to fucking rage. How fucking dare anyone treat Elena this way? "Fuck, baby. That's just…"

"Yeah. Well, that's a sad memory. I know it sounds bad, but she wasn't physically abusive outside of that episode."

"There's no excuse for physical violence, and you were a fucking *child*."

"I know. There isn't any excuse." She sighed softly before placing a kiss to my shoulder. "I did have a lot of good memories with her too. She seemed to be better in the summer, and we'd do things like go on picnics at the lake—all of us—and she was the one who taught me how to play the guitar."

We were both quiet for a minute, my hand still stroking her hair, and then she sighed again. "Go on, you tell me something sad now. Get all the depressing stuff out of the way first. By the way, I've never told anyone that story before. Only my aunt and uncle knew the truth—they encouraged me not to tell my mum."

"That's fucked up," I murmured.

"I know. There's a lot of things that I wish I'd done differently when I look back on them. Anyway, I can't change the past. Tell me your story."

"How am I gonna top yours?" The atmosphere was still heavy, so I tried to lighten it. "Do you want to hear about the time I cried because Santa brought me the wrong colour miniature Ferrari for Christmas?"

She stared up at me, then rolled her eyes with a smile. "Rich-boy problems."

"Oh, yeah. I was gutted. I wouldn't even get inside it."

"Wait, get inside it?" She arched a brow, and I smirked down at her.

"Yeah, it was a kids' version that you could drive around in. Proper replica of the real thing."

"Wow. Let me guess. You wanted it to be black, and it was red."

"Wrong." I shot her a smug grin. "It was red, and I wanted it to be yellow, just like my dad's one."

"So your obsession with black didn't begin at a young age," she mused. "It's very sweet that you wanted it to be just like your dad's, though."

"Take that back. I am not fucking *sweet*," I growled, and she laughed out loud, her whole body shaking.

"Your face!" she gasped between breaths. Patting my chest in a condescending way, she bit down on her lip, attempting a straight face. "You're right. You are very much not sweet. You're very manly and sexy and growly and other words ending with a Y. But all little kids are sweet."

"They are fucking not. Most are little shits, except for JoJo."

"Okay. *Some* little kids are sweet. You were obviously one of them."

"I'll give you fucking sweet." I yanked her on top of me and then rolled us so that she was pinned underneath me. We were both very naked, and it would be a shame not to make the most of it. "I'm gonna give you the sweetest fucking orgasm you've ever had in your life."

And I did exactly that.

33

Elena

"Tell me a happy memory now." Knox's voice was a low, lazy drawl. He eyed me from beneath his lowered lashes as he reached out and threaded his fingers through my hair.

"The first time I went on a plane. My uncle got a bonus at work, and he took us all on holiday to Tenerife. I was thirteen at the time. I remember being shocked at how fast the plane suddenly started to move, and then it lifted into the air, and I just remember staring out of the window, amazed at how small the trees and fields were getting. I had my first holiday romance there too."

"Holiday romance?" He raised a brow. "First kiss?"

I shook my head. "No, that was when I was eleven. My aunt and uncle's friends had a son who was a year older than me, and I had a bit of a crush on him. He looked a bit like Timothée Chalamet. I told him that I'd give him my bar of Dairy Milk in return for a kiss."

Knox's lips curved into an amused grin. "Bribery. I approve of it."

"Yeah, you would. You're the one who asked for sexual

favours in return for you keeping quiet about me snooping in your room."

His smile disappeared. "You know I wouldn't have actually forced you to do anything, right? Fuck, Elena. If there had been the slightest hint you weren't into—"

I reached out and covered his mouth. "Shush. I know. It was an excuse for both of us because we both wanted to fuck. Let's not deny it."

He smiled beneath my palm, and when I took my hand away from his mouth, he said, "What gave you that idea?"

"Hmm." I pretended to think about it. "Maybe it was the way your giant dick was trying to hammer its way out of your jeans."

"That's…very descriptive."

Returning his smile, I brushed my hand teasingly over his stomach, my hand dipping lower, but I stopped before I reached his cock. I didn't have another round of sex in me just yet, so I made the decision to move my hand away, ignoring his growl of protest.

"When was your first kiss?"

"I was eight. I can't even remember her name." He smirked at my eye roll. "Yeah, there have been that many girls."

"Of course. I'd expect nothing less from you. Give me a happy memory now—one that doesn't involve other girls, please."

"Why, are you jealous?"

"No." *Yes.*

"My little liar." Fuck, the way he called me that, it sounded almost fond. And the "my" part…I definitely wasn't complaining about that. He angled his head to brush a kiss across my lips. "Okay. This memory does involve another girl, but I think you'll be okay with it. It was the day JoJo was born. She came home from the hospital, and my mum showed me how to hold her. She handed her over to me, and I was so fucking scared. I mean, I'd never held a baby before, you know? But as soon as I was holding JoJo, she looked up at me, and she gripped my finger with a really tight grip, all her tiny fingers around mine, and I dunno, I was just really happy to have a baby sister. Before that, I didn't really care. I hadn't thought about what it would be like. It was, like, abstract or something."

I was melting. I was so fucking gone for this man it was ridiculous. "Knox. That's so—"

"Don't you fucking dare say it's sweet."

"As if I would." Widening my eyes, I gave him my most innocent look while he glared at me. After a minute or two of our silent staring contest, he cracked, the corners of his lips kicking up.

"Fuck." He scrubbed his hand across his face. His voice was tortured. "Why do you have to do this to me?"

"Do what?" I was genuinely baffled—one second, he'd been smiling, and now…whatever this was.

Pulling me into him, he spoke into my hair. "Making me fucking like you. I can't do this, Elena, not with you."

A lump came into my throat, a ball of hurt and disappointment, but I knew he was right. "You do the same to me." My voice lowered to a whisper, my lips ghosting across his collarbone. "I like you. A lot. Way too much. It's…I tried to stop it, but I can't."

"Fuck, baby. This is so fucked up. I know you've been lying to me. I know you're still lying and hiding shit from me. There are so many fucking red flags that I can't even see any other colour, but I can't stay away from you."

"Knox." Tears filled my eyes, and the lump in my throat grew bigger. I swallowed hard, the truth spilling from my lips unchecked. "I wish I could tell you the truth.

I wish you'd never met me, that you could live your life in peace without me in it. I wish that my mum and I had never come here, I really do."

"No." His voice cut through the room. "Fucking no. I'm happy you're here, okay? Fuck, I cannot believe the words that are coming out of my mouth right now, but the worst fucking times with you have still been better than the best fucking times with any other girl." Lifting his head, he stared down at me, his eyes flashing fire. "Any. Other. Girl."

My mouth dropped open, my mind reeling from his words. "*Knox*." That was all I managed to say before he lunged at me, kissing me until I lost both my breath and my mind.

When he released me, I dropped my head to his shoulder, speaking into his neck. "I was in your room that night because I was looking for something incriminating. Anything that could get you into trouble. Illegal drugs, papers, whatever. I'm sorry, so sorry. I promise you that I'm done with that. I don't want to hurt you anymore." Before he could say anything in reply, I continued my confession. I had to get it out. "I was meeting with that man because I needed money, and I knew I could sell things to him. It was wrong, I know. I sold him…it was one of the bags your mum bought for me. Believe me, I feel so fucking guilty for doing it, but I needed the money more. For the future. We had no savings, nothing. Now I have my job, and every penny is going into a savings account for the future."

Knox was silent for so long that I eventually forced myself to raise my head and meet his gaze. His expression was unreadable, but he didn't seem angry.

"Please say something," I whispered.

He shook his head. "I need time to process."

"I understand." It was time for me to leave. Drawing back from him, I began to lift myself out of the bed.

His voice stopped me. "Where do you think you're going?"

I glanced back at him. "I thought you wanted time to process."

"That doesn't mean you get to leave. You stay here until I say it's time for you to leave."

Some of the heaviness lifted from me. He still wanted me here, despite everything I'd just told him. Carefully lowering myself back down, I stayed a safe distance away, unsure whether he wanted me near him, until he huffed and tugged me into him again.

"It was me who sent you that text telling you that I knew your secret. And in reply to one of your other questions from our little game that night, yes, I did enjoy kissing you. Very fucking much."

"I already knew that. You've kissed me a lot lately." I met his eyes, and his gaze softened. Reaching out, he traced his finger across my lips.

"I'd do it all day if I could, and that's one of the problems I have." He paused, scrubbing his hand over his face. "Since you gave me an apology, I guess I owe you one for the shit I did to you."

I gave him a small smile. "I have to say, I definitely prefer this Knox Ashcroft to the one I first met. I can now understand why you have so many girls simping over you." With a sigh, I added, "I guess I've joined your collection of groupies."

"No you fucking haven't." The growl was back in his tone, and I loved it. "You're way better than those girls, baby. You're in a league of your own."

As soon as he'd spoken, he groaned. "What the actual fuck am I saying?" he muttered to himself. "If Ro and Tris could hear some of the shit I've said to you tonight, they'd probably disown me."

"No, they wouldn't. I bet they say all kinds of sickly sweet things to the girls they're into," I assured him, confident that I was right.

"No way. They wouldn't, and not only that...I can't picture either of them with a girl long enough to get to that point."

"Well, maybe that will change. You never know what's going to happen in the future."

"For fuck's sake!"

I startled at his sudden exclamation. "What's wrong?"

He shot me an impatient look as if I should magically know what he was thinking. "We're talking like you're my fucking girlfriend. And you're—we're not—"

"I know. But...maybe if things had been different, if we'd met under different circumstances, maybe one day I might have had a chance to be your girlfriend," I said quietly.

Closing his eyes, he let his head fall back against the pillow with a sigh. "Yeah. Maybe."

34

Elena

There comes a point in your life when you realise that your parents don't always know best. After this, you might get to another point where you have to actively go up against them, to stand up for your own beliefs. I'd spent the rest of the week mulling everything over in my head, but I could now admit that I'd known for a long time, deep down, that what my mother had planned to do was wrong, and I had to put a stop to it. Not because I was beginning to have serious feelings for Knox but because it was the right thing to do. Looking back on everything, it was patently clear that I'd let anger and grief cloud my judgement. I should never, ever have gone along with my mother in the first place.

That ended today.

I was going to speak to her tonight, as soon as my driving test was over, and if she refused to stop looking for ways to hurt the Ashcrofts, I was going to tell them everything.

I hadn't even had time to worry about my driving test because my thoughts were preoccupied with everything else, but now, here I was, about to start. I'd been given special permission to leave the school early, and despite the fact that Knox and I were still avoiding each other in school, he'd taken me completely by surprise when he'd cornered me around the back of Hatherley Hall to give me a good luck kiss, right before I was about to leave. A kiss that had somehow ended up with me sucking his dick and then him returning the favour with his incredibly talented tongue. I couldn't believe we'd done that on school grounds, but he'd assured me he knew all the blind spots the cameras didn't reach.

We were still wary around each other—him, especially, as he had every reason to be. He knew that I hadn't told him everything. I still wished things were different, but I couldn't change the past, only the future. And I had to prepare myself for the fact that I wouldn't have much longer with him. Whether my mum agreed to drop her vendetta or not, we'd be leaving. Even if, best-case scenario, she did agree with me and also agreed that we'd stay here to finish up my school year, that would be where Knox and I ended, even if we did carry on messing around with each other in the meantime. He was going off to university, where he'd be training to be a lawyer and hanging out with other people from his social sphere. I had nothing to offer him.

"Ready?" The driving test examiner's voice pulled me from my thoughts, and I gave a shaky nod, turning all my focus to the test. Soon, I'd find out if my hours of driving practice had paid off.

Taking a deep, calming breath, I started up the engine.

Cruel Crypts

I was glad that the sun was still out so I had an excuse to wear the huge shades that covered the redness around my eyes. Rationally, I knew that the number of people that passed their driving test first time was under fifty percent, but I'd been so hopeful that I was going to pass. My instructor had done his best to reassure me, and he'd even booked in another test attempt for me at the end of the following week, but my confidence had been knocked.

Now, all I wanted was a hug. That was it. Something so simple, but it was the thing I missed most about my uncle. He'd given the best hugs, warm and caring, always comforting me if I was upset.

My mum wasn't an option—as soon as I saw her, I was going to confront her about everything, and hugging would be the last thing on either of our minds. So instead of going straight back to the Ashcroft mansion like I'd planned, I'd asked my driving instructor to drop me back at Hatherley Hall.

The place where Knox was currently playing in a lacrosse game.

I arrived around ten minutes before the end of the game, according to the clock, just in time to see Knox racing across the field towards the goal. In the blink of an eye, Link Bellingham launched the ball at him, and he lifted his stick, swiping the ball out of the air and catching it. He didn't even pause for breath before he sent the ball soaring in a high arc, straight into the back of the net.

He was gorgeous like this, covered in mud, with a wild grin of triumph on his face as he fist-pumped the air and then was swarmed by his teammates. My breath caught in my throat as I leaned against the side of the stands, hopefully unnoticed by anyone else.

When the game came to an end, with the Hatherley Hall team victorious, I shrank back into the shadows around the back of the stands as the spectators began to disperse and then made my way across the grassy area next to the lacrosse field in the direction of the changing rooms.

My plan worked. I saw the moment when Roman noticed me as I drew level with the goal line, and he grabbed Knox's arm, giving a subtle nod of his head in my direction. Knox said something to him, and then he pulled off his helmet and jogged over to me, leaving the rest of the team to file inside the changing rooms.

He stared down at me, shading his eyes with his hand to stop the last of the sun's rays from blinding him. "Did you pass?"

I shook my head, biting down on my lip when it trembled, hugging my arms across my body.

"Take off your sunglasses." His voice was soft but commanding, and I drew my shades up onto the top of my head, letting him see my eyes.

"Fuck, Elena." He glanced down at himself, covered in mud, then at the changing rooms, then back at me. "Wait here. I'll be right back."

When he returned, I was leaning against the goalpost, my sadness temporarily forgotten as I watched him approach. So fucking sexy. Like, ridiculously. My body responded to him instantly, and dirty thoughts flashed through my mind.

"Here." Grabbing my hand, he placed something into my palm and curled my fingers around it. "You don't have to use fingerprints to get into the crypts. Open the panel underneath, and you'll find a keypad. I've written down the entry code, and you have the key to my bedroom. Close the door behind you, and it'll automatically lock, but you can still open it from the inside. Go and wait in my room for me, okay?"

My jaw dropped, and I forgot all about my ridiculous

libido. I was completely floored. He was trusting me with the code and his key, trusting me to be alone in his inner sanctum?

This was *huge*.

"T-thank you," I managed to whisper.

Giving me a long, scrutinising look, he released his grip on my hand. "I trust you. With this. I want to trust you with more than this, Elena."

"I know." The lump in my throat wouldn't go away.

His lips curved up in the barest hint of a smile. "Good. I'll see you soon."

I took a seat on the edge of Knox's huge wooden bed, topped with the softest mattress and a thick, luxurious duvet in rich, black fabric. Breathing in and out slowly, I pulled my phone from my bag. Before anything else happened, I had a call to make.

Glancing down at the screen, I noticed that I didn't have a phone signal, so I jogged back up the stairs and out of the crypts, propping the door open.

When the voice at the other end answered, I took a deep breath. "Hello. This is Elena Blackwood. Can I check if I'm still on the visitor list for Jason Myers?"

35

Elena

There was a soft knock at the bedroom door, followed by a low voice saying my name, and I climbed off the bed and let Knox in. He was freshly showered, his hair still damp. The second he dropped his bag, he wrapped me in his arms, and it was like I could breathe properly for the first time since I'd learned that I'd failed my test.

"How the fuck have I gone from wanting to throttle you to wanting to make you feel better when you're down?" he murmured into my hair. "Makes no sense to me."

I tightened my arms around him, smiling against his chest. "I have no idea, but I'm fine with the idea of a bit of sex-related choking, just saying."

His amused chuckle vibrated through me. "Yeah, I got that impression."

"Sorry you'll have to play chauffeur to me for a while longer. I've got another test booked at the end of next week." I paused as a thought struck me. "That's nearly the time when you stop giving me lifts anyway, isn't it? Your mum said you had to do it for what, four weeks? I guess I'll be cycling if I don't pass."

Gathering a handful of my ponytail, he tugged lightly so that my head tilted back. He lowered his head, taking my bottom lip between his, then released it. "You're not cycling. We'll work something out."

"Why do you care? You're not my boyfriend or anything."

"I'm aware of that." Releasing me, he walked over to his bed and took a seat on the edge. I turned to face him, leaning back against the door, watching as he rubbed his hand over his face. "Fuck knows why."

I smiled helplessly at him, and he frowned. "Don't look so smug." Tugging his phone from the pocket of his black joggers, he threw it onto the bed next to him and then crooked his finger at me. "Come here."

When I was standing between his legs, he wound his arms around me again, his hand running down the back and over my ass, squeezing it. "Fucking sexy." He met my gaze. "You came to watch me play—did you think I looked good?" An arrogant smile spread over his face, and I wrapped my arms around his shoulders, scraping my nails over the back of his head.

I shrugged, my own smile widening. "You were alright."

"I was more than alright. I was fucking exceptional."

"Do you mean exceptionally arrogant?"

He shut me up with a kiss.

"I've never had a girl in here before," he told me when we finally broke apart. Lifting his hand, he traced a finger over my lips, and I opened my mouth, letting it slide inside. I wrapped my tongue around the digit, watching as his eyes darkened while he tracked my movements with his gaze.

"I know you told me that before, but it surprises me," I

said honestly when I released his finger, running my hand down his chest and lower until it rested on the hard bulge there. His cock pulsed under my grip, and he groaned low in his throat.

"Fuck, baby. No. No one gets to come in here, like I told you, and even so, I don't like bringing my one-night stands into my private space. Here or back at my parents' house. That's—" He broke off with another groan when I eased his cock out of his joggers and then sank to my knees, running my thumb across the head and spreading the precum around the tip. "*Fuck.* Keep doing that. That's what the lower level of the crypts is for."

I stared up at him from beneath my lashes. "So… you're saying I'm special?"

He gripped my chin, tugging my head forwards until his cock rested against my lips. A smirk curved over his mouth. "Very fucking special. You're about to suck my dick in a place no one else has ever sucked my dick before. Open up."

By the time he'd come down my throat and then made me sit on his thighs and ride his fingers until I came all over them, I'd forgotten all about my earlier disappointment, my mind blissfully blank.

Eventually, I raised my head from where I'd been slumped against him, catching my breath. The sound of music filtered through my consciousness, a thrumming, heavy beat.

"After-game party," Knox said in answer to my unspoken question. "I can sneak you out of here when it gets busier, if you want…" He bit down on his lip. "Or… you can stay here if you want to. Stay the night."

This felt like a huge step, and I wanted nothing more than to stay, but I had to confront my mum. The familiar crushing guilt filled me again, and I knew there was no way

I could put it off any longer. It would have been completely selfish of me to stay when I was hiding something so big from the man I was beginning to fall for. Something that could hurt his family, badly, and I wanted no part of that anymore. I decided there and then that I was going to come clean to him. He deserved the full truth, even though I knew that it would mean the end of us. It was the right thing to do.

"Knox." I pressed my palm to the side of his face, rubbing my thumb across his chiselled jaw, his stubble rasping under my touch. "I need to go back to the house tonight. I need to speak to my mum alone."

Beneath my grip, his jaw tensed. "Why?"

"I…I can't tell you. Yet. But I will. I promise. Can you trust me to do that? Give me until the end of the weekend, and I'll tell you everything. No more secrets. No more lies."

His gaze was searching. I stroked my hand up the side of his face and then around to the back of his neck.

"I know you have no reason to trust me. But please. *Please*—"

"Okay. Fuck knows why I'm agreeing to this, but for some fucked-up reason, I actually believe you. Just don't let me down again. I can't fucking handle you lying to me, Elena. Not after I—" He cut himself off with a shake of his head. "I'll drive you home, and then I'll come back here. If you want me to give you until the end of the weekend, then I will. I'll stay away from you."

"Thank you." I pressed my body into him, lowering my head to the dip of his neck, resting my chin on his shoulder. "I know I have no right to ask you to trust me, but I just need this weekend." Tonight, I'd confront my mum. Tomorrow, I'd pay a visit to London. And then on Sunday, I'd deal with the remaining fallout, gather all of my information together, and tell the Ashcrofts everything.

Running his hand up and down my back, he sighed. We stayed like that for a while until I eventually raised my head to meet his gaze. The weight of everything was threatening to drag me under, and I knew with absolute certainty that he wouldn't let me near him once he knew everything.

He gripped the back of my head, pulling me to him as his mouth came down on mine. I kissed him back, tasting salt as I finally let my tears fall. "I'm sorry," I whispered, my voice cracking. "I'm so sorry."

"Shhh." He kissed me again, then held my face in his hands and kissed my tears away. "Baby. It's going to be okay."

I nodded, biting down on my trembling lip. It wasn't, not even close, but the way he was looking at me right then, like he really cared…like he saw me…I would've done anything to keep him looking at me that way.

And that was why I had to leave. Because I knew that he *did* care, and if I stayed, if we both let ourselves fall deeper, the hurt I'd cause when I broke him would be far, far worse.

"I need to leave." Climbing off him, I gathered up my bag and coat. "I'm going to make my own way home—I'll get a cab. I'll talk to you on Sunday."

He stopped me when I reached the door, coming up behind me and dipping his head to my ear. "Just so you know, you're the first and last girl that I allow in here. And I won't be going near the lower level of the crypts this weekend, so you don't have to worry about that either."

Fuck.

I had to get out of here.

Without another word, I slipped downstairs, unnoticed by the crowds, but I felt his gaze tracking me until I ascended the stairs and walked out of the door.

36

KNOX

Before I joined the party, I locked my bedroom door and then jogged upstairs, sending a text to my dad as soon as my phone signal returned.

ME:
Are you around this weekend?

After around ten minutes of hanging around the cellars with no reply, I made my way down to the others. Tristan waved me over, handing me a beer, then clinking his bottle against mine. "We did good today. Your goal was fucking epic."

I grinned. "Yeah, it was. I hope they got it on camera."

He snorted. "Freya was live-streaming the whole thing to her followers. Hit her up if you want it."

"*Fuck*, no. I'm not going anywhere near that girl." *Or any other girl.*

At my emphatic response, he raised his brows, opening his mouth to reply, but I was saved by Roman's arrival. Tristan's attention immediately turned to him, and I managed to sneak away from them both, although I was being trailed by two of the wannabe goddesses. I shot them a look that I hoped communicated that I very much wasn't down to fuck this evening, then made my way up the stairs, taking the occasional swig from my beer.

My phone buzzed when I reached the top, and I pulled it from my pocket. There was a message waiting for me from my dad.

DAD:

> Sorry, got held up in court. Look at the amount of paperwork I have to do

He'd sent me a photo that showed a huge pile of files teetering on the edge of his desk, a sheaf of papers fanned out in front of his hand, and his glasses resting next to a steaming mug of coffee.

ME:
> Are you at your work office?

DAD:
> Yes. Probably going to pull an all-nighter so it doesn't eat into my weekend

ME:
> If you want some company I can help

DAD:
> Aren't you celebrating your win?

I should be.

ME:
> Not really feeling it. Be there in 20

DAD:
> In that case, bring me Kung Pao chicken

"Knox!" I glanced up from my phone screen to see

Tristan on the stairs just below me, waving his own phone in my direction. "We're ordering pizza for everyone."

"I can't. Gotta help my dad with some paperwork."

He pulled a face. "What? But we're celebrating."

I sighed. "Yeah, I know. It's—"

Stopping me with a hand on my arm, he shook his head. "No, I get it. I know it's your future. Go and do what you need to do."

"Thanks, mate."

He shot me a sly grin. "I'm encouraging you for selfish reasons. It means I have less competition for the best pussy."

I laughed, saluting him as I backed away. "Enjoy. And get your own condoms."

"No promises!" he shouted after me.

"That hit the spot." My dad dropped the empty carton into his office wastepaper basket. "Thanks, Knox."

I gave him a thumbs-up before finishing up my final mouthful of rice. "I can't work on an empty stomach, not to mention I just finished playing an hour of lacrosse."

Wiping his hands on a napkin, he smiled. "True. Right, let's get to work. Your mother will have my head if I keep you here past midnight."

I studied the piles of paper in front of us. "What do you need me to do?"

He picked up the top sheaf and placed it in front of me. There was what looked like a phone number written in neat Biro at the top of the first piece of paper, followed by a printed list of numbers. "This is everything I have for the Stratford case. All I need you to do is go through these call logs and highlight any with the number I've written at the top. We can do it by computer, but I find it easier to see a pattern if it's printed out."

"I can do that." Helping myself to his desk drawers, I pulled out a yellow highlighter and began scanning the first sheet. Next to me, my dad reached for his glasses and then opened one of the manila files, studying the photos inside.

"What did you want earlier?"

I glanced over at him. "Huh?"

"In your text. You asked if I was free this weekend. Golf?"

"No…uh, Elena failed her driving test today. I was just thinking that if you were around at the weekend, maybe you could take her out in the Nissan. Might do her good to get a bit of extra practice."

He raised a brow. "Did you, now?" When I pulled a face, he smirked at me. "I'm sure I can sort something out. It's so nice to know you care."

"Shut up," I muttered. "Do you still think you'll win this?" Changing the subject from Elena as quickly as possible, I tugged off the highlighter cap with my teeth, then used a ruler to highlight a straight line on the call log.

"Yes." His voice was full of confidence. "This is an easy one. All the evidence is stacked in my client's favour."

"Good."

"Knox." The seriousness in his tone had me lowering the highlighter to the desk and turning to face him. His brow was pinched. "I think…I worry that you have certain expectations about things. I'm very, very good at what I do, but I want you to know that even the very best barristers in the country have to be prepared for losses. It's not an easy career, and I don't want you placing too much pressure on yourself."

"I know. Fuck, Dad, you're the best there is. I don't

even have a hope of measuring up. Believe me, my expectations aren't that high."

He gave me a small smile. "There's nothing for you to measure up to—you're your own person. And I want you to know that whatever happens, no matter how many cases you win or lose, I'm proud of you. I'm proud that you're my son. Even if you decide that this career isn't for you, I'll still be proud of you. Whatever happens."

Fuck, I was getting a bit choked up. I blinked, lowering my head and clearing my throat. "I, uh, I appreciate it. Thanks."

"Don't mention it." He laughed softly. "My win record wasn't so impressive when I first started out."

"Yeah, well, it is now. Your winning streak's unparalleled."

"That Myers case…I was sure I was going to win it." His gaze turned distant. "If I had, then I'd have made history by now."

"What happened?" We'd never really spoken about it in detail, but I figured enough time had passed that he wouldn't mind discussing it with me.

He sighed. "My client was on trial for murder. He'd specifically asked for me to represent him because he'd heard I was the best of the best. As you know, my fees are on the higher end. He sold everything to pay them—practically drove himself to bankruptcy. The evidence… some of it was circumstantial at best, and I really thought we had a chance of getting his charges reduced to manslaughter. I was never really sure if he did it… I've worked with criminals for many years, and there was something about him… It always felt like he was hiding something, though. Whatever it was, he's taken his secrets with him."

"What actually happened? With the murder?"

My dad raised his brows. "You want all the gory details?"

I nodded. "Yeah. I'm gonna have to deal with it in the future anyway, aren't I? Might as well make a start."

"Alright. Let me see what I can remember of the details. I'm not digging out the paperwork now—we've got too much to do here with this Stratford case—but if you're still interested later, then I can get something together for you."

"Thanks." Picking up my highlighter at his pointed look, I carried on scanning the pages for the number.

"The murder victim was found in an alleyway just after midnight by a dog walker who called the police. Let me think…" He grabbed a Post-it and began drawing on it with quick, slashing movements. When he was done, he placed it down next to my papers. "This is the alleyway. One end begins on a residential road, where my client lived, and the other end opens onto a larger road with a library on one side and a house on the other. There was CCTV here—" He tapped the paper. "—which was part of the library's camera system. The victim was found halfway down the alleyway, where I've marked an X. CCTV caught Jason Myers exiting the alleyway sometime after eleven thirty, if I remember correctly, and upon analysing the footage, it was determined that there was a high probability that a stain on the jacket he was wearing was blood."

"How could they tell? It could have been anything." I frowned as I highlighted another line.

"Exactly. Circumstantial. However, that wasn't the only piece of evidence against him. Forensics determined that trace amounts of his DNA were on the victim's clothes, and later, when the murder weapon was recovered from the scene, it contained a larger percentage, although the analyst testified that the weapon also contained seven other DNA profiles, including that of a dog. Mr. Myers lived nearby, and he often took a shortcut through that alleyway, including earlier that day, as confirmed by the same CCTV camera, so he could have touched the brick at any time."

"The murder weapon was a brick? How did they die?"

He shook his head at the enthusiasm in my voice. "You really want all the gory details, hmm? Yes, it was determined that the brick had come from the wall that ran down one side of the alleyway—there were several that were loose, and the wall was crumbling in places. The victim sustained several blows to the head. Heavy blows—the skull was severely fractured in multiple places, causing an intense brain bleed, and they ultimately died from a haemorrhagic stroke. It was an attack with intent to cause severe harm or even death."

"But why? Why would he do that?"

"That is a very good question without a very good answer." Leaning forwards, he reached for his mug, grimacing as he tasted it. "Cold coffee."

"I'll get you another. I need one anyway." Climbing to my feet, I stretched. "Fucking hell, sitting in that chair isn't good for the bruises I got during the game. I'm gonna need another ice bath later."

"Maybe you should ask Elena to rub some cream into your bruises," he suggested with a smirk.

"Dad. You can't say things like that to your son." Swiping his mug from the desk, I escaped the room before he could say anything else.

When I returned with two fresh mugs of coffee, I continued where we'd left off discussing the Myers case. "Did he ever admit to it?"

"Initially, no, only after I'd spoken in depth to the detective on the case and I met with him to go through his options. I explained how they would be investigating his family, conducting searches, and so forth—all the disruptive practices that have to be carried out as part of these things. He just...crumpled, for want of a better word, and admitted that he'd done it. Said it had been an accident, and he hadn't meant for it to happen. I asked why he hadn't called the police when he was at the scene, and he said he was too panicked, and he'd fled the scene as soon as he realised the victim was deceased."

I blew on my coffee to cool it before taking a sip. "But you don't believe that?"

"No. I don't. It was clear to me that he was lying. I tried to convince him that it would be better for him to tell me the truth, but he never did. Later, a tiny fragment of his jacket was discovered in the ashes of a bonfire at the bottom of his garden, and forensics managed to extract trace DNA that matched the victim. That linked him to the crime scene, but I don't know...it made no sense. He had no history of violence and no connection to the victim."

"Well, that's just shit."

He picked up his mug and gulped down a mouthful. "You could say that. I thought we had a case for charging him with manslaughter, but unfortunately, the jury didn't agree. And that was that. I probably shouldn't have taken the case on to begin with, but he was so desperate, and I thought it would be a good challenge for me. Too good, as it turned out."

"You can't win them all." I picked up the next sheet of paper and began scanning it for the phone number. "But I don't think you have anything to worry about here."

"I don't." His voice was confident as he turned back to the folder of photos, grabbing a legal pad and pen. "I'm going to win this Stratford case, and then George will have to cough up for my Scotch."

"Does he know how expensive your tastes are? A whole case is going to set him back at least a few grand, right?"

Tapping his pen against the pad, he shot me a conspiratorial smile. "Add a few more zeros onto that number."

"Bloody hell."

37

Elena

An instinct made me turn right instead of heading straight for my mother's room. I reached the corridor that led to Anthony Ashcroft's home office and immediately noticed that the door was ajar, a sliver of light visible in the darkened hallway. With quick steps, I made for the office and flung the door open.

"Mum!"

My mother spun around with a screech, clapping her hand over her heart. "Elena! What are you doing?"

"Never mind what I'm doing, what are *you* doing?" Papers were scattered everywhere, littering the desk and floor, and the filing cabinet in the corner of the room was wide open, a screwdriver lying on top next to the portable nanny cam. I'd only cleaned in here once before, but I distinctly recalled that it had been neat and tidy—no papers left out anywhere, and I was positive that the filing cabinet had been locked with a combination lock.

"I'm looking for evidence." Her eyes were wild. "We need evidence, Elena."

"No, we don't," I hissed, trying to keep my voice low,

although I was fairly certain that both Anthony and Maria Ashcroft were out, and I'd left Knox at Hatherley Hall. "Listen to me. *There is no evidence.* Anthony Ashcroft has no skeletons in his closet, okay? And even if he did, we are *not* going to ruin this family's life. Is that clear?"

I was shaking by the time I'd finished, mostly with anger and adrenaline and a tiny bit of fear. Confronting my mother like this was something that I'd never imagined I'd have to do, but there was no other way. She had to understand.

"How dare you—"

"Stop, Mum. We already went through all of this. As a courtesy that you don't deserve, and neither do I, I'm giving us both until Sunday to get everything together and make preparations for what comes next, and then you and I are going to leave. Disappear. And we're not coming back."

"No. He needs to pay!"

"He doesn't! He was just doing his fucking job! It wasn't his fault!" We were both shouting at this point, the need for caution forgotten. Tears were blurring my vision, and my mother's teeth were bared in a snarl, her entire face red as she exploded at me.

"I never! In all my life!" She gasped for breath, clutching at the desk. "You've betrayed this family, betrayed the good names of Myers and Blackwood!"

"Yeah? Well, I don't want your name! Jason Myers is a murderer, your sister is gone, and you don't deserve the name any more than I do. I was complicit in your plan, but I refuse to be part of it any longer. On Sunday, I am telling the Ashcrofts everything. Every. Thing. You'd better be gone by the time I do. I'll join you later…if they don't arrest me for what we've done."

"How can you do this to me? That man killed your

aunt. My sister. Your uncle is locked up, and they've thrown away the key, and we have nothing left! In the meantime, he gets to carry on his life in his fancy house with his perfect family and perfect life and millions in the bank. He has everything, and we have nothing. He *needs* to pay."

"He didn't kill her. She committed suicide."

She began to shake, her voice hoarse, cracking with every word. "I was the one who found her. You can't even imagine what that was like for me."

I took a deep, calming breath. "I know. And I know we lost everything. I know it destroyed us. That past year in Bristol just about killed me, living on the breadline with no money, not enough to eat or heat the house, having to survive in that area where someone would happily stab either of us so they could take our last tenner. I know what it was like, both of us crying ourselves to sleep at night, that haze of grief that we could never get away from. But we don't have to go back there. We can leave these people to their lives and make a fresh start somewhere else. I'm not going to do this anymore."

"I owe thousands to Pike! How do you expect me to pay that back? He'll send people after us if I don't pay."

"Maybe if you hadn't decided we needed fake IDs and references, oh, and our real identities buried, you wouldn't owe shady loan sharks anything." I bit down on my lip to stop myself from saying anything else because I had gone along with her plan to begin with, after all. I could see now that my heart had never been in it, which was why I'd attempted to stay away from Knox almost as much as I'd been drawn to him, but I'd still been in the wrong. That agonising grief and that twisted need for justice had brought us to this point, but now we were done. I wasn't going to let this go any further.

It was time to right our wrongs.

She slumped against the desk, all the fight going out of her. "There's no changing your mind, is there?"

"No. I'm going to tell them on Sunday evening. That gives you all day tomorrow and most of Sunday to get everything in order and make arrangements. You can leave before I tell them—and I'm saying that because you're my mum, and I do love you. I don't want to see the last of my family locked up. Hopefully, if I am arrested for falsifying documents or whatever, the police will be more lenient on me than they would with you, but I'm prepared to face the consequences."

"Fine. In that case, there's no time to waste." Grabbing the nanny cam, she came around the desk, sweeping past me out of the office, leaving me alone.

My tears fell in earnest as I began to straighten the room as best I could, piling up the papers and then carefully placing them back inside the filing cabinet. I couldn't do anything about the broken lock, but hopefully, Anthony wouldn't be working over the weekend, and I could explain everything on Sunday.

When I was done, I sank to the floor, drew my knees up, and cried until there were no tears left.

38

Elena

"This is a nice surprise." My uncle smiled at me from across the small table in the visitors' room. When did he get so old? His hair was fully grey now, and his eyes were dull, with deep, sunken circles beneath. The lines in his face were much more pronounced than they had been, and his skin had a sallow hue.

"I meant to visit sooner. It's…"

He shook his head. "No need to explain. I know how difficult it's been for you and your mother this past year. So, what's the reason for this visit in particular?"

I eyed him cautiously, shifting on the hard plastic chair. "How did you know that I had a specific reason?"

"Because I know you." His gaze softened. "Come on, tell me. I only get an hour here with you, and then I'm not allowed another weekend visitor for four weeks."

Despite the fact that I knew he was a convicted murderer, something inside me ached, seeing this shell of the man he once was. I still loved him, despite everything.

He'd been there for me and my mum, supporting us both financially and emotionally.

Until everything had fallen apart.

"Okay. Has my mum told you anything about her plans?"

He shook his head. "Plans? Last time I saw her, she said she'd have a surprise for me soon. Is that what you're referring to?"

As quickly and quietly as possible, not wanting to draw the attention of the prison officer that stood against the wall behind him, I gave him a rundown of everything that had happened—how she'd fixated on getting revenge on his behalf, selling the remainder of our possessions to fund new identities and false references, and how she'd planned to ruin Anthony Ashcroft's name. By the time I'd finished, his jaw was wide open, shock clear in his eyes.

Meeting his gaze, I pleaded with my eyes. "I need to fill in the blanks. I need you to tell me what happened. Please."

He blew out a heavy breath, his hands shaking violently. "I didn't kill that woman, Elena. Whatever else happens, you have to believe that."

"How were you convicted if you didn't do it?"

"Because I was there. I tried to stop her, but it was too late."

My stomach churned, dread rising up inside me. "Tried to stop who?"

He whispered two words that sent fractures through me, widening until I was ripped apart all over again. It hurt. So, so much.

"Your aunt."

"B-but how? What?"

His head bowed. "Your aunt and I were taking a late

evening stroll. We were…disagreeing…well, arguing, I suppose. She had some ideas in her head, and I was trying to discourage her. She accused me of things…things I'd never done. She said I'd been looking at other women. Having affairs behind her back."

Shaking his head, he exhaled sharply. "A woman was walking towards us, and I was so sick of the accusations she was throwing at me, I said, 'I'll give you something to accuse me of,' and then I looked directly at the woman in what I suppose was a suggestive way. Your aunt…she had one of her episodes. It was like the red mist descended. She snatched up a loose brick and jumped at the woman, knocking her to the ground, and then hit her over and over and over again. There was so much blood." His words became choked, and his eyes filled with tears. "I can still hear the sound of the brick connecting with the woman's skull. Her screams will haunt me to my dying day. The only reason I think that no one heard us was because the dogs at the house across from the library were causing a racket—probably foxes again. They'd often start barking madly at all hours of the evening, so no one would've thought anything of it."

"Didn't you try to stop her?" My arms were clasped tightly across my stomach in an attempt to make my nausea subside, but I could feel the bile rising in my throat.

"Of course I did! Your aunt was in a frenzy, but I managed to pull her off. By then, though, it was too late. She came back to herself as soon as I had her upright again, and she broke down like I'd never seen her break before. Honestly, Elena, it tore me to pieces. I told her to run back to the house and make sure that nobody saw her, and I'd deal with the rest. I said that if anyone questioned her, she was to say she'd been at home all evening. She'd been wearing leather gloves, so I hoped…well, I hoped there wouldn't be any evidence that she was there. When she'd gone, I tried to do chest compressions, tried to get the woman to breathe again, but it was too late. She was already gone." A tear tracked down his cheek. "Her name was Annie. She was only twenty-one, you know? Just graduated from university. She was about to start her life. And we took it away from her."

"I don't—I can't. I don't even know what to say." My voice was a shaky whisper.

"I threw the brick into a hedge, and I continued out of the alley, walking back round a circular route until I was home. Everything after that, you already know. Your aunt took her life the day I was sentenced, and the secret died with her. You're the only other living person who knows what really happened."

"*Fuck.*" I dug my nails into my palms, welcoming the tiny sting of pain. "Why did you do it? Why did you take the blame?"

"People do crazy things for love, you know. Things that you'd never think they were capable of. Good things, and sometimes, very bad things. She was my wife. They would have sent her to Broadmoor or something. I couldn't do that to her. I thought…I truly believed that Anthony Ashcroft would be able to help. Get me a manslaughter conviction so I could at least have some semblance of a life once I'd served my sentence. Make things right with you and your mother. And…there was another reason." He paused. "A reason that I'm not very proud of. You see, it was partly my fault that your aunt snapped. Not because we were arguing but because she was right. I loved her so much, and yet, I was also in love with another woman, and she was in love with me."

Cruel Crypts

"Who?" Even as I whispered the word, I already knew the answer. The final piece of this nightmare puzzle slotted into place to give me the full, bloody picture.

He met my eyes straight on.

"Your mother."

39

Elena

I blinked my eyes open slowly, glancing over at my phone. Nine twenty. I'd been asleep for just over three hours, and I was surprised that I'd even managed that after tossing and turning all night, my mind replaying all the revelations from my uncle.

My gaze caught on the notebook lying next to my phone. I'd written everything down on the train on the way home while it was still fresh in my mind, not wanting to miss any details when I spoke to the Ashcrofts. I wanted to speak to Knox first so I didn't blindside him with the news in front of his parents, and then, I'd face Anthony and Maria.

That would all come later, though. For now, I needed a shower and breakfast—sustenance to prepare me for what was going to be a very difficult day. Perhaps the most difficult day of my life, in a way.

When I'd showered and dressed in a soft pair of joggers and a hoodie from my old life, I glanced around my bedroom. I'd already decided that I wasn't going to take anything with me when I left, other than the few possessions I'd brought with me at the beginning. I was fully committed to this path, and that meant wiping the slate as clean as I could.

Logging into my bank account, I checked my balance for the final time. After visiting my uncle, I'd gone to the bank and withdrawn enough from my savings to cover the cost of a new Balenciaga bag—the same one that Maria Ashcroft had given me that I'd sold. It left me with very little in the way of savings from my job at the country club, but it was enough to get me away from here. I'd worry about the future afterwards. I'd survived a year of living in a block of flats crawling with the underbelly of society that people liked to pretend didn't exist, and I'd learned that I was stronger than I thought. I'd had to be. My mother had been incapable of doing anything, lost as she was in her grief. It made even more sense now, knowing what I knew—she'd lost her sister and no doubt felt guilt for the affair, and she'd lost the man that she was in love with, sentenced to a life behind bars.

When that was done, I navigated to my phone's settings, did a factory reset, and powered it off for the final time. It was another thing that had been given to me by the Ashcrofts, and therefore, it wouldn't be coming with me. I'd purchased a basic pay-as-you-go phone yesterday with the remainder of the money I'd withdrawn, which was currently tucked into the side pocket of my duffel bag, and that would do me for now.

Tucking the cash I'd withdrawn into an envelope, I glanced around the room for a moment before deciding to place it in the top drawer, along with the phone. They'd find it after I was gone. Then I straightened up my room, threw my meagre possessions into my bag, and left it next to the bed, ready for tonight. A lump came into my throat as I saw the pile of driving books stacked next to my bed. Books that I wouldn't need now.

I was loading my breakfast plate in the dishwasher when someone cleared their throat behind me.

"Elena. Are you busy?"

I turned to see Anthony propped against the kitchen island, a glass of orange juice in his hand. When did he get here? I hadn't even noticed him come in.

"Um, no. I'm not busy."

"Good. Come with me." He spun on his heel and began heading for the door without waiting for a response from me. I closed the dishwasher and followed him through the house to the side door that led to the garage. When we reached it, he gave me a smile. "Knox asked if I could take you out for some additional driving practice. I have an hour or so until I need to meet Maria and JoJo at the club, so I thought we could drive around for a bit, and then you can join us for brunch. I expect Knox will come, too, if I tell him you're going to be there."

No. I couldn't do this. Couldn't face them all and pretend that everything was okay when I knew I had to face them this evening. And I definitely couldn't face Knox while I was feeling so fragile. Not only that—I had so much to do today. Now I'd committed to telling the truth with the knowledge that it meant cutting all ties with the town of Nottswood, I had to make sure I tied up every loose end. I had to draft a letter of resignation for my employers at the club. Write letters to Katy and Will to say how sorry I was to be letting them down so close to the end of our music project, which was due at the end of the month. Aria too—we were friends now, and she deserved a proper goodbye. Most importantly, I needed to write a letter to the Ashcrofts to reiterate how sorry I was and another separate one to Knox. After that…I'd book a cab to take me away.

"Thank you for the offer, but—"

"No buts. I won't accept no for an answer, and it would be in your best interest if you agreed rather than trying to argue with a law professional." He gave me a tiny wink.

How could I get out of this? "Well, um, would it be okay if we did the driving and then I came back here? I've already eaten this morning, and I have quite a lot to do today."

"It's a deal," he agreed easily, grabbing the keys for the Nissan Juke and tossing them to me. Too easily, in my opinion. "Knox will be disappointed, though."

He really wouldn't, not after he'd heard what I had to tell him.

Nothing happened when I hit the button to unlock the doors. Frowning, I used the key to manually unlock the driver's side, but before I got in, I experimentally pressed the button to start the engine.

"What's wrong?" Anthony joined me, peering into the car and trying the same thing I had. His gaze flicked lower. "I forgot why we got Knox a different car until now. This kept happening for him too. The battery must be flat. I'll call our mechanic, get it swapped out."

A sense of relief filled me that I didn't have to do this after all until he said, "We'll take my car instead."

"What?" My voice came out as a horrified squeak. *No way* was he saying that I should drive his Lamborghini.

Waving away my concerns, he tugged the magnetic L plates from the Nissan and then began walking across the cavernous garage to where his hulking black beast of an SUV was waiting in the shadows. "You'll be fine. You're at test standard already. We'll take it nice and slow, and I'll be here to talk you through everything."

"I can't drive that!"

"Of course you can. It's all in your mind." Tapping the

side of his head, he gave me a reassuring smile. "Mind over matter. You can do this. Come on, we're wasting time."

Oh, fuck. I really wasn't going to be able to get out of this, was I?

When I'd made it down to the end of the driveway, crawling at a snail's pace, I hit the brakes for a second, just so I could wipe my sweaty palms on my joggers. There was so much power in this car, thrumming beneath my fingers every time I gripped the steering wheel, and all I could do was take it slow and hope that I managed to keep this beast in check.

"Turn right. We'll go out onto the country roads, where it'll be much quieter. There won't be many drivers around now. It's a Sunday morning."

I nodded mutely, flipping on the indicator and inching out into the road. As we turned, I thought I glimpsed the mansion's front door opening behind us, but my eyes were probably playing tricks on me.

When we'd been travelling at twenty miles per hour for a few minutes, I dared to press the accelerator a little harder. The needle inched up, first to thirty and then forty as we hit the open road.

"Good. You're doing well, Elena. Now we're on a straight stretch, let's see if we can get her up to fifty now. Nice and steady."

Anthony's praise warmed me inside, but it was tempered by the guilt that was overwhelming me. I increased the speed in tiny increments, forcing everything else to the back of my mind so I could give this car my full concentration.

"Careful up here. There's a bit of a sharp bend in about half a mile. Just ease off the accelerator a bit; the car will do most of the work. She handles beautifully."

"Okay." My fingers were aching from the death grip I had on the steering wheel, even though the road had been mostly straight so far. I swallowed hard, easing up little by little until the car slowed back down to thirty.

Slowly and carefully, I navigated around the bend, and Anthony tapped the dashboard as the road straightened up again. "Great work. There's a petrol station up ahead. Do you want to pull in and take a breather?"

"Please."

We came to a stop, and I closed my eyes, gulping air into my lungs. I heard Anthony's amused chuckle next to me. "Was it really that scary driving my car?"

"*Yes*," I said emphatically, and he laughed again before his face turned thoughtful.

"I was going to suggest turning back, but there are a few more sharp bends farther up this road. One of them can be a little tricky to navigate. Instead of heading back, how about I take over so you can see how I handle them?"

I couldn't agree fast enough. "Please. Thank you."

He climbed out of the car while I slid across to the passenger seat, and then he started up the engine. For the first time since I'd climbed inside the SUV, I began to relax the tiniest bit.

He indicated to turn back onto the road. "You know, I couldn't help noticing that you were looking a little peaky after driving. I think you could do with some sustenance, so I'm making the call. You're coming to the club with me." His words were innocent, but when I turned my head, I caught his smirk. "I'll phone Knox now to tell him that—"

His words were cut off instantly as everything erupted.

The zigzag sign warning of a sharp bend came up ahead, and at the same time I saw it, there was a loud crunch and a jarring impact. We were both jolted forwards, the SUV skidding across the road, out of control.

The car began making a loud beeping sound, and warning lights started flashing up on the dashboard.

"Fuck!"

I'd never heard Anthony swear before, and his tone…it was ice through my veins, freezing me. He spun the wheel, desperately trying to compensate for the slide, but it was too late. We hit the corner barrier of the road, and then we were weightless for a moment, flying through the air.

Then we came back down to earth, over five thousand pounds of weight smashing into the ground with a screeching impact, spinning over and over like we were on a corkscrew, the world twisting and blurring around us.

After that, there was silence.

40

KNOX

The first thing I saw when I reached the gates outside my house was Letitia Greenwood—no, *Black*wood—running down the driveway barefoot, her arms windmilling and an expression of panicked horror twisting across her features.

What the fuck?

I brought the car to a stop and wound down the window. "Letitia. What are you doing?"

She skidded to a stop, her head turning in my direction, but her eyes were looking straight through me. "Where's Elena?"

Elena? What? "What do you mean, where's Elena? Explain now," I barked. If Elena was in trouble—

"Thought…I saw her…driving Mr. Ashcroft's…car," she gasped out between breaths. "She can't! She can't! She's my baby! She's all I have left in the world…"

The woman descended into sudden sobs, and I gritted my teeth, my patience at an all-time low. How did someone as fucking amazing as Elena come from this snivelling bitch?

"Why would she be driving my dad's car? That makes no sense." Without waiting for her to reply, I gunned the engine and headed straight for the house. As soon as I came to a stop, I swiped my phone from my pocket, dialling my dad's number. It rang and rang and eventually went to voicemail. Next, I tried Elena's, letting myself into the house at the same time. I ran to her bedroom, hearing the call go straight to voicemail.

When I opened her bedroom door, that was when I knew that something wasn't right.

The room was neat—too neat. Everything was tidied away, other than a notebook on the bedside table in front of the small stack of books I'd bought her. I glanced down, and my gaze was drawn to the duffel bag lying on the floor next to the bed. Crouching down, I unzipped it and peered inside.

There wasn't much to be seen. Some clothes, a few books and papers, and a cheap-looking phone that was still sealed inside its box.

The clothes…these weren't the ones that my mother had given her. These were her originals—I recognised one of the hoodies, and even if I hadn't, the low-quality material would have given it away.

"What are you planning, Elena?" I asked aloud. Taking a seat on the bed, I dialled my mum's number as I picked up the notebook from the bedside table.

"Knox."

I didn't let my mother say anything else. "Mum, have you seen Elena? Or Dad?"

She was instantly alert—I could tell from her voice. "I haven't seen Elena. I believe she was sleeping when JoJo and I left the house early this morning, according to Letitia, at least. Your father is meeting JoJo and I here at the club for brunch in around forty minutes. Why, what's wrong?"

"I'm not sure yet. I just got to the house—spent the night at Hatherley Hall—and I saw Letitia running down the driveway screaming something about seeing Elena driving Dad's car."

"That makes no sense."

"Exactly what I said." I flipped the notebook open, skimming past scribbled pages—song lyrics, music compositions, little doodles of music notes and other music-related things that I didn't know the names of. Pausing before flipping to the next page, I had a sudden thought. "On Friday night, I asked Dad if he had any time this weekend to take Elena out for a driving lesson."

My mother sighed. "That's probably it, then. Letitia may not have recognised the difference between the Nissan Juke and your father's car, especially if she saw them from a distance." She paused. "Although I can't help wondering why she would be so upset about Elena driving. Did you check the garage?"

"Maybe she thought she'd crash it." Dropping the notebook to the bed, I strode towards the door, then stopped. An instinct made me turn back and pick it up before I left. When I reached the garage, I saw that the Nissan was parked in its usual spot, but my dad's SUV was nowhere to be seen. "The Nissan's here, but Dad's car isn't."

"Your girlfriend must have made quite the impression for him to trust her with driving his precious car when she hasn't yet passed her test." My mother's words were light and teasing.

"Not my girlfriend."

"Yet."

I became aware of the sound of someone shouting and

screaming, and I groaned. "Mum, I need to go and see what this woman's problem is. Can you phone me if you hear from Dad or Elena?"

"Knox. Her name is Letitia."

"Mum."

She sighed again. "Of course I will. Keep me updated on things your end."

Carefully bending the notebook in half, I tucked it into the pocket of my joggers, then headed back to Letitia, who'd made it back up the driveway and now appeared to be limping.

"Tell me what's going on, right fucking now." My patience levels were below zero at this point.

"She's g-going to be hurt…the car…didn't mean to… h-he's supposed to pay, not her," she hiccupped between sobs.

"Who's supposed to pay?"

"Your father!" she screamed. Tears ran down her blotchy face. "This is…all…his…fault!"

This woman was fucking unhinged, and I didn't have time to deal with it. I needed to find Elena and my dad *now*.

"Where are they?"

"I-I don't know."

"Where the fuck are they?" I roared.

"T-they turned r-right out of the driveway. I d-don't… know where they were going."

My phone was dialling another number before she'd even finished speaking. "Tristan? Change of plans. Are you already on your way? I need you at my parents' house."

"I'm driving down your road now. Be there in two minutes."

The sight of his Subaru BRZ had never been more welcome. When he reached us, I stepped over to his car, speaking in a low voice so that Letitia didn't overhear. I doubted she would have noticed anyway—she'd sunk down onto the gravel, still crying hysterically, punctured with nonsensical words. "I don't know what the fuck is going on, but I think Elena's gone somewhere with my dad in his car and for some reason it's making her mum freak the fuck out. I need to try and find my dad and Elena, but I need someone to keep an eye on her. I don't think she's, uh—"

He raised a brow. "Yeah. I see that. And you thought I'd be the best person to deal with a hysterical woman?"

"Honestly?" I stared at him. "No. *Fuck* no. But I knew you'd be closest because we'd made plans for this morning, and we're already wasting time discussing this."

"You fucking owe me for this," he groaned. "What do you want me to do?"

"Just don't let her go anywhere until I come back."

"I guess I can do that." His expression softened. "I hope everything's okay with your dad."

"Me too. Thanks, mate." Wasting no more time, I jogged back to my car and peeled away from the house, back down the driveway, and took a right.

As I drove, I tried calling both my dad and Elena again, but there was no answer. For lack of any other options, I pulled up the GPS app that allowed us to share our locations, but as usual, my dad's was set to private.

I banged my fist on the steering wheel. Fuck. I had no idea what was going on, but alarm bells were ringing very fucking loudly now.

Passing a petrol station, I slowed right down for the upcoming series of sharp bends that marked this part of the road.

The first thing I noticed was the set of skid marks, a thick black slash across the surface of the road.

The second thing I noticed was the crumpled parts of the metal barrier that hugged the corner.

The third thing I noticed was the heap of smoking, twisted black metal lying at the bottom of the slope.

The fourth thing I noticed before my car swept me around the bend was a flash of sudden orange brightness in my mirror.

Flames.

41

Elena

I blinked my eyes open. It took me a few seconds to get my bearings, but then it all came rushing back to me. The impact. Hitting the barrier. Rolling and rolling until we came to a stop…wherever we were.

I was upside down, and the blood was rapidly rushing to my head. *Fuck.* We needed to get out of here. Everything hurt, so much. I attempted to stretch out my arms and legs, wrestling with the airbags as I did so. It didn't appear that anything was broken, which was a minor miracle, but if I didn't get the right way up ASAP, I was going to pass out.

From next to me, there was a groan, and I turned my head to see Anthony. A trickle of blood ran down the side of his face, and his eyes were tightly shut, his mouth twisted into a grimace of pain.

"Anthony?" I immediately began coughing as soon as I'd opened my mouth and inhaled. Fuck. Fuckfuckfuck. There was smoke billowing out of the engine. We had to get out of here, *now*.

He groaned again in reply, his eyelids flickering but remaining closed, and instead of wasting any more time, I looked around me, thinking fast. Okay, I needed to get the right way up because, of the two of us, I was clearly in a better state. Stretching out my arm to the ceiling, which was now at the bottom of the car, I placed my hand against the surface, and braced both my arm and my feet, then unclipped my seat belt. Carefully, I twisted my body, lowering it down to a crouch, until I was the right way up. The car creaked ominously, rocking as I moved, and I crawled forwards as carefully as I could, uncaring of the shards of broken glass from the windscreen embedding themselves in my palms. The most important thing was getting free of this death trap.

I put my hand on the handle and pushed.

No.

The door wouldn't budge, thanks to the way the metal had bent and twisted.

For a moment, I panicked, my breaths coming fast and sharp in my chest, spots dancing in front of my eyes, but then a cough broke through my panic.

Anthony.

I had to get him out of here.

Bracing myself as best I could, I lowered myself down with my legs in front of me and then kicked at the glass of the side window. The car rocked, but I kicked again and again.

It wouldn't break. Fuck. What did I do? Tears filled my eyes, but I forced them down. The front windscreen wasn't an option—although it was now cracked and broken, it was still mostly intact, and behind it lay thick smoke, with the threatening orange glow of flames beneath, close to the engine.

My gaze darted around the car, looking for anything that would help.

The glovebox. I reached up, wrenching it open and feeling around inside.

My fingers closed around something—a handle. I yanked the object out of the glove compartment, and as the bright orange object came into view, this time, I did cry—with relief.

It was an emergency hammer. My uncle had always kept one in his car, so I recognised it instantly. It had a metal tip that could be used to break glass and a seat belt cutter at the other end.

The smoke was getting thicker, obscuring my view of the outside world. Flames were beginning to lick at the windscreen as I placed the metal tip at the glass of my side window, and I knew we didn't have long left. I swung the hammer as hard as I could, and the glass shattered but remained intact, but now I knew I'd be able to push it out. The car creaked ominously again as I desperately used my feet to shove the windscreen out of the frame, and then I was free. Cool, fresh air rushed inside, and I took a deep breath.

Anthony. I had to free him too.

Crawling over to his side and leaning across his unconscious form, avoiding the airbags, I attempted to open his door.

It opened.

Clutching the hammer in case I needed it, I crawled out of my window and then ran faster than I'd ever run, straight around to the driver's-side door.

I wrapped one arm around Anthony's waist and unclipped his seat belt. There was a whooshing sound as the flames roared, and at the same time, he collapsed onto me, knocking the breath from my lungs. Dropping the hammer, I *pulled*, adrenaline shooting through my body, infusing me with a strength I'd never normally possess. I dragged him along the grass, and the only thought in my mind was getting him as far away from the car as possible. I kept pulling, tears blinding my vision, my arms shaking with the effort.

There was a shout from up above that sounded like my name, but it was swallowed up by the sudden loud boom that echoed around us. A huge fireball erupted from the car, and even though I'd managed to get us a safe distance away, I felt the burning heat scorch my skin. Releasing Anthony, I collapsed back into the grass, the adrenaline leaving me in a rush, my body boneless and completely spent.

"Elena!"

My vision was swimming, but it looked like Knox was there. But that couldn't be right, could it?

"Elena! You're bleeding! Fuck, baby. Stay with me. Don't you *dare* fucking leave me."

I was bleeding?

I became aware of what seemed to be a long, throbbing pain radiating from my side. I placed my hand on it, and it came away wet with blood.

Oh. *Fuck*.

There was something wrong with my vision—it was getting hazier, and all I could see were tiny pinpricks of light.

And then I couldn't see anything at all.

42

KNOX

My entire fucking world had been turned upside down. It was like I was on a spinning wheel, rotating between shock, anger, hurt, and fear. The beep of the monitors should have soothed me, but they didn't.

My mum was reclined on one of the chairs in my dad's private room, JoJo curled up in her lap, both of them asleep. I should be trying to nap too, but I couldn't because every time I closed my eyes, I saw Elena pulling my dad from his burning vehicle, and I was too far away to help.

I'd come so close to losing two of the most important people in my life today. Even now they were both stable, I couldn't help the fear—that something might go wrong, that they might not make it. It was irrational—my dad had broken his ankle, and Elena had sustained blood loss from the cut on her side that the doctors thought had been caused by a large shard of glass. That had meant that she'd needed a minor transfusion. They both had various other cuts and bruises, but between them, there was nothing life-threatening. Regardless, neither of them were awake, and until I saw them open their eyes, I'd be fucking worrying.

I shifted in my seat, something digging into my leg, and I glanced down.

Elena's notebook.

Lifting it from my pocket, I smoothed it out and then opened it. Had it really only been this morning that I'd taken this from her room?

I began idly flipping through the book again, taking comfort from the sight of her words written there on the pages. Fucking hell, I was turning into such a sap. That was what this girl did to me.

My gaze caught on a familiar word, and I quickly turned back to the previous page. Lines of text filled the space from top to bottom, continuing onto the next page and the next. The very first line said:

My confession and heartfelt apology to the Ashcroft family.

Sitting back, I began to read.

"How are you feeling?" I took a seat at the side of my dad's bed.

He smiled tiredly. "I've been better. But it's nothing that a few nights' rest won't fix."

"Except for your ankle."

"Except that." Shifting into a more upright position, he reached for the cup of water that stood on the table next to him. When he'd finished drinking from it, he turned back to me. "I hear that I have your girl to thank for saving my life."

To my complete fucking shock and horror, I could feel

tears welling up in my eyes. How could I love and hate someone so much at the same time? How could I feel so fucking grateful but so fucking betrayed?

"Dad." My voice cracked.

His eyes widened. "Knox, what's the matter?"

I shook my head.

"Knox. I'm in a hospital bed, but I'm fine. Don't hold yourself back from what you need to say out of some misguided notion that you need to protect me while I'm in a fragile state." Despite myself, I snorted, and he cracked a proper smile. "That's better. Now, tell me what's going on."

I told him everything. Everything that Elena had written in her notebook, matching it up with what I already knew about Jason Myers' case, everything I'd discovered through my own investigations, and what had happened today. By the time I'd finished, my voice was so fucking hoarse that I didn't even sound like myself anymore.

My dad was silent for a long, long time, but eventually, he spoke. "You've given me a lot to think about. The first and most important thing is that we need to make sure that Letitia doesn't come anywhere near JoJo again."

I nodded. "I have Tristan watching her. In fact, I'd better text him."

"Good." He pursed his lips. "I don't think it's too much of a stretch to say that Letitia was involved in the accident today, going by the way she reacted to the news that Elena was in the car with me. I'll make a call to Detective Johnson—I'm sure we can gather enough evidence to charge her with fraud at the very—"

"Fuck! She gave Tristan the slip." I stared down at my phone, where a text had come through just thirty minutes earlier. My phone had been on silent since we were in the hospital, and I was fucking kicking myself.

"What?" My dad sat up straighter. "How long ago was this?"

"Uh, half an hour ago?"

"Hand me your phone. I guarantee that she'll head straight here—she'll want to see Elena. If we're lucky, we can kill two birds with one stone."

He made a call, telling me to keep the nurse out of his room in case he wasn't allowed to use it while he was on his "sick bed." In the meantime, my mum had woken up, and I quickly and quietly gave her a rundown of the situation.

"That poor, poor girl." She dabbed tears away from the corners of her eyes as I stared at her, open-mouthed. "She never stood a chance, did she? I can't imagine what her life must have been like for her own mother to be able to talk her into such an evil plan. But she did the right thing in the end, didn't she?"

"But...but...aren't you angry? Don't you feel, I dunno, betrayed?"

She shook her head slowly. "It's... Maybe my perspective is different, but during my modelling career and even beyond that, with the charities I've worked with, I've come across far too many girls with similar stories. Or...not similar in that way, but girls who have been taken advantage of, girls who have lost so much and cling to what they have left with all their might, even if it's wrong. Girls who have had their judgement skewed by those that are supposed to protect and love them unconditionally, girls who have lost everything and are incapable of coherent decisions because their trauma is too great. It takes time to work through everything, Knox. The fact that Elena has done it alone, without anyone to guide her..."

"I don't understand."

"I know you don't. Listen to me, Knox. I do feel angry

and betrayed—the same things you're feeling—but do you know what? Those emotions I feel are mostly directed at Letitia. Yes, Elena has done things wrong. She's lied to us all. She's been complicit in her mother's plan, yet I think we can all see how much she's changed in the weeks she's been here, and the fact that she was ready and willing to share everything with us counts for something. I'm not saying you should forgive her—far from it—but what I am saying is that maybe it's worth considering another point of view."

I slumped back in my chair. "Fuck," I whispered. "I don't know if I can do that."

43

Elena

The door to my room opened with a soft squeak, announcing my new visitor's arrival.

It was the person I'd least expected.

"*Mum?*"

"Oh, Elena." She raised a shaking hand to her mouth, crossing over to my bed and sinking down next to me. "I would never have forgiven myself if something had happened to you."

Behind her, I watched the door ease open again, slowly and carefully, avoiding the squeak, and I returned my gaze to my mother, watching out of the corner of my eye as two figures slipped into the room. One was so familiar to me that I'd recognise him anywhere, and the other, I'd never seen in my life, yet from the glimpse I allowed myself, I could see his uniform, and I knew.

He was here for my mother. I knew that beyond a shadow of a doubt.

My heart and mind were torn in two, but I was certain in my beliefs now. Blood wasn't always thicker than water.

"Tell me what happened, Mum. I just want to understand."

She crumpled, and it broke me. My brain *knew* that everything she'd done was wrong, but my heart still loved her.

"Please." A tear ran down my cheek, falling to the sheets.

Reaching out, she placed her hand over mine. "You scared me with what you said on Friday. Telling me that you were going to tell the Ashcrofts everything, and no matter how hard I tried to make you see sense, you wouldn't budge from your position."

"I'd already told you that I was against your position before that. I tried to tell you to stop then, but you didn't listen."

"You were wrong." Shaking her head, she stared down at the blanket covering my legs. "You were wrong then, and you were wrong on Friday. That's why I did what I had to."

"What did you do?"

Her eyes were full of tears as she met my gaze. "I never meant for you to get hurt. You were never supposed to be there. I…I knew your mind was made up. You'd given me until Sunday, and I needed to make the Ashcrofts pay. I contacted Pike—"

"You contacted the loan shark that you already owe thousands of pounds to? What made you think that would be a good idea?" I couldn't even hope to dial back the anger in my voice.

"Elena. Darling. I was running out of options. You wouldn't want your last remaining family member to end up in prison, would you?"

My fists were clenched so hard that I was ninety

percent sure that I'd drawn blood where my nails were digging into my palms.

"What did Pike do?" I asked instead of answering her question.

She stared at the wall, lost in her memories. "Of course he wanted more collateral. I gave him everything of mine that Maria had given me. Don't worry—I didn't touch anything of yours."

"You gave him your clothes?"

Something shifty entered her gaze, and I didn't like it. "Yes. Maybe...okay, look, I might also have liberated a few items from Maria's jewellery collection."

"What?" I gasped. I'd completely forgotten that anyone else was in the room—my entire focus was directed at my mother. "You stole jewellery from the woman who showed more generosity towards us than anyone I've ever met in my life?"

"Please, Elena. They're rich. This means nothing to them. Maria won't even notice that some of it is missing." Swiftly brushing the tears from her cheeks, she straightened up. "I contacted Pike, and once we'd agreed on a sufficient payment, he arranged for one of his associates to give Anthony Ashcroft's car a little nudge. It was supposed to be simple—I knew he was meeting Maria and Josephine for brunch at the country club, and he was going to have a little accident on the way. Then you came along and messed everything up."

"What was your plan?" I forced the question out, despite the fact that I wanted to scream or punch something. "Did you want to kill him?"

She laughed, and it was a laugh that I'd never heard from her. It was a laugh that chilled me to the bone.

"I wanted him to pay. Injured or dead—either would have been acceptable to me."

Something inside me snapped, an irreparable break. The pain was indescribable, tearing me apart, but I held it at bay, pushing back against the wave with everything I had. I could succumb to it later, when I'd carried out the final part of my plan.

Keeping my voice steady, I held her gaze. "I'm not a Blackwood anymore. I know I mentioned before that I didn't want your name anymore, but I'm telling you again now. My name is Elena Greenwood. That's the only name I'll answer to from now on."

Turning my head, I swallowed hard as I met the eyes of the policeman. "She's all yours," I whispered.

In the ensuing commotion, when both the policeman and Knox's attention were focused on my ranting and screaming mother, I managed to slip away. I shouldn't have left the hospital—I was supposed to rest for twenty-four hours after receiving my blood transfusion, but it was far more important that I got out of there.

They were better off without me.

Everyone was.

I needed a fresh start.

We all did.

Except for my mother. She needed to face the consequences of her actions. Just like I did. But I guess I was a coward. Or was I? I just wanted to get away so the Ashcrofts didn't have to face the person they'd made a home for, the person that had been lying to them all along.

Yes, I was a coward.

The cab detoured past the Ashcroft mansion, and I entered one last time. Just long enough to pick up my duffel bag, fighting the waves of dizziness that came from me not taking the prescribed twenty-four hours' rest after my blood transfusion.

At the front door, I looked around me, seeing the

mansion that I'd found so pretentious and intimidating at first.

The mansion that I'd come to love.

It wasn't the bricks and mortar; it was the people who lived inside that made it a home.

Anthony, Maria, Knox, and JoJo.

Knox.

The man I'd fallen in love with, against all odds.

The man that I didn't deserve, not in a million years.

He would be okay, I knew it. He'd become an amazing, successful lawyer, and he'd end up with a beautiful woman who deserved him and made him happy. Not someone who was so fucked up that they hadn't even done the right thing until the last minute, who'd lied to him from the beginning, whose only family members were liars and convicted criminals.

I reminded myself of the indisputable truth. He was better off without me.

They all were.

Pulling the door closed behind me, I swallowed the lump in my throat, dropping my keys through the letterbox.

This was goodbye.

44

KNOX

It had only been five days since Elena had vanished into thin air, but it was five fucking days too long.

I understood why she'd gone. All of us had received individual letters from her with a London postmark—me, my mum, and my dad, reiterating everything that had been written in the notebook and saying how sorry she was. She said she hadn't expected us to forgive her, that she wished that she could go back in time and never have met us. She thanked us profusely for making her feel welcome, and for all we'd done for her, and how she knew that she hadn't deserved any of it.

In my mum's letter, she'd written that Letitia had worked with children for years, and although Letitia's references were falsified to make it sound as though she'd been a nanny for other well-off families, she had, in fact, done a lot of other nannying work. I guess she'd included that to let my mother know that she'd believed JoJo to be in safe hands, because she also said that she would have stepped in if there was ever any issue with JoJo. She did also mention that after seeing the way her mother had deteriorated lately, if my mum hadn't been around to take JoJo last weekend, she would have told us all the truth even sooner.

As for my dad—she told him how sorry she was that his life had been put at risk by her mother's actions, how she would have never forgiven herself if anything had happened to him.

And mine? She'd left a lot unsaid. She said that I would make an amazing lawyer and a load of other shit about how great my life would be in the future, which was, quite frankly, fucking bollocks. My life was great already—or it had been, right up until last Sunday, when everything went to shit. And now she was gone, and things were the very fucking opposite of great.

Lucky for her, and for me, I could read between the lines, and if she thought I was going to just let her walk away, she was about to find out just how wrong she was.

"This is it." I pulled up outside the row of shops. "Above the fried chicken place."

In the rear-view mirror, I watched my mum wrinkle her nose. "She's spent five days too long here already. Go and get her."

Next to me, my dad patted my arm. "If she refuses to listen to you, carry her out of there."

I raised a brow. "As a legal professional, are you advocating kidnapping as an acceptable method of getting her to listen?"

"As a legal professional, I am not advocating kidnapping. As your father, I am advocating the use of any means necessary to bring Elena back home with us, where she belongs."

My mother climbed out of the car as I did and took my place behind the wheel. My dad still wasn't able to drive, thanks to his broken ankle, so my mum had offered.

"Good luck," she murmured. "I agree with your father—if she won't listen to you, carry her out of there by force."

"I might have to."

Adjusting the small bag that was slung across my body, I stepped up to the door that led to the flats, between the chicken place and a laundrette, and pressed the buzzer marked Flat 4.

There was no answer. I buzzed again, and again, and then I tried the next buzzer up. They didn't answer either. Fuck, where was she? It was Friday night, and I thought she'd be home. We'd driven to London as soon as my lacrosse game was over, and from the information we'd managed to gather, she should have been here.

"Excuse me." A dark-haired woman who looked to be in her mid-twenties appeared next to me, juggling three bags with a set of keys. "I need to get inside."

"Need any help?" I gave her a wide smile, the kind that I used a lot when I was younger to get out of trouble with my parents. "Let me get the door for you."

"Thank you." She returned my smile, and I took the keys from her, unlocked the door, and held it open for her before handing back the keys.

"No problem. Hey, do you know the girl who lives in flat number four? Elena? She's a friend of mine, and I was hoping to surprise her with a visit, but she's not answering her buzzer."

The woman nodded, and hope surged through me. "Elena. Yes. The new girl. Her flat's opposite mine. You won't find her at home tonight—she's working."

"Working? I didn't know—I mean, she didn't tell me she had a job already."

"Well." She glanced around us, lowering her voice even though we were the only two people in an otherwise deserted stairwell. "It's off the books, if you know what I mean. She only started there yesterday."

"Your secret's safe with me." I winked at her, and she smiled.

"If you want to surprise her, you can. The staff aren't supposed to have visitors when they're working, but the owners don't care." She shrugged. "If anyone asks, tell them Laura sent you."

"I will. Where can I find her?"

Nodding her head towards the street behind me, she said, "The pub at the end of the row. The Hog's Head. She's in the kitchens."

"Thanks." Wasting no more time, I backed out of the flat's entryway and jogged over to the car, letting my parents know what was happening. Within two minutes, I was pushing inside the dingy pub and heading straight for the door marked "Staff Only."

She wasn't in the kitchen, so I kept going down another corridor and through another door, ending up outside in a walled backyard with beer barrels stacked around the space. Literally no one seemed to even care that I was back here. It was fucking crazy. Although I guessed if they were employing people off the books, then it probably wasn't the kind of establishment that cared about patrons going where they weren't supposed to.

That was irrelevant, though, in light of the fact that Elena was here, working, when she'd only just been in hospital and had a blood transfusion. She shouldn't be here. She should be with—

The second I laid eyes on my girl, my heart fucking

jump-started in my chest, and everything I felt for her came rushing back to the surface.

"Elena."

Her head whipped around, and her jaw dropped as she took me in. Almost immediately, her eyes filled with tears.

"*Knox*? Wh—what are you doing here?"

I stepped closer, dying to touch her, but I held off, taking in her defensive posture and the way she was hugging her arms to herself.

"I've come to bring you home, baby. I've missed you. We all have."

She shook her head violently. "No. You can't. I— You know what I did. How can you, of all people, be standing here and saying that to me?"

"It's not just me." Reaching out, I tucked a strand of hair behind her ear, and she trembled at my touch. "My parents came too, in case you needed extra persuasion. I'm sure they would've brought JoJo as well, but she's currently having a sleepover with my aunt."

"But how? Why? After everything I've done? And how did you find me?" Her body was still shaking, and I didn't care about how I should or shouldn't behave anymore. I had to hold her. Wrapping my arms around her, I looked into her beautiful eyes, seeing the tears trembling on her long lashes.

"We found the phone. And the money you left for the handbag replacement. Those were the actions of a good person. A person trying to do the right thing, to make amends. And you saved my dad's fucking life, baby."

She shook her head again. "His life wouldn't even have been at risk if it wasn't for—"

I leaned in and kissed the words off her soft lips. "Don't you fucking dare blame yourself for that. The blame lies with your mother."

"That woman is no longer my mother. I renounced her. Disowned her, if you can do that to a parent."

A smile curved over my lips. "Yeah, you did, and I'm proud of you for doing it. As for your other question—how we found you...let's just say that both my dad and I have some useful contacts."

"So what now? Are you here to save me? I'm a charity case to your family?" Her voice was threaded with pain and bitterness, and it killed me.

"Fuck, no. You don't need saving. You can save yourself—you're a survivor. You're doing it right now. I mean, fuck. Five days, and you have a flat and a job, not to mention that you did all of this right after a blood transfusion. Although...I should mention that you shouldn't be doing anything after a blood transfusion, especially not moving to a new city and starting a job that requires physical activity." My jaw clenched, thinking of everything she'd been through. "You survived living with your mum for that year before you came to me, and I don't even know half of it."

She sighed against me, a soft, sad sound. "Why, then? I don't understand."

"Because we want you to come home. Because even though it's only been a month, which I realise is stupidly fucking fast, you've become a part of our family."

A sob tore from her throat, and I pulled her closer, lowering my head to her ear. "And I want you. I want you so fucking much. It's been hell not having you around. I missed you."

"Knox." Her arms finally came around me, and she was properly crying. "How can I just come back? After everything?"

"You're asking too many questions. Do you want to know something? Both my mum and my dad advocated me kidnapping you to bring you home, if it was necessary."

She laughed brokenly. "This is insane."

"Insane, but it's happening. Come on." I released her, wiped away as many of her tears as I could with my fingers, and then took her hand. She didn't protest as I led her back through the pub, out the door, and down the street. My Maserati was still idling at the kerb, and both my parents waved madly when they saw us. Embarrassing as fuck—they could've at least done me the courtesy of keeping the windows up, but no, they had to have them down, meaning we had an audience of three people in the chicken shop, plus a passer-by on the street.

"I see he didn't have to resort to kidnapping," my dad shouted at fucking foghorn levels, making even more people look at us. Elena took one look at the grimace on my face and started laughing, and *there* was my girl.

"Fucking hell. Quick, open the door. I need to get off the street." I crowded up against Elena's back as she slotted the key into the door that led to her flat, feeling her still laughing against me.

When we were safely inside her actual flat, I took a look around. No joke, if I stretched out both my arms, I could touch both walls. There was the tiniest excuse for a kitchen I'd ever seen, a bed, and one armchair, all in one room. Another door led to what I assumed was the bathroom.

"What the fuck is this place?"

She shrugged. "I sublet it from the people who own the laundrette downstairs. I pay in cash, weekly, and there's no contract."

"It should be condemned."

"You're such a snob." The tiniest smile appeared on her face, and I couldn't resist kissing her. "I missed you so much," she murmured when we broke apart. "I was trying to do the right thing."

"I know you were. But you're coming with us. Let's get your shit packed so we can leave."

My words were interrupted by her stomach rumbling, and my brows pulled together as I stared down at her. "When was the last time you ate?"

Biting down on her lip, she eyed me from beneath her lashes. "Um…yesterday?"

Thank fuck I'd had the foresight to bring something with me. It was better than nothing. Digging around in the bag that was slung across my body, I handed her a bottle of water, a bag of crisps, and a pomegranate.

She arched a brow at the pomegranate, and I shrugged. "It was the first thing I saw as we were leaving. I know you like the seeds, so I grabbed one from the fruit bowl on our way out."

The tremulous smile that spread over her face was everything. "Thank you. Really. I can't even… It's… Thank you."

I shook my head. "It's nothing. Come on. Let's get packed."

When she retrieved her duffel bag, I started picking things up to speed up the process. The sooner we got out of here, the better. There was a brochure on her bed, and I stared at it. "Adult education?"

She followed the direction of my gaze. "Yeah. I was getting ready to enrol. There's a place close to here that offers adult education, and they do a music A level. That's…it's the one I loved the most."

I shot her a grin. "Lucky for you, I think of everything. You're still enrolled at Hatherley Hall, so you can carry on with your A levels. As far as everyone knows, you've been home from school and work this week with the flu. Even my best friends don't know the full story, and believe me, I don't ever keep anything from them. Ever. The official line is that your mo—*ex*-mother left my parents' employment after a breakdown. She pleaded guilty to all the charges, so there's no trial, and we can keep it from getting out."

My best friends would hear the full story eventually, but I needed them to accept Elena first. To get to know her. To see what I saw every time I looked at her. As far as anyone else was concerned, I owed them nothing.

Pausing in the process of shoving clothes into her bag, she stared at me. "Knox, I'm coming back with you, but I can't come back to that school. I'm not taking any more money from your parents. I'll do A levels online if I have to, but I refuse to accept any more handouts."

My girl was so stubborn, something I loved about her, but if she was up against my mother, she'd lose. "Baby, first of all, your school fees were paid up front for the year, and people don't just get refunds if they change their minds. Secondly, have you met my mother? She lives to spend money on people. It makes her happy. You can't deprive her of that. JoJo's still little, and Cora's away at uni, so she doesn't have anyone else to buy those sexy dresses and jewellery for." My dick stirred as I remembered that dress she'd worn to the charity benefit, the way it had flowed over all those gorgeous curves, and that diamond choker at her throat.

"You look like you're thinking dirty thoughts, Knox." She dropped the clothes into her bag and took the two steps over to me.

"I am. I'm thinking very dirty thoughts. How I want you to wear that dress you wore to the benefit again so I can tear it from your fucking gorgeous body and then bend you over and fuck you in front of a mirror while you're wearing just your shoes and a choker."

"Fuck," she moaned as I ground my dick into her. "Yes. Let's do that."

"Tomorrow. After the party." I slid my hand over the curve of her ass, pulling her closer to me.

"Party?" Her head flew up. "What party?"

"Oh, yeah, I forgot to say. This is your official invitation to be my date to the Halloween celebration of the gods. Want to come?"

She bit down on her lip. "Should I? If I've been away all week, it might seem a bit…weird, maybe?"

"Nah, no one gives a fuck. William and Katy are coming, anyway—they've got a surprise for you, so you can't let them down." She was still chewing on her lip, and I raised a brow at her. "Go on. What's your other objection?"

"The…the loan shark that m—"

"Already taken care of. He happened to gain the attention of one of the top legal professionals in the country, and yeah, he won't be bothering you for anything. He's going to be far, far away from you. Anything else?"

Fucking finally, she shook her head. "I guess not."

"Good. Let's go home."

45

Elena

I couldn't believe that Knox had come to get me. And not only him but his parents too. After everything that had happened, they inexplicably wanted me in their lives, and I still couldn't help but feel like this was all a dream. I'd been so miserable when I'd left, and I'd cried myself to sleep every night, but I'd held out hope that eventually, I'd come out the other side.

Never in a million years did I think Knox would come after me, let alone his family.

But he had. *They* had. We'd talked all the way back, and I'd told him everything about my life that I'd been unable or afraid to say before, everything that I'd been holding back. When we got back to the house, he refused to leave me, taking me into his bed, where we'd continued talking, trading information about each other in a give and take that I never wanted to end. We hadn't even had sex, just talked until we both succumbed to sleep in the early hours of the morning.

And now I was here with Katy and Will, standing at the top of the stairs that descended into the crypts. They were a fitting backdrop for the Halloween theme, which spilled out into the cellar storeroom—pumpkins carved with grotesque features, skulls littering the ancient flagstones, and from somewhere, a smoke machine pumping a low cloud of smoke around our ankles, like an eerie fog from a horror movie. There was a general theme of "come in costume, but wear whatever costume you like," so I'd worn the dress I'd worn to the charity event, along with the shoes. I didn't have the choker, but Aria had used make-up to create a vampire bite on my throat, complete with dripping blood. Katy and Will had also only made slight concessions to the Halloween theme—Will with vampire fangs and fake blood dripping from his mouth and Katy with a vampire bite that matched mine, both courtesy of Aria.

As we descended the stairs into the crypts, we were hit by a wall of noise, dancing bodies filling the space with more smoke pumping into the atmosphere. Coloured lights pulsed across the cavernous depths, illuminating the Halloween decorations strung around the sides. At one side of the main crypt, there was even a DJ set up, pumping out music from huge speakers, and I shook my head in disbelief. Knox had informed me that the teaching staff had been persuaded to turn a blind eye to any celebrations coming from the A-level students, thanks to an extremely generous monetary donation, aka bribe, from Knox's and Tristan's parents—and the rest of the school was currently occupied with a far more sedate ball in the main hall. But it was one thing to be told about it and another thing to see a party of this scale in action.

"I've been given very specific instructions," Will told me, pulling out his phone and sending a quick text, his thumbs moving quickly over the screen. "You have to come with us to the DJ booth."

"Uh, okay." I shrugged and then followed him and Katy through the crowds until we popped out next to the speakers. The music was so loud here it pounded through my skull, but I liked it. It made me feel alive.

"I was going to pick you as my next murder victim, but I see that a vampire managed to get to you first," a low, smooth, and sexy-as-fuck voice said in my ear. I turned to see Knox, dressed in a tight, deep blue T-shirt that clung to his muscles, black jeans, and black boots, his face covered by a hockey mask.

"*Friday the 13th?*" I guessed.

Next to me, Will pointed at my throat and then flashed his fangs with a grin. "I'm the one who got to her first."

I bit down on my lip to hide my smile at the way Knox growled, pulling me into him. "She's mine. Get your own fucking girl."

"Already did." He wrapped his arm around Katy's waist, and this time, I did smile, glad that Will was feeling comfortable enough to tease Knox...even if it wasn't the best idea.

I elbowed Knox in warning, and he leaned down to me, his mask knocking against my cheek. "You're mine. *Only* mine." Raising his head, he turned back to Will. "You're up next. Just know that the only reason I'm letting this happen is Elena."

He rolled his eyes. "Yes. I know." Then he sighed. "Thanks, though. I—we appreciate it."

Knox's voice softened. "You're welcome. Get up there."

Will and Katy disappeared behind the DJ booth, and I stared up at Knox, wishing I could see his face behind the mask. "What's going on?"

"You'll find out in a minute. Be patient." I just *knew* he was smirking.

Instead of segueing into another song, the DJ cut the music to a collective cry of outrage from the crowds.

There was a screech of feedback from the mic, and suddenly, Will's voice was booming from the speakers. "Hatherley Hall students, we have a Halloween treat for you!"

"Go prefects!" someone screeched from right behind me as Will paused dramatically.

"This song was originally written and composed by me, Katy Peterson, and Elena Greenwood. The version you're about to hear was produced by myself, with credit to Knox Ashcroft. Enjoy."

As cheers filled the air, Will stepped back, and the DJ took his place. A low, heady beat filled the cavernous space, and then the melody kicked in.

"Is that our song? Knox, it's our song!"

"Yeah, it is. Remixed by William, with the hook taken from 'Lost in the Moment.' What do you think?"

"I can't believe this. This is amazing. Fuck, it sounds so good, doesn't it?"

He nodded. "Yeah, it does. Notice how William gave me credit?"

I cocked my head, staring at him. "You made him do that, didn't you?"

"Maybe, maybe not." He gripped me around the waist and then spun me around so that my back was to his front. Lowering his hands to my hips, he began to move us to the music. "Yeah…I like this song. Like the way you move to the beat."

"Mmm." I tipped my head back against him. "Something about you just pulls me in/ I can't explain, where do I begin/ I'm lost in your eyes, your smile, your touch—"

"You wrote those lyrics about me, didn't you, baby?"

I repeated his words from earlier. "Maybe, maybe not."

His hands slid around my waist as he ground his hardening cock against me. "I know I'm your muse."

"Oh, really? What else do you know?" I pressed back into him, rolling my hips.

"I know that ever since I laid eyes on you tonight, all I could think about was taking you into my bedroom, stripping you out of this dress, and fucking you until you can't walk. Then doing it all over again on the tombstones, down in the dark, maybe with that spreader bar. Or maybe with me tying you down. I know how much you like it, baby."

Fuuuck. "Knox," I moaned. "What's stopping you?"

"Obligations. As one of the hosts, I need to be seen at the party. It's in my honour, after all. A double celebration —Halloween and me finally moving in here." He ran his hand up my stomach, his thumb rubbing teasingly over the underside of my breast. "I never thought I'd say this, but I'll miss being at home in a way. No. Fuck. Okay, the truth is, I'll miss *you*. But I'm going to make the most of every minute I can get with you, even though I'm back here."

It struck me then that we were here in the crypts, surrounded by his friends, and he was openly dancing with me. He'd even told Will I was his, and now here he was, talking about what would happen now that he was boarding at Hatherley Hall.

I wanted him to be mine so, so much, and maybe, just maybe, he felt the same way too.

The dancing crowds had thinned out, and somehow, I'd found myself with a group of students clustered together on the sofas, playing a version of truth or dare that involved no truths, but you had to take a shot if you refused a dare. I could blame the fact that I was playing it on the three vodka drinks I'd had, but in reality, it was because Knox had finally taken off his mask, pressed a soft kiss to my lips, and then asked me to join him and his friends, and I couldn't say no to him.

All three gods and their usual group of friends and lacrosse team members were there, along with Aria, who was perched on the arm of the sofa next to me, sending the occasional rude gesture in Tristan's direction and receiving a mouthed insult in return. He and Roman both had girls on their laps, as did a number of the other guys. Several of them had been masked earlier, but now the masks were gone, and they were all drinking. Knox had taken a seat opposite me on the same sofa as Tristan but left a space between them, and my jaw clenched as I noticed Freya slide in next to him. I knew she was into him. Although I trusted Knox, even though there was nothing official between us, I didn't trust her at all.

"Link, I dare you to get your dick out right here." Roman smirked at Lincoln.

Blaine raised his brows. "Is this the kind of thing the lacrosse team gets up to when the rest of us aren't around?"

Aria made a fake puking sound, covering her eyes. "Tell me when it's over. I don't want to be scarred for life."

"You want to see mine instead, baby?" Tristan called over the noise. Her hand flew away from her eyes, and she glared at him. He smirked, his hands going to his crotch. "On second thoughts, no. Your eyes look like they'd burn laser beams through my junk."

"If you wanted to see it, all you had to do was ask. You didn't have to dare me," Lincoln shot back, jumping to his feet. He swayed a little as he stood. Bloody hell, he was already drunk.

"We've all seen it enough times after lacrosse," Knox interjected. "Been there, done that."

Shouts, cheers, and whistles came from all angles as Lincoln turned in a slow circle, flexing and generally showing off, and I caught Knox's eye. *I like yours better*, I mouthed, and he mouthed something back that I thought was, *I'm gonna fuck you with it later*.

When Lincoln was sitting back down, Freya piped up. "My turn. Knox, I dare you to kiss me. Properly."

Knox's gaze flicked to mine and then back to Freya. I held my breath, my heart pounding. I'd said earlier that I trusted Knox, but I had a moment of panic and hurt when he angled his body towards her, lowering his head.

I couldn't breathe.

He opened his mouth.

"No," he said, and he swiped the huge bottle of vodka from the table, sloshing some into a shot glass and then downing it. He slammed the glass back on the table and looked straight at me, fire in his eyes.

"My turn. Elena. I dare you to come over here and answer my question."

I licked my suddenly dry lips. Everyone was staring at me. "What's the question?"

"You'll have to come over here to find out. Do you accept the dare, or are you gonna take a shot?"

Taking a deep breath, I held his gaze. "I accept."

46

KNOX

Elena rounded the coffee table, and I stood. When she was right in front of me, I ran my hand down her arm, fucking loving the way she shivered beneath my touch.

"Elena Greenwood. Will you do me the honour of—"

"Oh, shit! He's proposing!"

I threw my middle finger up at my friend-slash-pain in the fucking ass Tristan, who was grinning maniacally at me, before I spoke again. "Okay, fuck. Yeah, that did sound way too much like a proposal."

Elena's eyes danced with amusement, and all I wanted to do was kiss her. But first, I had to ask the question. I raised my voice. "No one fucking interrupt me this time." Sliding my fingers between hers, I tugged her closer. "How would you feel about being my girlfriend?"

Shock flared in her gaze.

"Elena."

"Um." She cleared her throat. "I'd feel…like that was a good idea."

I grinned at her, taking in her flushed cheeks and bright eyes. "Will you be my girlfriend, then?"

It seemed to take forever, but eventually, she gave me a shy smile and nodded. "Yeah. Yes. Definitely."

I planted a hard kiss on her lips, then turned to the rest of the group, or as many of them as I could take in at once.

"I'm officially off the market."

There were cheers, along with noises of protest from some of the girls. My two best friends grinned at me, genuinely happy for me, and I returned their grins. It was a relief that they were okay with it. Especially Roman—I hadn't been sure how he'd take it. He'd been very anti-relationship since…since the summer we were fifteen and Quinn Farrow had disappeared from our lives. He'd never discussed what had happened between them, but all I knew was he'd changed after she'd left Hatherley Hall for good. As for me, I'd never seen the appeal of monogamy, but now Elena was in my life, and I got it. And when she'd left… I'd missed her more than I knew it was possible to miss someone, and that had to be a crystal-clear sign. This wasn't about being tied down; it was about making a commitment to a person you really fucking wanted to be with, to the point that you couldn't even imagine being with anyone else.

Still holding Elena's hand, I began tugging her away from the sofas. "Got to seal the deal now."

Elena's cheekbones were an even deeper shade of pink after my words, but she laughed, turning back to our friends. "If I can't walk properly tomorrow, blame Knox." I noticed that she was mostly directing her comment at Freya, and I smirked, dipping my head to her ear as we headed for the stairs.

"I love this side of you."

"What side?"

"The jealous side. Not that you have anything to worry about. I'm all yours, baby. When I asked you to be my girlfriend, it was purposely public so that everyone knows you're mine."

She turned her head, pressing a kiss to my jaw. "Mmm. I liked it earlier when you got jealous of Will saying he'd bitten me. He didn't, by the way."

"You liked that, did you? I know he didn't get his mouth anywhere near you because you wouldn't let anyone else get close. You're too into me." I pulled her through the archway.

"No desecrating the tombstones!" Tristan shouted, but I just utilised my free hand, flipping him my middle finger as we continued to move towards the locked door that led to my own private space.

"He's a bit too interested in our sex life for my liking," Elena said, amusement dancing in her gaze as she took in the finger I was directing at my friend. Her eyes returned to mine, and they darkened in a way that had my dick fucking throbbing. "But going back to what you just said, you're right. I'm into you. Very into you."

Unlocking my bedroom door with one hand, I trailed the other up her stomach and onto her breast, hearing her breath hitch as I stroked my thumb over her nipple. "I'm gonna be into you in a minute."

"That was the worst…line…ever," she breathed as I manoeuvred us both inside my bedroom and shut and locked the door. The noise of the party was instantly muffled, and I could hear her unsteady breaths. Now I had both hands free, I continued palming her lush tits as I walked her into the centre of the room, my cock throbbing against the curve of her ass.

"You look so fucking good in this dress, but you're

going to look even better out of it." I lowered the straps, peeling the dress away from her body until there was a pool of sapphire-blue satin at her feet.

"And the lines keep coming," she muttered, but her pupils were dilated, and her nipples were so fucking hard they could cut glass. Fucking beautiful. My fingers skimmed across her waist and then down to the scrap of deep blue silk that covered her pussy. I tugged, dragging the material down her legs until she was bared to me in nothing but a pair of heels.

Yeah. So. Beautiful.

I stepped away from her, over to my chest of drawers. Opening the top drawer, I closed my fingers around the slim velvet box. "The vampire bite looks good, and it gives me ideas for later, but I think we can improve on it."

I went back to her and opened the box, lifting it up so she could see inside.

She gasped. "Knox, is that—"

"Not quite the same, but I think you'll like this better." I lifted the collar from its box and spun her around, pushing her long hair over her shoulder so I could fasten it around her neck. It looked very similar to the diamond choker, but it was essentially a thin strip of the softest leather studded with diamonds all along the outside.

When it was in place, I turned her back around. The diamonds lined her throat, a perfect row of iridescent sparkles against her flushed skin.

So fucking sexy. My cock had never been as hard before as it was right now, and I needed to be inside her, to claim her, to own her, to make sure she knew that she was mine.

"This is too much. I can't—"

Cutting off her words with my mouth on hers, I repositioned us so we were standing in front of my full-length mirror—or at least, mine for now, because I'd liberated it from the lower level of the crypts earlier today. I turned her around again so that we were both facing the mirror and then directed her to put her hands on the back of the chair that I'd purposely placed in that exact spot.

"Bend over. Keep your hands there. Don't move." I released her, walking around the chair so I was in front of her with my back to the mirror. From this angle, she should be able to see both my front and my back.

I took my time stripping out of my clothes, fucking loving the way she was white-knuckling the back of the chair, her breaths coming hard and fast as I exposed my body to her. Was there anything better than wanting someone so fucking badly and knowing that they wanted you just the same in return? It was more than that too. The other F-word was involved. *Feelings*. Yeah, I had so many fucking feelings for this girl it was honestly blowing my mind. I'd never felt this way before, never even come close. Not even remotely.

When I was as naked as she was, I moved around behind her, admiring the curve of her back and ass before sliding my hand down between her legs. *Fuck*. She was so wet and ready for me.

"I'll take my time with you later. But right now, I don't think either of us can wait, can we?" I ran my free hand up her back, then curved my fingers around her throat. The diamonds were cool against my overheated skin. When I squeezed lightly, she gasped.

"Need you inside me." She pushed back against me, my cock sliding between her legs, my length dragging along her wetness. "Please."

"I fucking love it when you beg." Removing my hand from around her throat, I slid my fingers through her hair and then curled them around the back of the collar, tugging lightly. "More."

"Fuck, Knox," she moaned, grinding back against me, shamelessly rubbing her pussy all over my dick. "*Please*. I need you."

I positioned the head of my cock at her entrance, and we both straight out moaned as I began to push in. "Look in the mirror, baby. Look how fucking hot we look. Look at how much you want me. How much I want you." I punctuated my final word with a hard thrust, filling her all the way, and I watched her reflection as her mouth fell open, her eyes so fucking wide, pupils completely blown.

"Fuck me, Knox. Hard. Please. Please. *Please*." Her words were gasps, her head falling forwards as I gripped her hip and began pounding in and out of her. She moaned over and over again, and when I could tell she was getting close, her breaths stuttering and her movements becoming more frantic, I tugged on the collar again.

She came. Just like that. Her pussy throbbed around my dick, so fucking tight and wet and hot, her eyes falling shut as I watched her in the mirror, and it was the hottest sight I'd ever seen. The orgasm was ripped out of me, my dick shooting inside her, filling her with my cum.

"Ohhh. That…" She slumped forwards, curling over the chair, and I went with her, needing to stay inside her for longer, to keep this connection.

"…was so fucking good. Epic." I finished her sentence for her, my own voice raspy and breathless as I came down from my high. "You're amazing, Elena."

I curved my arm around her waist and lowered us both to the floor. She let her head fall back against my shoulder, and I placed my lips to her neck, right above the diamonds.

Her fingers threaded through mine, pressed to her waist, and she sighed. "Knox. You make me so happy."

"Same, baby. So fucking happy." I took our clasped hands up across the swells of her gorgeous tits, a slow drag over her curves. Then I slid my free hand lower, onto her clit, making her bite down on her lip, her eyes fluttering closed. "How about we go down to the lower level and play with your sexy-as-fuck body until I'm hard again, and then we can go for round two?"

The moan that came out of her mouth at my words told me that she had no objections at all.

47

Elena

"My dress." I eyed the crumpled heap of satin discarded on the stone floor.

Knox followed my gaze, his brows pulling together. A second later, a slow smile spread across his face. "We'll get it dry-cleaned. In the meantime, I have an idea." He crossed over to his wardrobe, flinging the door open. When he emerged, he held up a bundle of navy fabric with royal blue trim. "Number 26. My lacrosse jersey. What do you say?"

I stared at him. "You want me to wear that?"

"Yeah, I fucking do. You're mine. What better way to show it? I'd ask you to wear my helmet too, but I don't want to hide your gorgeous face." Stepping up to me, he murmured, "Lift," and I lifted my arms, letting him slide the shirt down over my body. It came down over my thighs, long enough that it wasn't indecent, and as I rocked back on my heels, Knox groaned, palming the huge bulge in his jeans.

"Fuck. You in my clothes with those sexy-as-fuck heels and that collar. You look so fucking hot, baby."

"You're not too bad either." I let my gaze sweep over my man's sexy body, all the way up to the angular lines of his face, his perfectly mussed hair, his sinfully soft lips curved upwards, and his dark eyes burning with fire as he held my gaze. My heart skipped a beat. How did I get so lucky after everything we'd been through?

"Ready?" He tilted his head towards the door.

"Bring your mask," I told him, and his smile widened into a wicked grin. Swiping his mask from the floor, he crossed over to me, the mask dangling from his fingers. He dipped his head to my ear.

"You're so fucking perfect for me, Elena."

Before I could reply, he tugged me out of the room, locking the door behind us.

The party was still going strong when we stepped back into the main crypt, Knox steering me through the crowds with a possessive arm wrapped around me. Before we could reach the door leading to the lower level, Tristan appeared in front of us.

"Knox. We have a situation."

Knox stiffened against me. "What is it?"

Tristan glanced around us. "We need to talk in private." He turned on his heel, heading for the entrance to the lower level. Knox didn't seem to be in any hurry to let go of me, and so I found myself in a new room I'd never been in, all stone walls and a low ceiling, dimly lit, much like the other rooms—except this one didn't have any tombs or gravestones. Rather than taking a seat on the futon to his left, Knox leaned back against the wall, wrapping his arms around my waist with my back to his chest, his mask still clasped between his fingers.

"Quinn Farrow is coming back to Hatherley Hall," Tristan announced, and from behind me, I both heard and felt Knox's sharp intake of breath.

"Does Roman know?"

Tristan shook his head. "Not yet."

"Fuck," Knox muttered. "When?"

"If my sources are correct, she'll be here on Monday."

"Okay." Tightening his arms around me, Knox breathed out heavily. "This weekend is supposed to be about celebrating. We should wait to tell him. It's just going to put him in a shit mood, and he doesn't need that. He deserves to have a good time tonight."

Tristan nodded. "I agree. I just wanted to give you a heads-up."

"Who's Quinn Farrow?" I ventured.

"A girl who used to go to school here. She's got some history with Roman." Knox pressed a kiss to the side of my head. "I'm sure you'll meet her at some point, but it's nothing you need to worry about right now."

Before I could reply, the door swung open, and Roman Cavendish entered the room.

Silence fell.

Roman's gaze flicked between me, Knox, and Tristan. His brows rose. "Private party?"

I was the first to recover, and it was because I suddenly knew what I needed to do. Straightening up, I untangled myself from Knox's grip, meeting first Roman's eyes, then Tristan's. "Can I speak to you both?"

It was a long, halting story, with interjections by Knox, and by the end of it, I was completely wrung out, a lump in my throat and tears in my eyes, Knox cradling me in his arms on the edge of the sofa. "I understand if neither of you want anything to do with me, but I promise you…I swear on my life…I'll never, ever knowingly do anything to hurt Knox or his family again. They mean everything to me."

Roman and Tristan exchanged wary glances, but eventually, Tristan nodded. "It's clear that since you've been around, Knox has been less of…" He paused, trying to find the words.

"Less of an asshole?" Roman suggested, smirking at Knox, who gave him the middle finger.

"Fuck off, both of you. We want a fresh start, okay? We've been through a lot of shit, and none of us can judge Elena, because…because…fucking hell, if we'd been through what she's been through—"

"We get it." Tristan straightened up, looking at me before turning to Knox. "We'll hold back judgement. It's a fucked-up situation, but…yeah. Elena has been a victim in this too. And we know you, and we know you don't do relationships, so I'm thinking that your girl has to be someone special."

"He's important to me. I—"

Knox placed his palm across my mouth, stopping my words. "Shhh, baby. They know what we mean to each other." He cleared his throat. "Are we done here? I need to spend some quality time with my girl."

"We're done." Tristan nodded at him. "Just to be clear, we're happy for you both." He jerked his head in the direction of the door. "Ro. Coming?"

Roman pushed off the wall. "Yeah. We're done here." He yanked the door open and disappeared, with Tristan shooting Knox a pointed glance before he followed Roman, closing the door behind them both.

"It's more difficult for Roman, with the whole Quinn thing." Knox tugged me in the direction of the exit. "But that's not our problem to worry about right now." His fingers closed around the door handle, and as he stared down at me, a sinful smile tugged at his lips. "I hope you're ready."

Then, he covered his face with his mask.

48

KNOX

I took a step back, admiring my handiwork. My cock was pounding so fucking hard at the sight in front of me. The crypt was lit by a combination of dripping wax candles and hidden recessed lighting, sending dancing and flickering shadows across the lines and curves of ancient stone, illuminating the cobwebs that stretched across the arches of the ceiling. In the centre of the room, the huge tombstone was draped in heavy black fabric, and spread out on top of it, her arms and legs bound by scarlet rope, fully nude aside from the diamond collar that sparkled at her throat, was Elena.

"I have never seen anything hotter in my life," I rasped, drinking in the sight in front of me.

"I want to see you," she moaned, arching her back, thrusting her gorgeous breasts upwards. "Please."

"I fucking love it when you beg." Stepping closer, I tugged off my T-shirt, keeping my mask in place, and then curved my fingers around the band of my jeans. I watched in satisfaction as her pupils dilated even further, her lips parting as she dragged her gaze down my body.

"More. More, Knox. Please."

"Mmm, yeah." I flicked open the button of my jeans and lowered them a little, enough for her to notice the fact that I hadn't bothered with underwear. "More?"

"*Yes.*"

I dropped the teasing and removed my remaining clothing, leaving just the mask, the cool air brushing over my skin as I stood in front of the tombstone, my cock hard and heavy, glistening with precum.

"It's funny how things change." Sliding a finger up Elena's side, continuing until I reached the collar at her throat, I lowered my head. "When I first had you here, right on this tombstone, I never imagined you'd be the one to make all my fantasies come true."

She blinked up at me, her long lashes fluttering. "What fantasies, Knox?"

"Having someone right here on this tombstone, bound and helpless and so fucking willing to let me do what I wanted to them. This is even better than I imagined, though, because it's you, baby."

"I want this. I want you. My masked man." Her arms were bound above her head, but she struggled against the restraints anyway, wanting to touch me. I'd let her, soon, but for now, I wanted her helpless beneath me. My dick was leaking precum, needing to be inside her, but before that happened, I was going to drive her wild.

I smiled beneath my mask, not that she could see. "Lie back and enjoy." Tugging at the collar enough to make her breath hitch, I used my free hand to trace decreasing circles over the swell of her breasts, teasing her with light strokes, never enough to satisfy her. When she was moaning and panting, I tugged on the collar again as I dragged my thumb over her pouty lips. Her mouth opened, and I slid it inside.

"Suck for me, baby. Get it nice and wet." She complied immediately, and my dick throbbed as I removed my thumb, inserting my index and middle fingers and instructing her to suck. When I removed them, I stepped back, moving to the end of the tombstone, between her spread legs, which were tied down with a series of intricate knots that I was very fucking proud of. It gave her enough room to writhe around, like she was doing now, but she wasn't going anywhere. I wrapped my fingers around my cock, slowly stroking up and down.

"Knox. Please."

"Do you want my cock?"

"Yes. *Yes.*" Her eyes were glassy, her nipples were peaked, and at the apex of her thighs, her wetness glistened in the candlelight, making my mouth water. My girl was so fucking ready for me.

But she'd have to wait. Releasing my aching erection, I slid my hands up the inside of her legs, stopping at the tops of her thighs. I spread my fingers, stroking over her soft skin, never touching where she wanted me to. This was torture for us both, when all I wanted was to be inside her, but getting to play with her delectable body while she was bound and helpless was so fucking intoxicating.

I finally dragged my thumb over her clit, two fingers sliding through her wetness at the same time, a combination of her arousal and my cum from fucking her upstairs. She arched upwards with a cry, the restraints hindering her movements.

"More. I need more."

My fingers entered her, so fucking slowly, stroking inside her tight, wet heat, and I groaned, losing my fucking mind at the sensation, knowing she'd feel so fucking incredible around my dick.

"Is that what you want?"

"Need. You," she panted, and I couldn't deny her any longer. I withdrew my fingers, climbing onto the tombstone and lining myself up. Her body was so soft and warm beneath me, flushed and beautiful, her gaze fixed on me, her silky hair spilling over her shoulders and across the black fabric like a dark waterfall. She was the most gorgeous woman I'd ever seen in my life, and I was the only one who'd ever get to see her this way.

When I pushed inside, the moan that fell from her lips was so fucking intoxicating. I wanted my mouth on her. Wanted her hands on me. Wanted to fill her with my cum.

It seemed like she felt the same way because she gasped out, "Knox. Untie me. Please."

Withdrawing from her, I untied her restraints, and when she was free, she twisted on the tombstone, moving onto her hands and knees.

"Fuck me like this. With the mask on. Just for a minute. Then I want to touch you. Kiss you. Feel you inside me."

Whatever my girl wanted, she was going to get, if it was in my power to give it to her. I entered her in one long, slow thrust, planting one of my hands on the surface of the tombstone and the other clasping her hair in a makeshift ponytail. Pulling it as I thrust forwards, I was rewarded with a breathy moan as she pushed back against me.

"You like this? Being fucked by a guy in a mask?" I tugged on her hair again, lowering my voice. "I could be anyone. Holding you down, having my way with you."

A gasp fell from her lips, and she shuddered beneath me. "No. Not anyone. You. Your dick. Your body. Your voice."

"Yeah, baby. Me." I thrust forwards again, feeling her tighten around my dick. "No one else can fuck you the way I do. No one else will ever fuck you again. You're mine, and I'm never letting you go."

"Fuck. I need—I need to touch you. To kiss you."

"You can have it, Elena. Take what you want from me."

I let her manoeuvre me so that I was the one lying on the surface of the tombstone, on my back with my knees bent. I stroked my cock as she straddled me and then held it in place as she sank down onto me. When she was impaled on my length, she reached forwards, removing my mask and dropping it to the floor. Her smile was so fucking soft as she stared down at me, all wide golden-brown eyes with blown pupils.

"You're so beautiful, Knox. Like a god. Being here, in this crypt with you like this, it feels…" Her words trailed off, but I nodded.

"I know." *It feels different to anything I've ever experienced before. So fucking special. A new beginning for us both.* I reached for her, pulling myself into a seated position and wrapping my hand around her throat over the top of the collar. "Come here. Kiss me."

Her lips met mine, her mouth opening to me, our tongues sliding together as we lost ourselves in a hot, fucking filthy kiss, all moans and panted breaths, our hands all over each other's bodies as she rolled her hips down and I thrust up into her. The candles flickered and crackled, dancing shadows playing across the room as we fucked. Cool air played across our heated skin as our thrusts sped up, and my hands clasped Elena's hips, directing her movements, both of us racing towards the edge.

I slid my hand down between us, stroking across Elena's clit. Her hips stuttered, and her pussy clenched around me as she came on a long moan, her head falling back as she lost herself in her orgasm. It was seconds before I followed her over the edge, her body still shuddering as my cock pulsed inside her, filling her with my cum. I buried my head in the side of her throat, sucking a bruise into the skin above her collar so everyone would see the physical proof that she was mine.

Her fingers stroked across the back of my neck and up into my hair as I wrapped her in my arms, letting her fall into me, holding her up. We held each other, breathing in and out, taking in this fucking incredible connection that had built between us, that I'd never even imagined with anyone before. She pressed a soft kiss to the side of my jaw and then raised her head.

"You're a beautiful man with the body of a god and a big dick, and you know exactly how to play my body." A smile crossed my face, but she covered it with a finger. "I haven't finished yet. Not only that, you're intelligent, and great company, and you have the biggest fucking heart that only those that are close to you get to see. I feel so privileged to be a part of your life. To be yours."

This woman was fucking everything to me. When she removed her finger from my mouth, I brought my hand up to brush her silky strands of hair behind her ear, gently stroking my thumb down over her cheekbone and across her jaw.

"I could say exactly the same about you. You're so fucking beautiful, inside and out, you take my breath away. I'm the privileged one because I get to call you mine. I'll never, ever let you go."

"Never," she agreed.

We sealed our promise with a kiss.

Waking up with Elena next to me…we'd done it before, but this time, it felt different. New. Better. This time, there were no secrets and lies between us. This time, we had a real connection, and she was my girlfriend.

"Hi." She gave me a sleepy smile, then pressed a kiss to my jaw. My heart fucking exploded, all the feelings that she was giving me overwhelming me in the scariest but most amazing way.

"Hi." I couldn't even hide the way I was feeling, staring down at her. My girlfriend. *Mine*.

She could read it in my eyes, I could tell, because hers went impossibly wide, and a flush came to her cheeks. Her smile grew bigger, and she ducked her head, placing another smiling kiss against my skin.

"Come here." Tugging her up, I rolled us over so she was on her back beneath me, my arms on either side of her. I dipped my head to kiss her. "You give me so many feelings that I don't know what to do with."

"Good feelings?" Her question was whispered against my lips.

"Very fucking good." I kissed her again. "The same feelings that I know you're having for me."

She huffed out a soft laugh. "You presume a lot, Knox."

"But I'm right, aren't I?" I lifted my head slightly so I could meet her gaze, a smile spreading across my face.

Her cheeks darkened, and she stared right back at me. She was silent for a long time, and then she gave a tiny nod. "Yes. I—I'm falling for you, and I just…I hope you'll catch me."

My chest fucking ached. This girl was everything. "I'll always catch you, Elena, and I know you'll catch me too."

"Always."

I lowered my head to hers and captured her mouth in a kiss, sealing our promise between us.

It was a new beginning. A fresh start.

And I knew the best was yet to come.

49

Elena

TWO WEEKS LATER

I jumped to my feet, clapping and cheering alongside the other students, families, and friends of the Hatherley Hall lacrosse team. A few minutes ago, Tristan had scored a goal, taking us ahead for the first time in this game, and now Knox was racing down the field, the ball cradled in the head of his stick, heading straight for the goal.

"I can't watch." I covered my eyes. From my left, I heard Aria laugh, and then her fingers were peeling my hands away.

"You won't want to miss Knox's goal. Keep your eyes on your boyfriend."

Blowing out a shaky breath, I nodded. "I know. I won't hide. It's just that this is so stressful. I can feel his tension from here."

"You can help him work it out after the game." She smirked at me, and I laughed.

"Mmm, I'd love to, but we're having dinner with his

family tonight, celebrating JoJo's third birthday. But after that, I am *definitely* helping him to work it out."

"The car is always an option. Or sneak down to the crypts after everyone leaves. Or there's the tower..." She trailed off, glancing down at the field.

"Really?" I raised my brows. "Is this based on personal experience?"

She shrugged, miming zipping her lips shut. "I don't kiss and tell. But you're right. Family comes first." There was a pause, and then she added softly, "Or they do, if you're close to them. And if they're nice people."

I didn't reply to her comment straight away because Knox was drawing closer to the goal. It felt like the whole crowd was collectively holding their breath, willing him to score. Or miss, for the fans of the opposing team.

He suddenly moved to the right, his body a fluid line as he flung the ball, sending it sailing straight past the goalkeeper and into the net.

The crowd went wild, and I went wild with them, shouting and cheering, so proud of the man that I loved. His teammates piled on him, and from my position close to the edge of the pitch, I watched a wide smile spread across his face.

He emerged from the pile of players, running across the field, and then he stopped close to the stands. He pointed directly at me with a gloved hand, placing his other hand over his heart. *I love you*, he mouthed.

My jaw dropped, my breath catching in my throat as I stared down at him. He *loved* me? Swallowing hard, I blinked back the sudden tears in my eyes. *I love you too*, I mouthed back, meaning every word, placing my own hand to my pounding heart. He smiled widely, his eyes sparkling up at me, and then jogged back to his teammates to continue the game. I watched him go, my heart swelling, overflowing with everything I felt for him. How did I get so lucky?

"Who knew Knox Ashcroft had a sweet side?" Will peered around Katy, who stood to my right. "It's weird."

"It's not weird." Katy elbowed him in the ribs. "It's sweet."

I laughed, knowing how much it riled my boyfriend up when anyone referred to him as "sweet." I'd definitely have to tell him later. Turning back to Aria, I picked up the thread of our earlier conversation. "I'm lucky that they're nice people, and they've accepted me. Is…" I trailed off, unsure how to voice my question, but luckily, she seemed to understand what I was trying to ask her.

"I meant in general, it's good to have family to support you. People who aren't assholes. Especially with all the shit you went through. I'm happy for you, even if your taste in men is, uh, not the best." A grin spread across her face, and when I shot her a mock glare, she laughed. "Kidding."

"My taste is amazing, in fact. But thanks. They've been so good to me, even after everything, and I just feel so glad they gave me a chance. Same with you guys. You're the best." I'd given Aria, Katy, and Will a condensed version of my story, and despite my fears, they hadn't judged me, hadn't even treated me any differently than before. "It should be a good weekend. We've got Knox's older sister, Cora, coming down tomorrow for a little family party, plus a load of their other relatives. I'll be meeting the rest of the family, which is quite daunting, I can't lie, but I hope they like me." I was also due to have my second therapy session over the weekend, which Maria had set up for me, but that was something I wanted to stay private. Everything was still too raw, and I had a lot of unresolved grief and trauma to unpack.

Aria gave me a reassuring smile. "We're friends for life

now. And don't worry about Knox's relatives. Of course they'll like you. You're impossible not to like, and it's obvious to anyone with eyes that you make Knox happy. He actually smiles now. It's weird." We both laughed, and she continued. "You call it a little party, but I bet Knox's mum has hired caterers, right?"

"Yep. And children's entertainers. Hopefully no clowns, though." I shuddered.

"I agree with you. No clowns." She pulled a face. "Tell me all about it on Monday. That reminds me—on Monday, you can officially meet my new roommate and old friend, Quinn. You'll like her, I know it."

My gaze tracked Knox jogging down the field, his gaze intent behind his helmet. He was so gorgeous in his lacrosse uniform, clinging to his body after his exertions, his muscles shifting and rippling as he moved. With an effort, I refocused my brain on my conversation with Aria. "Um. Sorry, got sidetracked for a second. Quinn…yeah. What's the thing between her and Roman?"

Aria sighed. "It's not my place to say, and I really don't know the details. But long story short, Quinn used to board at Hatherley Hall. She moved away when we were fifteen, and Roman refused to talk about her afterwards. I know they used to hang out, and…I don't know. There are rumours. There seems to be quite a bit of animosity surrounding them."

"Like there is around you and Tristan?" I nudged her with a grin, and she rolled her eyes.

"He may be one of your boyfriend's best friends, but that doesn't mean I have to like him. His ego knows no bounds. Seriously, he actually believes he's a god. I've got no time for people like him."

"Hmmm." It seemed to me like she enjoyed riling him up. Maybe she was in denial. "If you say so."

"I do say so. Now, concentrate on the game. It's almost over, and you don't want to miss the end."

With a smile, I returned my attention to the field, my gaze fixed on player number 26.

When the game was over, Hatherley Hall had won, 10-8, and two of the goals were thanks to Knox. I was proud of the team and so proud of my boyfriend.

After saying goodbye to Aria, Katy, and Will, I wound my way through the dispersing crowds, along with the partners and groupies of the other lacrosse players. When we reached the changing rooms, I fixed my gaze on the doors, my heart beating faster as I waited for Knox to come out.

As soon as he appeared, dressed in navy sweatpants and an oversized Hatherley Hall hoodie in royal blue, I ran for him.

Dropping his bag at his feet, he swept me up into his arms, spinning me around as he kissed me.

"I'm so proud of you. You were amazing out there." I placed kisses all over his face, and he laughed before capturing my mouth with his.

"Yeah, I was amazing. But so were you. My favourite supporter."

"Your number one."

"My number one," he agreed, dropping a final kiss to the tip of my nose before he released me. "Come on, let's go home."

"I knew you loved my music." Knox gave me a smug smile as he brought his Maserati to a stop outside the Ashcroft mansion, sending up a spray of gravel. "You were singing along then. I saw you."

With a shake of my head, I unclipped my seat belt. "That's not my fault—that song gets stuck in my head. Why does it have to be so catchy?"

He eyed me, clearly unconvinced. "Baby. You're in denial. Don't pretend that you don't love it."

"Nope. Sorry to disappoint you."

I caught his smirk as he exited the car and smiled to myself.

When I joined him next to the car boot, he shouldered his duffel bag, picked up the bag with JoJo's gifts in one hand—an elaborate Duplo castle, plus a ridiculous amount of dressing-up clothes and shoes that I'd chosen—and slid his fingers between mine with the other. We walked hand in hand to the front door, and even before we reached it, it was being pulled open and Maria was throwing her arms around us both. We were joined seconds later by Anthony, carrying JoJo in his arms, and as soon as JoJo saw Knox, she squealed, reaching out for him.

"He's so good with children, isn't he?" Maria nudged me, then gave Knox an indulgent smile as he dropped the bags and lifted JoJo onto his shoulders.

"Very good. He'll make a wonderful father one day, don't you think?" Anthony joined the conversation with a smirk that was so much like Knox's on his lips.

I looked at each of them in turn, my brows raised. "Hmm. Let's revisit this conversation in, say…seven to ten years."

They both laughed, and Maria linked her arm through mine to follow Knox and JoJo down the hallway while Anthony picked up the discarded bags. We headed into the kitchen, where we tended to eat more often than not, even though the Ashcrofts had a huge dining room. On the kitchen table, a huge fairy-tale castle cake topped with three sparkling candles stood, waiting to be lit.

Knox placed JoJo on her booster seat at the table, dropping a kiss on the top of her head, and then returned to me, taking my hand. "Come and sit next to me."

We sat down opposite JoJo, Maria next to her, and Anthony at the head of the table. After we'd sung Happy Birthday and JoJo had blown out the candles, Maria served up slices of the cake while Knox gave his dad a rundown of the lacrosse game, and I entertained JoJo by playing a game where we attempted to copy each other's movements. I felt so content right then, a part of the family that had welcomed me into their lives against all odds.

Placing the cake fork down on his plate, Knox leaned into me, curling his arm around my shoulder. He placed his mouth to my ear, speaking too low to be overheard by anyone else. "I love you so fucking much."

Turning my head, I met his eyes. "I love you too," I whispered. It was the first time we'd spoken the words aloud to each other, and I leaned into him, sliding my fingers between his, still in disbelief that everything had worked out for us, despite our circumstances.

He brushed his lips over mine softly, a promise of more to come later tonight, when we were alone in the dark, just the two of us, sharing our bodies and our souls.

Drawing back, he smiled down at me, and I was struck all over again by just how lucky I was to be here by his side.

"I'm so glad you're here," he murmured.

I smiled back at him. "Me too," I said.

EPILOGUE

Elena

9 MONTHS LATER
AFTER GRADUATION—A-LEVEL RESULTS DAY

"This is it, then." Seated in front of my laptop, I clicked the link that would take me to my results page. Behind me, Anthony and Maria collectively held their breaths, while JoJo sat at my feet, staring up at me with huge eyes as she clutched an Iron Man figure in her palm.

When the page loaded, I stared at it in disbelief. "I passed all my A levels," I whispered.

"Not only that, but you now have a confirmed place at London Southwark University. You're going to study that degree in music and business that you've worked so hard for." Maria leaned forwards, squeezing my shoulders. "We're so proud of you."

Anthony stood, patting my shoulder. "We are. Very proud of you, Elena."

"Proud," JoJo echoed, waving Iron Man in the air. I smiled, my heart full to bursting.

"I couldn't have done it without you all."

Across the dining table, Knox shook his head violently, his dark eyes shining with fierce pride, and I melted. "That's all you, baby. I never had any doubt that you'd do it."

"Your turn, now. Don't keep us in suspense, son." Anthony clapped his hands together as he rounded the table, stopping next to my boyfriend, who had his own laptop open in front of him.

"I'm glad I insisted on you going first." Knox gave me a soft smile. "It means that whatever my results are, I can be happy knowing that you've got a bright future ahead of you."

A lump came into my throat. *This man.* Every time he did or said something so soft and genuine, it made me melt. It was a side of him that was so private, and I'd never take it for granted.

"Knox! My heart can't take this. Please, put us out of our misery," Maria gasped dramatically as Anthony bit back an amused smile. From the way everyone was acting, it was clear that they knew exactly what I did—there was no way that Knox wouldn't get exactly what he wanted.

"Okay. I got…" Knox paused, dragging the moment out. "Elena. I hope you're prepared to share a living space in London."

"You got in!" I flew out of my chair, racing around my table to throw myself into his strong arms. He caught me, tugging me into his lap as he pressed kisses to the side of my face, angling his laptop screen so I could see it.

"Yeah." A huge grin spread across his face. "I did it. I got into the London School of Economics. One of the best law programmes in the country."

Anthony, Maria, and JoJo all descended on him, and I disentangled myself from his arms so they could congratulate him properly, happiness bursting out of me. Our two universities were both in central London, close together, and that meant we could share the beautiful warehouse flat Anthony and Maria had sourced for us—supposedly as an investment, but they'd made it clear that they wanted us to live in it while we were based in London.

I still wasn't ready to accept things without giving something in return, despite their insistence that I owed them nothing and I was like another daughter to them—and that was something that still made me choke up with overwhelming emotions. The fact that they accepted me and treated me the way they did was something I'd never, ever take for granted. Anyway, along the lines of paying my way, I'd applied for a student loan, and I had a part-time job interview that I'd planned to go for whether or not I got into LSU. It was at a music shop fairly close to the university, and as well as being open during the day to sell instruments and music paraphernalia, it hosted open mic nights. The hours were flexible, and I was determined to get the job.

Life was good. Better than I could have ever hoped for, other than my ex-mother being jailed recently. I hadn't been able to face her—wasn't sure I ever could again. But I'd written a letter to her, getting out all my thoughts on paper. It wasn't a letter for her; it was for me, to help me process everything. I'd also continued seeing the therapist that Maria had recommended, one she'd personally used, and she was helping me to unpack the complicated feelings that I had surrounding my uncle. He'd had an affair, yes, and he'd lied in court, covering for my aunt, but at the end of the day, he didn't deserve to be locked up for life. Knox's dad had visited him once, and they'd had a long talk, and he'd referred my uncle to another legal professional to look at a possible appeal of his sentence.

Whatever happened, it was out of my hands. I needed to focus on the things I could control, not those I couldn't. My priorities were Knox, his family, our friends, and now, our upcoming degree courses and move to London.

When I looked up again, Anthony was pouring champagne into four brimming glasses, and Maria was handing JoJo a cup of what looked like sparkling apple juice.

Anthony raised his glass. "To Knox and Elena."

We all drank and exchanged yet more hugs.

A hand wrapped around my wrist, and a mouth dipped to my ear.

"Come with me."

I went, because I'd follow Knox to the ends of the earth.

We stepped outside, and he wrapped me in his arms again. "There are so many stars tonight. I should be appreciating them, but I want one last night in the dark. One more time in the crypts."

I glanced up at him, smiling. "If you can get us in there, I'd like that. It seems fitting. We shared our first kiss in the crypts. You were cruel to me, and I hated you, but we wanted each other even then, didn't we?"

He returned my smile as we headed towards his SUV. "You've always been impossible to resist. I wanted you then, and I want you even more now."

When we reached the Maserati, he glanced over at me. "Want to drive?"

I shook my head with a smile, climbing into the passenger seat. Driving again after the accident had been a long, slow process, but I'd gradually rebuilt my confidence, with Knox supporting me every step of the way, and I'd eventually managed to pass my driving test. I much preferred it when my boyfriend drove, though. He made me feel safe. Protected.

As we headed towards Hatherley Hall, I glanced over at his profile, drinking him in all over again.

"What you said about wanting me then and now. It's even better now."

His lips curved upwards. "Yeah, baby. It is. And it'll only get better."

I placed my hand on his thigh, palm up, and he slid his fingers between mine.

"I love you, Knox," I whispered.

The smile on his face widened. "I love you, too, Elena."

Fixing my gaze on the road ahead, his hand still warm around mine, I reflected on everything that had brought us here. It had been a long, difficult journey, but we'd made it.

When we'd first met, Knox had been one of the gods of Hatherley Hall. Now, that part of his life was ending, and this amazing man that I was lucky enough to call mine was ready to begin a new chapter.

He had a bright future ahead of him, and I'd be with him every step of the way. My best friend and the love of my life. The person that knew me the best, out of anyone in the world.

And I knew he felt the same way, too, because he let me know every single day.

THE END

THANK YOU

Thank you so much for reading Knox and Elena's story! If you want to know what's coming next, sign up to my newsletter for updates or come and find me on Facebook or Instagram.

Check out all my links at https://linktr.ee/authorbeccasteele Feel free to send me your thoughts, and reviews are always very appreciated ♥

Are you interested in reading more from this world? You can find out more about Roman's cousins and dive into the mystery and suspense surrounding them in The Four series, beginning with The Lies We Tell:

https://mybook.to/tlwt

Becca xoxo

ALSO BY BECCA STEELE

Hatherley Hall Series
(M/F new adult academy romance)
Cruel Crypts

LSU Series
(M/M college romance)
Collided
Blindsided
Sidelined

The Four Series
(M/F college suspense romance)
The Lies We Tell
The Secrets We Hide
The Havoc We Wreak
*A Cavendish Christmas (free short story)**
The Fight In Us
The Bonds We Break
The Darkness In You

Alstone High Standalones
(new adult high school romance)
Trick Me Twice (M/F)
Cross the Line (M/M)
In a Week (free short story) (M/F)*

Savage Rivals (M/M)

London Players Series

(M/F rugby romance)

The Offer

London Suits Series

(M/F office romance)

The Deal

The Truce

The Wish (a festive short story) *

Other Standalones

Cirque des Masques (M/M dark circus romance)

Reckless (M/M soccer romance)

Mayhem (M/F Four series dark spinoff) *

Heatwave (M/F summer short story) *

Boneyard Kings Series (with C. Lymari)

(RH/why-choose college suspense romance)

Merciless Kings

Vicious Queen

Ruthless Kingdom

Box Sets

Caiden & Winter trilogy (M/F)

(The Four series books 1-3)

*all free short stories and bonus scenes are available from https:// authorbeccasteele.com

**Key - M/F = Male/Female romance

M/M = Male/Male romance

RH = Reverse Harem/why-choose (one woman & 3+ men) romance

ABOUT THE AUTHOR

Becca Steele is a USA Today and Wall Street Journal bestselling romance author. She currently lives in the south of England with a whole horde of characters that reside inside her head.

When she's not writing, you can find her reading or watching Netflix, usually with a glass of wine in hand. Failing that, she'll be online hunting for memes or making her 500th Spotify playlist.

Join Becca's Facebook reader group Becca's Book Bar, sign up to her mailing list, check out her Patreon, or find her via the following links:

- facebook.com/authorbeccasteele
- instagram.com/authorbeccasteele
- bookbub.com/profile/becca-steele
- goodreads.com/authorbeccasteele
- patreon.com/authorbeccasteele
- amazon.com/stores/Becca-Steele/author/B07WT6GWB2

Printed in Great Britain
by Amazon